Kathleen M.
9/23/10

Final Fling

Kathleen M. Fraze

ISBN:197370398X
ISBN-13: 978-1973703983

To Mike, who puts the fling in Ireland.

Also by the author:

Final Straw

Final Exam

Final Breath

Final Bid

Final Stretch

Final Leap

Final Sale

Final Trick

PROLOGUE

Cold waves crashed ninety feet below me as I clung to the wet black rock of the cliff with fingernails and toes and looked up into the madly sincere eyes of my murderer.

She leaned over the stone wall six feet above my head. “I'm truly sorry about Scooter,” she shouted into the Irish wind. “She wasn't meant to die.”

Then she heaved a rock over the wall, and it smashed onto my left hand.

I jerked in pain, lost my grip and slipped toward the angry gray waters of the North Atlantic.

PART ONE

CHAPTER ONE

In the late spring of 1957, Dwight D. Eisenhower was president, gasoline sold for 31 cents a gallon and the interstate highway system was still more paper than concrete. There was a U.S. highway running north-south through our town and a state route cutting east-west, and they crossed in the center of downtown, which was still where Mother and other ladies did their shopping and the lawyers and doctors and dentists and insurance agents kept their offices. The university was still just a college barely touching the eastern city limits, and the main industry in town was the Heinz plant, which sucked up the produce from the surrounding farms and spewed out truckloads of ketchup each fall until the air reeked with processed tomatoes and vinegar.

There were a couple of boarding houses fronting the campus, but back then, most of the houses – two stories with an attic and a single-car garage – were still whole and home to working families, some struggling, some not. Most moms stayed home and raised the kids. Those who also held a job were considered most unfortunate.

There was no diversity back then – well, there was a lot of sniping between the Protestants and the Catholics, but they were all *Christians,* and Jews and Muslims and Buddhists and atheists were a foreign concept – so the city schools didn't take a "spring break." They blatantly shut down for Easter week, and the kids ran wild in a hellish preview of summer vacation while their moms dyed eggs, snapped up milk chocolate bunnies and chicks at the drugstore and sweated over the Easter ham.

On the Saturday between the solemnity of Good Friday and the joy of Easter Sunday, two 6-year-old neighbor girls sneaked their bicycles out of their respective garages and met at the schoolyard for a spin around the block. Back in the fall, they had still been using training wheels, so their mastery of two-wheelers was tenuous. If their mothers hadn't been so distracted by the holiday, they would have strictly forbidden the girls from their adventures, but there were table linens to wash and church outfits to prepare and Easter baskets to hide, so the girls were able to slip away and wobble around the playground on their bikes.

But after a while, one of the little blondes discovered the smooth ride on the flagstone sidewalks, and that was much nicer than the pebbly old blacktop around the school, and both girls took off, sailing past houses and over driveways and even daring to bike across a street or two. The sun was blazing, nearly as warm as summer, and they giggled like little girls do as the wind danced through their hair and they zipped around the neighborhood with a freedom they'd never felt before.

They weren't dangerously adventuresome girls. They never drifted more than a five-minute dash from home. And when they finally stopped in the middle of a block to catch their breath, they were still in familiar territory. Between them, they knew every other family on the block. To the left was the route home. To the right was a seductively mild hill down to the highway.

They didn't even discuss it. They both remounted their bikes and turned to the right and coasted downhill in bliss.

The breeze caressed them and they forgot to ride their brakes. Maybe they were even blinded a little by the afternoon sun. They cruised and squealed in delight, and one little girl pulled ahead of the other as they barreled down the slope.

In the end, they both knew they were in trouble. They were racing much too fast. The handlebars bucked under their fingers as spring-dormant lawns sped past them in a blur. Their laughter turned into frightened shrieks as they gripped the handlebars and their feet slid off the pedals.

The highway, clogged with furiously belching semis, rushed at them. The little girl in front tried to drag her feet on the sidewalk, and that slowed her some as she attempted to steer around the corner, but the girl in back was helplessly picking up speed as her bike aimed straight for a semi loaded with hogs.

The truck driver caught sight of them out of the corner of his eye and tried to brake. The big rig wheezed and shuddered but couldn't stop, and powerless to save the girls, the driver squeezed his eyes shut and waited for the thud.

It didn't come. As the first girl wrenched herself into the turn, she tipped, and the bike slid onto its side and skidded into the devil strip. The second bike slammed into her back wheel and the impact was just enough to keep it from sailing into the highway. Both girls were thrown off their bikes and they landed hard, but neither one fell into the path of the truck.

They were bloodied and bruised, and each broke an arm, which they later showed off in matching casts. The first little girl was hailed as a heroine for inadvertently blocking her friend's headlong dash into oblivion. The second little girl was pampered by family and friends for her miraculous escape. A photographer took their pictures, and their harrowing story was displayed prominently on the front page of the town newspaper. Their shocked parents forgot to scold or punish them for their misdeeds, and their mothers saved the best pieces of chocolate just for them.

It was the best damned Easter ever.

CHAPTER TWO

"Slow down, Jo," Mother grumbled. "They won't start without us." And she stubbornly planted her hiking staff into the trail and stopped to cough delicately into her fist.

"Aw, geez," I groaned, "we should have *never* agreed to this."

"Nonsense," Mother wheezed. "It will be fun."

The prospect of watching your 70-plus mother pass out on a remote park trail is never fun, so I obediently stopped and waited for her to catch her breath.

It was a deceptively mild Sunday afternoon in mid-March, and we were retracing a hike we had taken thirty years before with my Girl Scout troop to plant trees on a hilltop overlooking the river. It wasn't a *high* hilltop. The elevation in our county doesn't change that much. Most of the land is relentlessly flat, which was why family farms used to be so profitable. But there are some mild hills along the river, and that was where thirty years ago, my troop leader had bartered with a farmer to let the Scouts plant pine seedlings so we could all earn some badge or other. I vaguely remembered trudging up the hill with my fellow Scouts and throwing dirt at each other as we studded an otherwise unremarkable hilltop field with little pine trees. Then we promptly forgot about our excursion into nature as we graduated to more exciting adventures – like boys.

Eventually, the farmer's hilltop was absorbed by the local park district, and one day an enterprising ranger discovered the pine grove, which still sheltered a neglected plaque acknowledging the efforts of our troop back in 1964. Since we were coming up on the thirtieth anniversary of the planting, the ranger got it into her head that there ought to be a celebration, and after much digging through musty records, she located our troop leader and the list of girls who had participated, and she sent out invitations to all of us to return to the hilltop and reconnect with nature.

I was inclined to ignore the offer. I'm a cop, and I prefer to reserve my precious days off for nothing more challenging than a romp in bed with Dave. But Mother, who had served from time to time as an assistant Scout leader for both me and my younger sister Maureen, was intrigued by the invitation, and browbeat me into accepting. Since Mother lives with Dave and me, the opportunities for browbeating are endless. I never had a chance.

I tried to coerce Dave into going, too, but he mangled a knee in the waning days of Vietnam and successfully argued that a hike up a hill was not in his best interests. His son Adam and Adam's girlfriend Emily also share our crowded house, but they conveniently had other plans for that Saturday. So there I was, alone on a hillside with Mother, climbing to a reunion with girls I hadn't seen in decades and wondering just why I was wasting a warm spring afternoon in the woods when I could have been doing something much more productive, like scrubbing out toilets.

I should have brought the dog.

Mother eventually allowed that she was ready to go on, and we slowly snaked our way up the hill. The trail was soft – it had been a rainy spring – and I fussed at Mother, offering her my arm. She indignantly shooed me away. She had broken a hip the year before, and I had alarming visions of her tripping over tree roots and destroying all the fine handiwork of her surgeon. But she was determined to get to the pine grove under her own steam.

We had started out early from the trailhead by the river, but we were going so slowly, we had been passed by several ladies of a menopausal age, and I was sure we were at the back of the pack. The ceremony was supposed to start at 2 p.m. It was already a quarter past.

"Ah, that's much better," Mother sighed as her hiking staff dug into a dry stretch of trail littered with pine needles. "Doesn't that smell lovely?"And she stopped to sniff.

The scent of pine was strong, and I realized in surprise that instead of passing through meadows, we were suddenly surrounded by trees that towered darkly above us. Where I remembered grass dappled with wildflowers, there were now rows of ramrod straight pines that had flourished to the point that they had joined in a green canopy that blocked the sun and obliterated the undergrowth. We were in a 30-year-old forest with a dirt floor cushioned by a thick layer of decaying needles.

I shook my head. I *knew* we were on the hilltop, but the transformation over the decades was befuddling. Nothing felt or smelled like I remembered.

Voices filtered through the trees, and we could see a clutch of ladies up the trail, hugging each other and gabbing. There weren't nearly as many as there should have been – there had been at least three dozen girls in my troop, doggedly planting a hundred seedlings under the stern eyes of our troop leader and two assistant moms. There weren't even a dozen ladies milling now along the trail.

A plump white-haired matron spotted us and eagerly waved at Mother and me to join the pack. There was no escape now, so I doggedly led Mother to our reunion.

The woman who had waved to us was my old troop leader, Mrs. DeWitt. She was Mother's contemporary, but she had weathered the hike well. She was much heavier and much more wrinkled than I remembered, but there was still the old tone of command in her voice as she greeted us, and since we were the last two on the guest list to arrive, she immediately ordered the "girls" to gather round for the ceremony.

The ladies shuffled into a line, with Mother and Mrs. DeWitt in front of us, and a 30-something woman in park uniform took center stage to welcome us to the Girl Scout Forest.

The ranger was flushed with importance, and she launched into an exuberant speech about nature and conservation and the wonderful deed we had done by planting a forest at the top of the hill. While she talked enthusiastically about saving the environment, a girl who must have been a park district intern scurried around and snapped photographs.

As the ranger gushed platitudes – at length – I surreptitiously studied the ladies who were lined up with me and tried to place them.

The very tall woman was definitely Diane Hearne, who would have been a basketball star if the school district had indulged in girls' sports back in my day. She was still tall, but a basketball of fat had lodged in her belly and I doubted she dribbled much anymore.

Standing beside her, looking bored, was a woman with salt and pepper hair in a severely unflattering cut and the big plastic eyeglass frames that were popular that season. I identified her immediately as Sandra Porter, who had been just as bored back when we were Scouts. She had always distanced herself from the rest of us, and I was somewhat surprised that she had bothered to show up.

But then wasn't my presence just as puzzling? I hadn't kept in touch with any of these girls, and here I was, just like Sandra, fidgeting in the shade and willing the park ranger to get *on* with it.

Next to Sandra were two co-conspirators, still as thick as the day we planted the trees. One was Marilyn, Mrs. DeWitt's daughter, and the other was Patty. They were best friends who had reigned over the "in" crowd through junior high and high school. They were the most popular among the teachers and fellow students, always on the honor roll, always winning spots on the cheerleading squad, always elected to Student Council and rotating leads in the annual choir musicals. They had their pick of the best dates, and I still instinctively hated them.

Two ladies I couldn't quite place stood next to them, and Ginny Reed anchored the line. She had been universally pleasant, although we all agreed in the restroom that she was quite slow. That hadn't prevented her from learning the joys of sex. She didn't graduate with us because she was knocked up by then by her equally slow-witted boyfriend. They were married after *he* graduated, and produced seven more kids. He had risen to assistant manager of the local grocery chain, and she occasionally clerked at the drugstore. By all accounts, they scrambled from paycheck to paycheck, and once in a while, one of their kids appeared on my radar for some stupid juvenile prank. But whenever I showed up at her doorstep with a miscreant in tow, Ginny was smiling. She was content with her brood, even when one of them misbehaved, and she never held it against me when the kids got into trouble. She waved at me happily from the end of the row, and I self-consciously waved back.

There should have been more, even after thirty years. There should have been more girls standing on that hilltop – but many had married and followed husbands to jobs out of town. Others couldn't be bothered by a Girl Scout reunion.

And several were dead.

Too many, I later figured out. And the revelation almost killed me.

But on that March afternoon, death wasn't in my thoughts – unless throttling the ranger to shut her up counted.

When she finally wrapped up her speech, she invited us all to introduce ourselves. The two women I couldn't remember were Christine Pope, who used to run the cash register in the school cafeteria in exchange for a free lunch, and Marci Gibbs, who had the gym locker next to mine and indisputably the most stupendous *natural* breasts in our entire freshman class. They had, most distressingly, drooped over the last three decades.

There were some discreet hoots as I introduced myself as a police detective. Perhaps my fellow Scouts remembered my early experimentations with controlled substances.

The ranger unveiled a new plaque dedicated to our trees, and Mrs. DeWitt led us in a disjointed recitation of the Girl Scout pledge, and then we were freed to attack the picnic table loaded with cold cuts and macaroni salad and Girl Scout cookies.

Mother was happily tethered to Mrs. DeWitt. They had many children and grandchildren to chronicle, including my long-dead daughter Elizabeth. I circled the pack, balancing my paper plate of food on one hand and nibbling on Dutch loaf with the other, and finally found a somewhat sturdy log where I could plant myself.

Ginny Reed, now Edgerton, accosted me first. She parked herself on the log beside me, and as she noshed through two weighty sandwiches, she brought me up to date on all of the kids, four of whom had already produced grandkids and two of whom were living on welfare. The American Dream had not been kind to her family – her smile was missing several teeth – but she laughed heartily over memories of our troop's escapades, and I found myself in envy of her good cheer. Pooling my paycheck with Dave and Mother, I had climbed several rungs up the economic ladder from Ginny, but she seemed remarkably happy with the hand she had been dealt. She had a small home in the southwest corner of town, none of her kids was currently in jail and she still had her health, if only she could give up the cigarettes.

She was eventually supplanted on the log by Sandra, who really had nothing to share with me but found the log a fine place to rest while she observed with disdain the others milling around the food table. Sandra was the one who dolefully reminded me of the dead – Nikki, who had been killed in a traffic accident at 16; Debbie, who had died of an allergic reaction to anesthesia at 20;

Becky, who had been ravaged by breast cancer; Carol, who had hanged herself in the agony of divorce.

I shuddered at the recollections. I hadn't thought of our troop as doomed before, but Sandra made a forceful case. The trees had survived better than our Scouts had.

The intern was desperately trying to herd us around the plaque for a group photo. Normally, I shun such endeavors. The ranger was promising to have our reunion written up in the local newspaper, and a cop just doesn't need her face plastered in the news. I don't *want* the public to recognize me. But Sandra was such dismal company that I leaped at the opportunity to ditch my plate in the trash bin that someone had obligingly hauled up the hill and let myself be jostled into the front row.

Marilyn and Patty were arm in arm behind me.

"I know a lovely hairdresser who could take care of that gray," Patty whispered into my ear.

I grimaced as though I'd just been felled by an attack of gas.

And *that* was the shot that was displayed on the local news page two days later.

* * *

The reunion broke up quickly when the cookies were gone. Ginny headed back down the hill with Diane, the tall one bobbing down the trail with the short one. Sandra, as was her nature, stalked off alone in the opposite direction, to take the long loop back to the trailhead. Christine and Marci scooted away before they could be drafted for cleanup detail, which was pretty much how they had operated during our Scouting days. In an instant, it was just Mrs. DeWitt and Mother, and Marilyn and Patty and me, and the ranger breathlessly assuring us that if we'd just pack up the leftovers and police the grounds for trash, a maintenance crew would come by eventually to haul away the table and the garbage and donate the extra food to the town shelter.

And then she and the intern disappeared down the trail, too.

"Typical," Patty said.

"I am *not* picking up Ginny's trash," Marilyn huffed.

"Or Sandra's," Patty said.

"Oh, we'll have this cleaned up in no time," Mrs. DeWitt said. And she clapped her hands in the same authoritative way she had used on us back in the day.

We "girls" just rolled our eyes.

But old habits die hard, and we hopped to it while Mother and Mrs. DeWitt cheerfully supervised from my log.

Somehow I ended up on trash detail while Marilyn and Patty bagged the leftovers that Patty wasn't popping into her mouth, but as I wandered between trees, I also wandered in and out of their conversation enough to bring myself up to date. Marilyn had matured into attractive but brittle. She was lean, bordering on gaunt. Her hair was still a blond helmet, but I cattily suspected it was expensively maintained. She had gone into nursing, but hadn't settled for an R.N. She had earned a master's in business administration as well, and now ran the regional office of the state health department. Prospects for a promotion to the capital were good. She had collected two husbands over the years, and a child from each. The husbands were gone and the children nearly so. She talked like she was ready for a third spouse and maybe even another child – *if* they didn't get in the way of her inevitable promotion.

Patty had aged more softly, with a rounded face and thighs, but still worth a second look from men Dave's age. Her hair was now more frosted than blond, but it flew around her head in artful strokes that I was sure were most expensive. She, too, had obtained a husband and a child along with a degree in physical therapy. Like Marilyn, she had discarded her husband, the child was a prodigy weighing an offer from Harvard, and the degree had led her to the local hospital, where she was in charge of the therapy department, but perhaps not for long. A bigger hospital in a bigger city was courting her, and she was seriously considering a move.

All of this was divulged for the sole purpose of putting me in my place, I was sure. I was only a cop. And though they were too considerate to bring up *my* disastrous attempt at motherhood, I thought the intent was clear. *They* had successfully reproduced. I had not.

Dave would have said I was paranoid. But he hadn't grown up with these girls. They were obviously devoted to each other, just as they had been in school, but the rest of us – well, now, only *me* on trash patrol – didn't measure up.

I sighed as I tied up the last bag. I had a job I enjoyed, a man who inexplicably adored me, a quasi-stepson following in my professional footsteps and an elderly mother still in possession of most of her faculties, her fascination with this reunion notwithstanding. After all these years, did I really need the approval of two girls from my past?

Mother summed it up succinctly as we followed the girls and Mrs. DeWitt down the trail. We broke free of the pine forest and into a meadow basking in the sun as it sloped down to the river, and I felt 30-year-old memories of classroom snubs sliding off my shoulders. The air was warm, the breeze dancing over the early wildflowers was delightful, and I had sudden visions of coercing Dave into dragging the grill out of winter storage.

Marilyn was making a particularly caustic remark about Diane Hearne's big belly and Patty was laughing in appreciation.

Mother uncharacteristically leaned on me as we followed them around a bend in the trail, but her eyes were twinkling as she looked at me.

"They are *such* bitches," she said.

I laughed, patted her wrinkled hand where it gripped my arm, and safely led her home.

CHAPTER THREE

The little blond girl was 8 years old when her parents decided to load the family into the big blue Ford Fairlane and drive to Arizona to visit her aunt and uncle and multitudinous cousins. It was a long, arduous trip of marathon driving broken each night by a few hours of uncomfortable sleep in a cheap motel. The trip took three and a half days, with the little girl crammed into the back seat with her two little brothers, and the journey felt like it would take forever, especially when her parents squabbled in the front seat over her father's speed down the highway and her mother's frequent need to find a bathroom. The little girl felt hot and gritty when the car finally pulled into a subdivision on the edge of the desert, and as the family tumbled out of the car, she felt the heat sucking the life out of her tiny heart.

But her aunt and uncle had a wonderful surprise. They had dug up their small back yard for an aquamarine gem of a swimming pool, and the little girl jumped into it immediately. She spent nearly their entire vacation paddling through the water, so much that the sun bleached her hair white and baked her skin a nutty brown. She dived fearlessly off the board and learned how to propel herself nearly the length of the pool with one ecstatic jump.

It was on their fifth day in town, with the adults lounging in lawn chairs and guzzling beer as they ignored the many cousins, that she made a particularly stunning leap into the pool – one that took her to the very bottom, where she scraped her knuckles before twisting upward toward the hot scorching skies of the desert – and she unexpectedly kicked a soft, round object, knocking it out of the depths and back to the light.

She was annoyed as she bobbed gracelessly to the surface – her lovely dive, the one she had solemnly instructed her mother to watch, had been sabotaged by debris in the pool, and she was already making excuses in her head for her poor performance. But when she shook the water out of her eyes, she saw the adults frantically fishing her 2-year-old cousin out of the deep end, where she had inadvertently kicked him.

The toddler had fallen into the pool unnoticed while the adults imbibed. He surely would have drowned if the little girl hadn't unceremoniously booted him to the surface.

Her uncle hauled her out of the pool and hugged her fiercely to his chest. "Oh, my God," he sobbed drunkenly into her hair, "you're a hero!"

And the adults proceeded to make a bigger fuss over her accidental heroics than they did over her cousin's near brush with death.

She reigned as a queen over the final days of their vacation. Her brothers and cousins were in awe. Her aunt and uncle plied her with presents and treats. Her parents viewed her as a young goddess. She had saved the boy, and she was rewarded handsomely.

It was the best damned vacation ever.

CHAPTER FOUR

I sat outside the drunk tank on Monday night and stared through the bars at a sorry specimen of humanity.

I had the night shift that month, which meant more hands-on policing than usual. Ellen Graham and Berger were on days, and Jamal and Henry were anchoring the afternoon shift, so I had no detecting backup. It was just me and the patrols, including Adam, guarding the town overnight, and it was up to me to sort out the particulars that had landed Louie Brandon in the tank.

I don't normally deal with the nightly haul of drunks. That's why God invented patrolmen. Back in the early days, before Bradley could install me as a detective without raising too many eyebrows, I had been afflicted by drunks nearly every night on patrol. Most were students raising hell downtown, and if they didn't vomit all over my squad car, I usually cut them some slack. I wasn't so old then that I couldn't remember the joy of cruising the bars on Saturday night after a long week of mind-numbing classes, and I had been inclined to let the jolly drunks blow off steam. Usually, I would drive them to their dorms and kick them out on the doorstep with a blazing lecture to shape up or else.

But there had been other drunks – usually townspeople or older students with cars – who managed to total their vehicles around telephone poles and, if they survived, my tolerance would take a nosedive. Drunks in cars hurt innocent people, so I had little sympathy for *them*.

And there had been a fair share of belligerent drunks who took their booze out on the wives and kids waiting for them at home. I had no warm and fuzzy feelings for those guys, either.

Louie Brandon looked like he might fall into that category.

But there I was on Monday night, trying to get his attention when by all rights, he should have been the uniforms' problem.

It was my dental hygienist's fault. She was a chatty lady in her 50s, and even though she used medieval implements of torture to scrape my teeth clean every six months, she did it with great care and a minimal amount of lecturing about my bad dental habits. So when she loaded up my mouth with sharp pointed objects and asked whether I could keep an eye out for her boy Louie, what could I do but nod frantically? She had a load of hurt at her disposal.

Louie wasn't a bad boy, she assured me. He'd been mixed up with a crazy crowd as a teenager – well, she was a single parent, she sighed, what could she do? – and there'd been some evidence of drugs and borderline felonious assault, but he'd grown up a lot in the last year, ever since his girlfriend had produced a son. Louie had never finished his degree, but he was the assistant manager now at the video store, and he and his girlfriend were working hard to establish a home for their baby and her son by a previous unfortunate relationship. They were renting a nice duplex away from campus, and Louie was even talking about going back to school. And he only *occasionally* lapsed into drink.

She would consider it a personal favor, she told me as she stabbed at my gums, if I'd keep watch on her boy in the unlikely event that he ever landed back in the drunk tank.

I was a hostage, trapped nearly upside down in a dental chair as she wielded the lethal accoutrements of her trade, and I feverishly promised to do good by her boy.

Unless he murdered someone.

"Louie?" she laughed. "Never. You can spit out now."

Which I did. And promptly forgot about Louie Brandon.

Until that Monday night after the Girl Scout reunion, when Quinlan and Adam hauled him in, and with vaguely maternal instincts, I scanned their preliminary arrest report and recognized Louie's name.

A rash promise made in the throes of dental misery suddenly came back to haunt me.

Adam had graduated from the police academy in December and was serving his six-month probation. That meant he wasn't allowed to ride alone. He had been paired up with Quinlan that month, and it wasn't a bad arrangement. Quinlan could be a hot dog, but he had developed a keener sense of self-preservation since becoming a dad, and he had served me well as backup on more than one occasion. If I had to entrust the well-being of Dave's son to anyone on the force besides myself, Quinlan was a safe choice. He liked Adam and was politically savvy enough to know it wouldn't hurt him any to keep my boy out of trouble.

He also didn't mind too much when I nosed around his arrests. He'd been around long enough that his ego wasn't seriously threatened.

Adam, however, was annoyed when I interrupted them at the coffee pot and asked about Louie Brandon.

"It's a righteous bust, Jo," he huffed.

"I'm sure it is," I said equably. "But why bring him in instead of running him home?" And I looked pointedly at Quinlan.

"He blew a 1.5," Quinlan said, "and he was belligerent." And the smile he gave me said there was no way a guy who was nearly twice the legal blood-alcohol limit was going to get a pass.

I nodded. "Good move."

Adam's shoulders relaxed.

"Mind if I talk to him?" I asked.

Adam's blood pressure shot right back up.

But Quinlan calmly stirred some powdered creamer into his coffee. "You know the guy?"

"I know his mother," I amended.

"Ah," Quinlan said, and that explained everything to him.

Adam was still trying to prove himself – to his father and to the department – and my relationship with Louie's mother severely threatened his self-worth. "You're gonna cut him loose," Adam said, and his voice dripped with accusation.

"I'm just going to talk to the guy," I said blandly.

Adam looked at Quinlan for help. "She's gonna cut him loose."

Quinlan smiled expansively and clapped Adam on the shoulder. "Doesn't matter. We did *our* job. We brought him in." Quinlan was wise in the ways of office politics, and since no one doubted his judgment or his balls, he could be generous.

Besides, he also knew I was the mistress of the overtime budget.

Adam was too consumed by the need to establish himself as someone other than my "stepson," and he was bristling. "She's gonna let him *go*," he repeated around gritted teeth.

"Saves us paperwork," Quinlan said. "Did I show you that gun I lifted off that guy at the convenience store last week?" And he abruptly steered Adam to the property room for a look at some really fine weaponry.

I made a note to myself to pad Quinlan's uniform allowance and went down to the drunk tank to introduce myself to Louie Brandon.

It wasn't his best day, so it wasn't fair to judge him by first impressions. He was slouched on a bench as far away from the toilet as he could get, and the look he gave the two frat boys in residence for underage drinking kept them huddling as far from him as *they* could get. He wasn't overtly threatening them, but in their fog, even they could see they didn't want to get in his face.

If he had been standing, he probably would have been tall and gangly. A stained flannel shirt hung on him loosely, but the impression wasn't emaciated, just lean. Skinny legs in jeans were splayed out in front of him, ending in a fine pair of pointy boots that could have done some damage if he were so inclined.

I told myself to remind Quinlan to relieve prisoners of the lethal weapons on their feet.

At least Quinlan had confiscated the guy's belt.

Brandon had black hair that hugged his neck in sweaty clumps. It probably washed up into a devilishly curly tangle that a woman could ecstatically twist around her fingers. He had a couple days' growth of beard, which was ruggedly appealing, and dark eyes that smoldered with drink. He was unencumbered by glasses and had pretty much outgrown acne. His mouth was a little too mean for my tastes, but with a shower and twenty-four hours to sweat out his hangover, he would probably be quite attractive.

The smell wasn't so great, but in all fairness, that could have been the toilet and the two boys in the corner instead of him. The drunk tank never loses the stench of bodies fighting off too much booze.

"Louie," I said, showing my hands so he could see I wasn't taking notes that could come back to haunt him, "I'm Detective Ferris."

His eyes slid from the center of the cell over to me and I could feel him evaluating what he saw – a fortyish woman in glasses and curly salt-and-pepper hair, a hint of pre-menopausal poundage straining her sweater and jeans, maybe reminiscent of his fourth-grade teacher. Too old to interest him and too young to be his grandmother. He dismissed me as inconsequential and his eyes slid back to the center of the cell.

"Shall we talk?" I asked pleasantly.

He just grunted at the ceiling and closed his eyes.

"Louie," I said, and rapped on the bars with my knuckles, "look at me."

His eyes opened a fraction and skittered toward me. They were red with the impending hangover, but they were still fierce. I understood immediately Quinlan's reference to "belligerent."

"What the fuck you want?" he slurred.

"I'd like a good look at you," I said. "So I can report your condition to your mother accurately."

His eyes flickered a little – maybe in anger, maybe in embarrassment. Since he was well past the age of emancipation, I figured it was anger.

"Meddling bitch," he growled, and dismissed both me and his mother by lazily closing his eyes again.

My own anger suddenly shot in hot spurts up my throat. My doctor had recently put me on acid reflux drugs, and until that moment, I couldn't fathom why. But I was immediately hot. His mother and I weren't best buddies, but she treated me well and I generally considered her a nice lady. His abrupt dismissal of her good intentions rankled.

So I dislodged some paper from my back pocket – his rap sheet – and said coldly, "You aren't a first-time offender. We press charges, this won't go well for you."

Brandon snorted, with his eyes still closed.

"Underage drinking – three times as a juvenile," I recited. "Suspicion of assault – two times as an adult. DUI, three charges, one conviction. You lost your license for twelve months when you were 18. Drunk and disorderly, three times since you were 16. Another charge will probably be enough to get your boss's attention. He'll definitely fire your ass. How is *that* going to go down at home?"

Brandon condescended to open one eye. "I was *not* disorderly. I was feelin' good. Your shit-ass patrolmen overreacted."

"You blew a 1.5," I countered. "That is *not* overreacting."

"Was I hurting anybody?" he asked, suddenly very much into the conversation. His body tensed up in self-righteousness. "I had a few beers. I was goin' home. No harm in *that*. But your *patrolmen* had to get in my face."

"After you threatened to eviscerate the barmaid," I said.

He was still trapped in an alcoholic fog. "Say *what*?"

I read from the arrest report. "You said you would carve out her guts."

"Well, yeah," Brandon agreed. "She shortchanged me."

"So, of course, you threatened her."

"Wouldn't you?" he demanded.

"I might try another avenue of persuasion," I said diplomatically.

"You got no balls," he said, then curled up on the bench and chuckled at his own joke.

He was not doing much to grab my sympathy, his mother notwithstanding.

Monday is not a busy night for drunks in our town. Most students are still drying out from the weekend, and the townspeople are generally tucked into bed by midnight because they have to go to work in the morning. So there were no miscreants lined up in the hall, waiting for their turn at incarceration. I could let Brandon and the frat boys spend the rest of the night in the tank without fear of violating anyone's civil rights over issues of overcrowding.

But I *had* made that silly promise to Brandon's mother, so I took another stab at rehabilitation.

"We hold you overnight and haul you into court in the morning, you're probably going to miss work," I pointed out.

"I got a late shift tomorrow," he said, unconcerned.

"Maybe you won't get into court until late," I said.

He shrugged, but it wasn't quite as nonchalant as he'd hoped. My antennae quivered. Maybe the video store job was more important than he wanted to let on. Maybe this bust was a bigger complication in his life than his record indicated. Maybe there was a world of trouble waiting for him at home if he added another drunk and disorderly to his sheet. Maybe the love of his life would walk – snatching away his son.

But just as I was entertaining conciliatory thoughts of letting him go, he pulled himself to his feet and charged the cell door.

"You think you know *anything*?" he spat, grabbing the bars and glaring at me with eyes that burned with too much whiskey. "You think you can lock *me* up? You and my mother – you think either of you got any right to tell me what to do? How to raise my boy? When to go to work? How to spend the money *I* earn? You're pathetic – all of you!"

And the spit of his indignation sprayed between the bars.

Well, that did it for me. I was willing to cut the guy some slack for the sake of my dental health, but he was an ungrateful moron, and it just wasn't worth alienating myself from Adam and disrupting the peace on my own home front.

So I pocketed his rap sheet. "You need to think about how you're gonna make bail," I said. "Maybe your mother."

His descriptive response was not complimentary.

"Or your father," I said stiffly.

"Fuck you," he said, with more intensity than warranted.

I've been told to fuck myself by more prisoners than I can count, so I wasn't particularly offended. But I was surprised by the vehemence of his response.

"Your dad is out of the picture?" I asked.

"He's *dead*," Brandon said, and with great effort, he pried himself off the bars and shuffled back to the bench. "Dead and burned up long ago," he muttered as he sprawled on the bench and stared malevolently at the frat boys.

I was plotting my escape, already planning excuses for his mother, but the word "burned" stopped me cold. "Burned" did not have a good history with me.

"Your father died in a fire?" I asked.

"Incinerated," Brandon said as he made himself comfortable on the bench. "What's it to you?"

"Nothing," I said.

"Fucking bitch," he said, and crossed his arms and glared at the small world of the drunk tank.

I shivered.
And went up to the squad room to write up his release.

CHAPTER FIVE

"You undercut me, Jo," Adam seethed, and his eyes were red hot.

"I was exercising my discretion as a supervisor," I countered, and primly dunked a piece of toast into the perfectly fried egg Mother had just planted in front of me.

"Bullshit," Adam said. "You made me look like an idiot." And he was so angry, he didn't even glance at the plate Mother had loaded up for him.

We had both clocked out at seven and, since we were sharing the ride to work, Adam was forced to fold himself into my hatchback for the trip home. Usually, it was an animated drive as we rehashed the night's adventures – or lack of them. Everything on the job was new to Adam, and his enthusiasm reignited my own passion. We were normally chattering away at each other in excited police code as we spilled through the back door into the kitchen. And Mother was almost always waiting for us with a hot breakfast to take the edge off the night shift. (Well, her prime purpose was to feed herself, but by making enough for us, too, she usually got an earful of all the gritty inside details that cops normally shield from the public. Mother is an unapologetic voyeur and is not above using food to get information.)

But this Tuesday morning, neither Adam nor I was brimming with the third-person horror stories that titillated

Mother's evil side. Adam was royally pissed that I had negated his bust by freeing Louie Brandon, and I was determined to pass it off as a good call, totally unrelated to the future well-being of my gums.

Mother picked up on the tension immediately and was nonplussed. I had been Adam's champion ever since he had declared his intentions to be a cop. The two of us were a united front against Dave's objections, even though it occasionally put a very big damper on my sex life. Dave and Mother and Adam's girlfriend, Emily, all had qualms about Adam's chosen profession. I was the one who backed him up, even when by all rights, Adam should have been disinclined to like me. After all, I was the one who had supplanted his mother in his father's life.

But we had hung together, through his criminal justice degree at the university and his tour at the police academy and now his probation as a rookie in the department. Dave still entertained hopes that Adam could be persuaded to follow another career path, but I knew better. Adam had the soul of a cop.

He just didn't like it too much that I could veto his decisions.

So even though Mother's cooking was nearly as seductive as Emily's chest, he sat at the kitchen table with his arms crossed and his jaw jutting defiantly, and dared me to defend myself.

I've trampled on many uniformed toes in my career, so I wasn't exactly quaking in the face of his wrath. But it did disrupt the peaceful routine of our household, and Mother charged in immediately to referee.

"Jo," she said sternly, "what did you do?"

"My job," I said, and smoothly slipped Barney a hunk of bacon. The dog nearly swooned.

"Do you agree?" Mother asked Adam.

He was so indignant, he couldn't answer.

And his breakfast chilled on the table.

Mother abandoned all pretense of objectivity. Anyone who ignored her bacon and eggs was in dire straits and obviously needed her protection. So she parked herself on Adam's side of the table and gave me the look she had used for forty-two years to squeeze many true confessions out of me.

I was marginally outnumbered. Dave would have lined up with me, but he had already left for class. Emily would have draped herself all over Adam, but she, too, was on campus. The cats were apolitical, but since I was handing out bacon, Barney was slobbering all over my lap. So I wasn't entirely without an ally.

"Adam," I said calmly as I swirled another piece of toast through the eggs I loved but my doctor despised, "you did your job. You busted a drunk. That's all you need to worry about."

A drop of golden egg yolk fell onto my knee and Barney deliriously lapped at my jeans. I patted his head for not deserting me.

Adam glared. "Quinlan and I *both* did our jobs, and you let the son of a bitch go."

"Jo," Mother intoned in disappointment. And she looked like she clearly regretted wasting her morning preparing breakfast for me.

I carefully wiped my greasy fingers on a dish towel. "You're going to make a lot of busts," I said, purposely looking Adam in the eye and avoiding Mother. "Sometimes they'll fall apart in court. Sometimes they'll disappear because they aren't worth our time to pursue. You have to get used to it. As long as you do *your* job, it doesn't matter what happens down the line."

"Bullshit," Adam repeated, but he grabbed a fork and stabbed at his eggs. The smell of grease was distracting him.

Barney immediately transferred his affections to Adam's side of the table, where the possibility of food dropping accidentally to the floor seemed much higher. Barney is a good judge of moods and who isn't paying proper attention to the efficient transfer of food to mouth.

"I could understand if the drunk tank was full," Adam said, waving his fork and inadvertently flipping a hunk of egg white onto Barney's snout. "Sometimes you gotta let guys go so the really bad drunks are off the street. I *understand* that."

And Mother helpfully nodded in his defense.

"But Christ, Jo, it's Monday night – "

"Tuesday," Mother automatically corrected. She's on a day shift and doesn't understand.

"It's Monday," Adam insisted inelegantly through a mouthful of egg, "there's only two other guys in the tank. There's no way you had to let Brandon go because it was too crowded."

"You're right," I said, and nibbled daintily on a piece of bacon.

Barney reconsidered switching his allegiance to Adam and swirled back around my knees.

Mother listened keenly to our exchange. So far, Adam was scoring all the points that mattered to her, and she raised an eyebrow at me.

I ignored her.

"We had him dead to rights, Jo," Adam pushed. "He's got priors, he's drunk on his ass, he probably beats his girlfriend. How can you let scum like that back on the street?"

"He beats his girlfriend?" Mother asked, shocked.

"We don't know that," I said hastily.

Adam snorted.

Mother shook her head. "That's so unlike you, Jo," she said.

"She's trying to wash me out," Adam said angrily. "She's made a deal with Dad and she's going to make sure I don't get past probation."

"Oh, Adam," Mother said automatically, "Jo wouldn't do that."

But there was a flicker of doubt in her eyes – well, after all, my first allegiance was to Dave, and I should have known she'd recognize it. I suddenly had to justify myself to her, if only to ease the iron grip of remorse suddenly squeezing my chest.

"For God's sake, Adam," I finally cracked. "It was the fire, okay? Use your goddamned head. I cut him loose because of the fire."

"Fire?" Adam squawked. "He was drunk and disorderly. There wasn't any fire." And he looked at Mother for backup.

But Mother had become very still.

And I was suddenly tossing the rest of the bacon at Barney with trembling hands and trying to douse the flames burning my lungs. I wasn't in my safe kitchen anymore. I wasn't even in the tank with a raving drunk. I was spiraling down into hell, and Adam's protests were just part of the noise as I fell.

Mother reached out and grabbed my hands, and her voice called me back before the flames could lap up my legs. "Tell me about the fire, Jo."

I stared through the smoke in my head at Mother. Her eyes were wide and haunted behind their bifocals, but she was solid. I *knew* she was real. The images searing my brain were not.

We leaned into each other over the table. Our eyes were locked. Adam was abruptly excluded.

"Brandon's father," I said hoarsely, my throat raw from smoke inhalation. "He died in a house fire."

Mother closed her eyes and aged ten years. "How old was the son?" she asked quietly.

"Ten," I said. I'd dug through the records during the night and had found the report moldering in the basement of the station. It was sparse. The detailed records would have been filed away in the fire department next door. But there was enough of a police report to sketch out what had happened. Brandon and his mother had been out of the house when his father had fallen asleep with a lighted cigarette in his hand.

Just like my husband Steve.

Except Brandon's father had been considerate enough to kill only himself.

My husband had killed our 4-year-old daughter, too.

Mother slowly opened her eyes. "The boy – he's been troubled?"

"In and out of court since he was a teen," I said.

"No father to help him," Mother sighed.

"Only his mother," I said, "alone."

Mother was pale. In my more selfish moments, I liked to think I carried the burden of Elizabeth's death myself, but I was wrong. A part of Mother had died in that fire, too. And she knew *exactly* why I had let Louie Brandon go.

Mother wearily squeezed my hand. "You did the right thing."

I nearly cried in absolution.

Adam was indignant. "This is wrong, Ma," he protested. "She undercut my case!"

"She saved a boy's soul," Mother said.

Adam gaped.

Mother smiled wanly and patted his cheek. "Close your mouth when you chew, Adam. You are most unattractive."

Adam snapped his mouth shut. He knew the tide had inexplicably turned.

So we made a temporary peace.

* * *

"It is probably unwise," Dave observed as he sipped on a Jack and Coke, "to let criminals go free because your daughter is dead."

It was Tuesday night, and we were defiantly hunched on the deck in scarves and down jackets, sipping a night cap outdoors because the thermometer had bounced up to 60 that afternoon and we had declared the arrival of spring, night temperatures be damned. I had the evening off, but Adam did not, which was why Dave and I had the dark and chilly deck to ourselves.

"You talked to Adam," I said, still marginally lucid. I was on my second drink, and the edges were blurring, but I could carry on an intelligent conversation.

Well, intelligent in *my* mind.

"We often talk," Dave admitted.

"About cop stuff?" I asked.

"Unfortunately," Dave said, and sipped some Jack. Dave's views leaned precipitously to the left, and though that didn't prevent him from *sleeping* with a cop, it did make the idea of *fathering* a cop as distasteful to him as the thought of fathering a Republican. When Adam had landed on our front porch three years earlier after dropping out of a West Coast school, Dave had fantasized about steering his son into a profession that would lift up the downtrodden masses. He had been forced instead to foot the tuition for a degree in criminal justice, which in Dave's mind equaled criminal persecution (present company excepted). There had been many arguments at the dinner table over Adam's career choice, and many nights when I had stomped off to bed, angry and bruised by Dave's caustic (but generally accurate) view of my police brethren. But Dave had had the wisdom to avoid crossing the line between engaging in vigorous debate and issuing ultimatums to his son. Adam had doggedly pursued his badge, and since it was the first time the boy had ever disciplined himself to reach a goal, Dave had stoically kept most of his angst to himself (and me).

But he still had wistful dreams that someday Adam would realize the error of his ways and use his education to further the rights of his fellow man.

Dave had no such wistful fantasies about me. I was a lost cause.

But as the old saying goes, I can suck the chrome off a trailer hitch.

And Dave happily knows it.

"So," I said, staring up at the stars, "Adam thinks I'm trying to wash him out to make you happy?"

"He did," Dave agreed. "But I disabused him of the notion."

"That was very noble of you," I said.

Dave leaned over and patted my hand. "Anything for my honey."

I smiled sloppily into my drink. It was good to know he had his priorities straight.

"But you probably shouldn't let a drunk go free because of Elizabeth," Dave said to the clouds swirling around the moon.

I would have bristled at such a suggestion from anyone else. But Dave has held me tight through too many flaming nightmares, and he more than anyone else but Mother knows how much the death of my daughter colors my judgment. She has been dead fifteen years now, but her eyes – and the fact that I wasn't home to save her – still haunt me.

I am not haunted by the death of my husband. He killed our baby. I sincerely hope he is tormented by everlasting flames.

A counselor once told me I needed to purge my soul of such thoughts and forgive him.

Dave strongly encouraged me to drop the counselor.

So I knew Dave was in my corner. And I could lower my defenses and safely ask whether he thought I'd blown it with Louie Brandon.

Dave carefully topped off his glass with the last of the Jack. He was several drinks ahead of me, and at our age, that meant there was no sex in our immediate future. So he didn't need to couch his answer in terms that would shuck me out of my jeans.

"Louie Brandon?" Dave said. "He's an inconsequential drunk. Other than pissing Adam off, it's no big deal whether the guy walks."

"Pissing Adam off is no big deal?" I countered.

Dave's smile was lopsided but endearing. "Boy's gotta learn he won't always get his way."

"So you have my back?" I asked.

"Indubitably," Dave said – or something like that.

I relaxed over my own drink.

"But I worry," Dave said, picking at the edges of my satisfaction. "Letting a drunk off 'cuz his dad died in a fire is one thing. But letting really bad guys go free because of your daughter is something else."

I chomped down hard on the edge of my glass. Fortunately, it did not shatter. "I don't do that," I protested.

Dave looked at me with liquid eyes. He really was quite drunk. "Are you sure?" he asked.

My brain stumbled over recent cases – some of which were petty and some of which were fatal – and I couldn't think of anyone but Louie Brandon who had been helped or hindered by the fact that I had lost a daughter to fire. Her death had nearly unhinged me, but it had been many years ago. I felt fairly confident – with a good bit of alcohol to sustain me – telling Dave that Elizabeth rarely came into play on the job.

"You're sure?" Dave asked, and he drained his glass as he waited for my answer.

My mind hopscotched over my history (after so many years on the force, there were many arrests in my past) but only Louie Brandon stood out as someone I had turned loose because of our shared loss. Even mildly drunk, I acknowledged that my daughter's death had probably played a subconscious role in my decisions ever since the fire. But Brandon was the only defendant I'd ever sprung specifically because he had lost someone to a fire.

The decision was so novel for me, I was absolutely positive as I swore to Dave that Brandon was the one and only.

"Well," Dave said as he capped the bottle of Jack and made moves to decamp, "as long as you don't make a habit of it."

I leered and clumsily groped his thigh. "There's only one thing I make a habit," I said, and gave him a come-hither look.

Dave dislodged my hand from his nether regions. "In your dreams," he said regretfully.

And we retired to the bedroom, where we curled up with an assortment of pillows and chastely snored through the night.

CHAPTER SIX

It was a sunny day in May, and the 10-year-old blond girl was mad. Her best friends from school were all meeting downtown to see *The Absent Minded Professor,* but she wasn't allowed to go. She had to stay home instead to watch her brothers while her mother took the new baby to the doctor for some silly shots, and it just wasn't *fair.* Her *dad* could've watched the boys. He wasn't going to work lately because of something called a strike, so he was home all the time. *He* could've made the little brats behave while she huddled in the dark with her friends and gorged herself on popcorn. But noooooooo. *He* was too busy climbing ladders and digging through the gutters, trying to stop the leak that had sprung up in the dining room ceiling. *He* couldn't be bothered with the *kids.*

So the little girl fumed and swatted her brothers on the head as soon as her mother drove away with the baby and the coast was clear.

Her brothers wanted to play tag, which was no fun at all 'cuz she was bigger and could always catch them, no problem. But there was nothing good to watch on TV and no potato chips in the cupboard to steal and no friends of her own to play with 'cuz they were all at the movie, and besides, the weather was so warm, she was itching to go outside, so even though today she really hated the little monsters who lived in her house, she said okay, one game of tag, and she even let them run out the back door ahead of her ’cuz at least that would stretch the game out a little longer.

One brother dashed behind the garage, but there were spiders back there, so she didn’t chase *him*. The other boy tore around the corner of the house, out toward the street, and since that was where freedom lay, she raced after him.

He scurried around the back of the house, giggling because he thought he could get away from his big sister. Like a cat, she toyed with him, slowing her pace enough to let the confidence well up in his chest. He was only 4 years old. This wasn’t even a contest.

She let him slip around the corner ahead of her, counted to three, then barreled after him, propelled by thoughts of how she’d grab him by the collar and triumphantly make him IT. The little snot would never be able to tag her back.

She slid around the corner, and there was the ladder, leaning precariously against the house, and her father, the bum, perched on the upper rungs as he dipped his gloved hands into the muck of the gutters.

She didn’t even stop to think about it. She was suddenly so consumed with rage that he was placidly executing his stupid chores while *she* was forced to baby-sit her brothers instead of going downtown to the theater that she simply slammed her shoulder into the ladder and bounced off toward the rose bushes.

There was a squawk of surprise from the roof line as the ladder shuddered, and then almost in slow motion, the ladder slid along the gutter as her father windmilled against the nothingness of spring air. Then the ladder crashed to the ground, and her father sailed across the bright blue sky and landed with a sickening thud in the grass.

Her world telescoped to three square yards of ladder and grass and her dad, splayed across the aluminum rungs, with one leg twisted at a painfully odd angle, and his head solidly planted in the ground.

"Oh!" she breathed, and a tingle of fear crept up her spine. What had she done?

Her brother, drawn by the mighty sound of the crash, peeked around the corner of the house, and his eyes grew wide. "Daddy?" he said. And his face twisted between the mischief of tag and the inexplicable sight of his father sprawled in the grass.

The little girl sucked in her breath and tiptoed to her father.

His eyelids weren't quite closed, but his warm brown eyes were gone. She saw nothing but white beneath the lids. And a tiny stream of blood trickled from the corner of his mouth. Her dad, who could bounce back from *anything* when they wrestled with him in the living room, lay motionless in the yard.

Her brother scooted up to her side. "What's wrong with Daddy?" he asked.

"Nothing," she said, and angrily nudged her father's ribs with the toe of her tennis shoe. "He's foolin'."

Only her father didn't budge.

She wasn't even sure he breathed.

The 6-year-old crawled out from behind the garage. His eyes were saucers of fright. "Is Daddy hurt?" he asked, and his voice quivered.

The 4-year-old clung to her leg and started to cry.

The 6-year-old cried, too.

Panic clogged her throat. What should she do? What should she *do*? She was all alone with two crying babies, and her father looked *really* bad. She must have killed him.

Well, it wasn't her fault, a little voice chimed in her head. It was *his* fault.

True, she thought, but what would she tell her mother? And had her brothers seen what she had done?

Oh, boy, she was in a jam. Bigger than anything she'd ever done before.

But before her world could collapse, a lesson popped into her head. A safety class at school that had been very boring, because everyone knew emergencies never happened to anyone but on TV. But there had been film strips and songs and slogans, and copies of a cartoon poster that everyone got to take home. Her mom had taped it onto the refrigerator door, and filled in the blanks with emergency telephone numbers.

'Cuz if anyone got hurt, she was supposed to ...

CALL THE POLICE!!!!

The little girl shoved her brothers off her legs and tore into the kitchen, grabbed the telephone and stretched the cord all the way to the refrigerator. Her mind was suddenly crystal clear, and her fingers didn't fumble once as she dialed the number her mother had written in bold Magic Marker. She knew *exactly* what to do.

When the operator answered on the third ring, the little girl's voice was breathless but her words were explicit. "My daddy's hurt. He fell and hit his head." And without being asked, she recited the address – twice.

The operator prevaricated. "Is there an adult to help you?" she asked. "Your mother? A neighbor?"

"No," the little girl said firmly. "My dad needs help *now*." And her tone of voice was so definite, the operator promised to send someone right away.

The little girl stayed on the line to spell her name and repeat her phone number, just like she'd been taught to do. Her brothers had followed her into the kitchen and were sniveling around the phone, but she shushed them and calmly answered the operator's questions.

Soon, she heard sirens squealing up the street. "I gotta go now," she told the operator, and slammed down the receiver.

By the time the firetruck howled to the curb, she was standing on the sidewalk, ready to lead the firemen to the back yard and her dad.

He was still lying motionless where he had fallen, and he was very pale and his lips were blue. The little girl stood back and wisely let the firemen have their way. She grabbed her brothers and held them hard by the shoulders so they wouldn't get in the way. And that was how the neighbor lady, alerted by the sirens, found the kids and took charge. A great weight lifted off the little girl's shoulders. She had done all she could do, the neighbor assured her. Now it was up to God.

And he must've liked her dad, 'cuz the firemen hustled him to the hospital and he didn't die after all. He had a broken leg and a terrible bump on his head, and little blood vessels had leaked into his brain so that his balance was never quite the same, although he did go back to work after the strike was over. However, he never again climbed up to the roof to clean out the gutters.

The little girl waited in some trepidation for him to come home from the hospital and yell at her for knocking over the ladder. She was *pretty* sure she could convince him it was an accident 'cuz, after all, she was just a *kid*, and no one could think a *kid* would do such a nasty thing on *purpose*.

But she never had to defend herself. As she waited nervously in the driveway, her dad crawled out of the car, his leg in a cast and his head bruised and bald where the doctors had shaved it for the stitches, and the very first thing he did was awkwardly spread his arms. "My little heroine!" he said happily. "My little girl saved my life! Come give your dad a hug!"

She couldn't *believe* her good fortune. Not only was her crime a secret, but her dad thought *she* had saved the day. And in relief, she flung herself at her father and cried hysterically as he wrapped his arms around her.

The family made a great fuss. She was toasted and praised by all the relatives, and got a telephone extension *all her own* for her bedroom because she had proven how level-headed and trustworthy she was by saving her dad.

Other family members eventually forgot her heroics, but her dad never did. He was fond of reminiscing at family dinners about the day his daughter saved his life.

"Oh, Dad," she'd say, and blush. "It was nothing."

But it was a very big something indeed.

Because the little girl learned, if she worked it right, she could make bad things happen and still be a hero.

CHAPTER SEVEN

Some folks just don't have any luck.

Or they're criminally stupid.

Or a little bit of both.

The week after I endangered my relationship with Adam by springing Louie Brandon, Adam and Quinlan caught a traffic accident downtown. Quinlan grimaced when Herchek nailed them for the call. It was half an hour to shift change, and the paperwork alone would run them into overtime. That would normally be a good thing, because Quinlan couldn't keep it in his pants and there was another baby on the way. A paycheck padded with overtime was a cause for celebration in his household these days.

But it was also a new month, and since the three of us had rotated from nights to the day shift, Quinlan had been hoping for a little happy hour at the Farmhouse before settling in for an evening of dirty diapers and his wife's nausea. So his dismay over a traffic accident that didn't even promise mangled body parts as a diversion was understandable.

Adam was ecstatic over the possibilities. It had been a slow shift and there had been nothing but routine patrols to occupy their hours on the clock. Even the student bars had been relatively tame, biding their time until the last classes were dismissed and the hordes descended downtown.

So Adam was chomping to take the call, and Quinlan obligingly tossed him the keys to the cruiser. The siren was wailing before they even cleared the parking lot.

Herchek winced as Adam burned rubber. “Boy needs a good case,” he said, digging a pinkie into his ear in a vain attempt to restore his hearing.

“Boy needs to grow up first,” I said pointedly. I’d just wrapped up a string of assaults at the Laundromat and was trying to clear the paperwork in time to meet Dave for a rare dinner sans Mother.

“Well, there’s your problem,” Herchek said as he shook his head, hoping to dislodge decades of ear wax and other debris. “You still think of him as a boy, not a cop.”

“*You’re* the one who called him a boy,” I replied tartly.

“Jo,” Herchek sighed, “everyone’s a boy compared to me,” and his bones literally creaked as he settled himself back at the public service counter.

I guiltily watched him from my desk. Herchek was as old as dirt. He could have run off with his pension years ago and lived quite moderately in a warmer climate where he wouldn’t be required to let drunks barf on his shoes and outraged citizens berate him with their complaints. He could have been a jolly granddad bouncing babies on his knee and regaling timid daughters-in-law with horrific stories of real crime. But instead he ran the squad room, juggling hot dog detectives like Jamal and Henry with brash uniforms like Quinlan and woefully untested rookies like Adam, and somehow he made it all work so every call was covered with a minimum of delay and a maximum of professional courtesy. Watching Herchek orchestrate the patrols during finals week was akin to watching a maestro conduct a symphony. Herchek always knew when to cue in the brass.

But his hair was white and his hands were nearly crippled with arthritis, and I feared the day was not too far off when his desire to protect and serve would simply run out.

We'd be in a world of hurt when that happened.

But it wasn't going to happen *today*, so I refocused on my computer screen, and Herchek amused himself with the afternoon newspaper spread out on the counter and we let the chatter from the dispatcher waft comfortably over us. There were no dead people on either of our plates. Life was good.

Which was why I jumped when my cell phone buzzed in my pocket.

Few people have my number. Just Bradley, because he's the boss, and Mother, because her bones are fragile, and Dave, because he likes to breathe heavily in my ear when he's feeling frisky, and Adam, because he's a rookie and I've pounded it into his head that if he's ever in trouble, I'm the first person he should call, before even Herchek.

So, except for Dave's raunchy appetites, there was no good reason for my cell phone to be ringing, and I flipped it open with some trepidation.

It was Adam, and my blood pressure burst up into my ears at the sound of his voice. I suddenly had visions of him hiding behind his cruiser as drug dealers sprayed him with shotgun pellets, and there was no way I'd *ever* be able to explain that away to Dave.

But, no, Adam was in full possession of his body parts. The traffic call he and Quinlan had answered was just a fender-bender, and no one was visibly injured, although tempers among the three drivers were hot.

"So what's the problem?" I snapped. Now that I knew he wasn't under fire, I was irritated by the interruption.

"No problem," Adam assured me, "but I thought, given your history, you might want to be in on this." And his tone of voice was suddenly too agreeable, like a teenager who's about to stick it to his parents.

"What history?" I demanded, and I had a queasy vision of Mother causing a three-car pileup. I'd *never* live that down.

But Mother wasn't anywhere near this accident scene.

It was worse.

One of the drivers was Louie Brandon.

I groaned – and Adam almost chortled over the phone.

"Don't let him leave," I instructed.

"He's in the cruiser," Adam said.

"And don't brain him before I get there," I said sternly.

"The thought never crossed my mind," Adam said.

But we both knew he was lying.

* * *

The accident was at an intersection on Main Street, a few blocks north of the center of town. One oblivious driver had started a left turn, and an oncoming car had clipped his back end, driving him into a third car waiting obediently at the cross street. By the time I arrived, all three cars had been pushed to the side and traffic was muddling slowly through the intersection, but bits of chrome and glass littered the road, and I clenched my teeth as I inched through the debris to the curb. New tires were *not* in my budget.

Two red-faced men were waving their arms and spitting at Quinlan in indignation. Adam was leaning against the cruiser, prepared to leap in if anyone crossed the line. Fat chance. Quinlan is all muscle. *No* one was going to ruin his day.

"Run it down for me," I said as I joined Adam at the cruiser.

He kept his eyes on Quinlan, like a good backup should. He was primed, but had the sense not to wade in and tip the delicate balance between Quinlan and the bad guys. "The gray-haired jerk was making the left turn," Adam said. "The other guy hit him. They disagree as to who's at fault."

"Quinlan outweighs them both," I said. "I'm sure he'll sort it out."

"Kinda fun to watch, though," Adam said, and the smile twitching his lips was a hundred percent cop. He was itching for an excuse to help out his partner. Short of that, he'd settle for a good story to tell back at the station.

"And Brandon?" I asked.

Adam jerked his thumb at the cruiser without looking away from Quinlan. "He's the innocent third party. Just minding his business waiting for the light, and his car gets totaled."

We watched Quinlan stiff-arm one of the drivers, who was lunging. The driver staggered back and fumed. His opponent smirked, but Quinlan gave him a look that dared him to ratchet things up a notch.

The opponent declined.

Adam and I chuckled softly. Quinlan hadn't even broken a sweat. He really was the heir apparent to Henry.

As much as I was enjoying Quinlan's performance, Louie Brandon sulking in the cruiser was my prime objective. I diplomatically asked Adam whether he'd mind if I had a word with the man.

Adam shrugged elaborately. "It's why I called you." And his voice was so perfectly nonchalant, I knew it was killing him.

"Good call," I said, and reached for the door handle.

"You want me to sit in?" he asked.

"You're Quinlan's backup," I said. "Don't let him pull a Henry."

Adam almost smiled. He'd *love* it if Quinlan popped and escalated the situation. So as much as Louie Brandon rankled his soul, he let me slide into the cruiser alone.

In the cop world, I'd owe him.

I took the passenger seat in front.

Brandon was bristling in the back, safely caged.

He should have been merely agitated. His car was a wreck, but he was clearly an innocent victim. No one was holding *him* at fault for the accident. Once Quinlan and Adam wrote up the report, he'd have a free ticket to his insurance agent. No points on his license and a new car in his future. He should have been calmer.

But as soon as he recognized me, he was ragging. “What the fuck am I doin’ in this cruiser? I didn’t do nothin’!” And despite the tone, his voice was free of alcohol fog and fumes.

“You’re here,” I said equably, “precisely because you aren’t at fault.”

Brandon shook his head. “That makes no sense, lady.”

“Look at those guys,” I said calmly, pointing through the windshield at the culpable drivers. “They’re hot and they’re ready to punch someone out. You want no part of that.”

Brandon squared his shoulders. “I can handle *them*.”

“I’m sure you can,” I said, “especially since you’ve got twenty years on both of them. But you mix it up with them, you go from victim to perpetrator.”

“They totaled my car!” Brandon protested.

“And so far, the fault is all theirs,” I said. “Let’s keep it that way.”

Brandon fumed in the rearview mirror. He had cleaned up nicely since the last time I’d seen him, and the righteous anger in his eyes gave a dangerous edge to his tough good looks. I didn’t think he was the type who smiled gently in bed. I knew younger ladies who wouldn’t mind.

Brandon decided to calm himself with a smoke and pulled a pack out of his pocket.

“Uh-uh,” I said, almost like a schoolmarm. “Not in the cruiser.”

“Am I under arrest?” he challenged me.

“Not yet,” I said evenly.

“Then screw you,” he said, and promptly lit up.

I sighed. The boy had no manners. Why in God’s name was I bothering with him?

The smoke from the cigarette was a sharp reminder, and I held my peace.

Eventually the tow trucks showed up. Brandon groaned as he exhaled. “This is gonna cost me my job,” he said, as though – despite his rudeness – I should care.

“I’ll write you a tardy slip for your boss,” I said.

Brandon snorted. “It isn’t just *today*, lady. We got only one car.”

“And the insurance company will replace it,” I said reasonably.

“In *months*,” Brandon said as he flicked his butt out the back window. “What are we supposed to do in the meantime? I got to get to *work*. My *lady’s* got to get to work. And the *kids* gotta get to day care and the doctor’s. We supposed to walk them across town to the doctor’s and the drugstore?”

“There are such things as taxis,” I pointed out.

“You pay for one lately?” he countered. “That’s a week’s worth of formula.”

“Or buses,” I reminded him.

“Only if you’re a university student – which I’m *not*.” I couldn’t tell whether he was proud of the fact or resentful. Maybe a little of both.

“Okay,” I agreed, “life sucks without a car, but you can walk.”

“You try carrying two kids,” he huffed.

I’d collapse within half a block, but I was twenty years older and not quite as trim. His excuses were beginning to irritate me.

Maybe I just needed to scrape him out of my life and find a new dental hygienist.

We watched in blessed silence as the tow truck drivers attached their chains to the mangled cars. Maybe Brandon was rationally plotting out ways to schedule transportation until the insurance check arrived. Maybe he was realizing that if he’d stopped a foot closer to the intersection, he might be as dead as his car. Maybe he was vowing to live a good and pious life here on after.

Or maybe he was just thinking of blowing the milk money on a shot and a beer.

Adam popped open the driver's door and slid in without a word to me. He swiveled his head to Brandon and said, "They're taking your car to Eddie's shop down on South Main. He won't be able to fix it, but he might take it off your hands for the parts."

Brandon just grunted.

Adam kept his tone neutral, and only I saw the twitch in his left eyebrow. It was killing him to be civil. "You sign the statement you gave us and you're on your way." And he passed his clipboard over the seat.

Maybe Adam was distracted by thoughts of Emily. Maybe he was nervous with me in the cruiser. Whatever – he misjudged the distance and the clipboard popped into Brandon's knee and cartwheeled to the floor.

"What the fuck?" Brandon squawked as he grabbed his knee.

Adam instantly raised his hands in apology. "My fault, man. I'm really sorry."

I rolled my eyes.

"You *oughta* be sorry," Brandon growled. "Damn near took my *knee* off."

"I'll call the paramedics," Adam immediately offered.

"And sit here another hour? No fucking way," Brandon said, and he fished the clipboard off the floor. He scribbled his signature and leaned forward to pass the clipboard back to Adam. It would have rammed Adam behind the ear, but he'd seen it coming in the rearview mirror and jerked out of the way. The clipboard sideswiped the head rest instead and tumbled onto the console.

"I am *so* sorry," Brandon said.

Adam ground his teeth and stared steadfastly out the windshield, his neck muscles red and bulging against his collar.

"Christ," I muttered, and plucked the clipboard off the console.

"May I go now?" Brandon asked acidly. "I'm late for work."

I waved him out of the cruiser. He bolted without wishing us a good evening and raced down the sidewalk. Tardiness must have been a serious issue with his boss.

Provoking a witness was a serious issue with me, so I blistered Adam's ears for playing games with Brandon. Adam took it silently because he knew better, and I didn't soften it for the sake of home peace because I knew better, and then I slipped out of the cruiser, nodded to Quinlan to let him know I was out of his hair, and trotted to my car. If I hurried, I could grab a shower before dinner and up the odds of a big fat dessert from Dave.

Main Street was getting jammed with townspeople fleeing before the students swarmed downtown, so I turned onto a side street that went in the general direction of home. A block away from Main, I spotted Brandon hustling around dawdlers on the sidewalk, his face red with exertion. He was obviously busting his butt to get to work, and that made me feel a little guilty for keeping him in the cruiser so long. So even though he could have done some serious damage to Adam's head with the clipboard, I pulled to the curb just ahead of him and rolled down the window.

"Need a lift?" I called to him.

His head jerked to the street at the sound of my voice, and for an instant there was a look of hope on his face. Then he recognized me and scowled.

"No way I'm showing up at work in a cop car," he said. "I got enough trouble."

"Does this look like a cop car?" I asked, waving at the dents and dirt on my 10-year-old hatchback.

Brandon put his hands on his hips as he surveyed my ride.

"It *is* pretty crappy," he agreed.

My face soured.

"But you owe me," he decided.

And before I could retract the offer, he yanked open the door and folded himself into the front seat. "Jesus," he growled, "you got a family of pygmies or what?"

Louie Brandon had not inherited his mother's keen sense of customer service. But I kept my mouth shut, knuckles white on the steering wheel, as I pulled away from the curb. If good deeds were easy, cops would be superfluous.

Brandon worked at a video store out by campus. I knew my town and how to get around it, but I valiantly let him dictate directions. And I didn't bitch when he lit up another cigarette. I had been hooked once and remembered the god-awful need. But when he reached forward to change radio stations, I automatically slapped his hand away.

"What the fuck?" he sputtered.

"My car, my music," I said crisply.

"That's putrid," he protested.

I silently prayed to the gods of the British Invasion to forgive him.

"Christ, don't you even have a police radio? At least *that* might be interesting."

I pointed to the extra dials and gizmos on the dashboard.

"Well, turn it *on*," he prodded.

"I am officially off duty," I said primly. "I don't *want* to know what's going on."

"Aw, c'mon," he said, and he was suddenly like an eager kid, earnest and pleading to play with the new toy. Years dropped from his face as he lost the sullen attitude, and I got a glimpse of why his mother might love him.

I sighed. "Flick your butt out the window first," I sternly directed.

The cigarette sailed to the pavement in a rain of glowing ash. Brandon smiled at me like a perfectly obedient little boy.

So I flipped the switch and the car was immediately flooded with the chatter that had become the background noise of my life. The dispatcher was juggling afternoon traffic calls with a skirmish in the high school parking lot. Nothing really tense, but Brandon sat mesmerized and didn't notice that I was taking the scenic route to his job. If I was going to be his reluctant guardian angel, I needed to see a few more sides of his personality.

Henry's unmistakable voice rattled the air waves.

"Code 7?" Brandon repeated after him, his brow furrowed. "What's that? A robbery?"

I chuckled. "Out of service," I said. "Officer on a lunch break."

"You can do that?" Brandon asked, truly incredulous. "Stop everything and eat?"

"We get lunch breaks like everyone else," I said.

"Hmph!" Brandon sniffed, just like a taxpayer.

Adam barked over the radio with a Code 12.

Brandon recognized his voice and stiffened. "What the hell is *he* doing? Talking about me?"

"Maybe," I said blandly. "Code 12 means returning to the station. Probably to write up your accident report."

"He better get it right," Brandon said, threatening to slip back into sullen.

"You're in the clear," I reminded him. "Don't sweat it."

"Easy for you to say," he snorted. "You *got* a ride." Then he scanned my interior. "Such as it is."

I pondered defending the honor of my car, but there was a new burst of traffic over the radio and Brandon tuned into the perceptibly more somber tone. "Code 10," he repeated. "What's a 10?"

I sighed. "Coroner's case," I reluctantly admitted.

Brandon's eyes widened. "Oh, man, there's a body? Whaddya think? A shooting? A stabbing? Should we *go* there?"

"Probably not necessary," I said as I signaled the turn into his video store. "Not at that address."

"What's wrong with the address? You scared to go there or something?"

"The address is perfectly respectable," I said as I blithely stopped the car in a no-parking zone. "It's a nursing home. It's not unusual for people to die at a nursing home."

"Gotcha," Brandon said, nodding. "Good to know so you don't waste your time."

"Speaking of – " I said, tapping my watch. "Aren't you late?"

"Aw, fuck," Brandon groaned as he was abruptly wrenched back into his world. He kicked open the passenger door – I couldn't reprimand him because most of my passengers had to kick it – and hit the pavement. He did remember to slam the door shut behind him, but he didn't look back or say anything to me. By the time he slipped into the video store, he had effectively transformed himself from pain in the ass to contrite employee.

I doubted his boss would buy it.

CHAPTER EIGHT

Adam and I didn't cross paths again until breakfast the next morning. By then, he had conveniently forgotten the little matter of provoking a witness and was more interested in provoking me. The entire household – Emily in barely there pajamas, Mother in wig and robe, Adam in uniform and Dave and I in jeans – had managed to hit the breakfast table at the same time, and there was a noisy scramble for toast and pancakes and sausage as crumbs flew across the kitchen into Barney's mouth. Emily handed out juice and I poured coffee as everyone kept an eye on the clock. Adam and I had twenty-two minutes to shift change, and there wasn't time for a blowup.

So I was irritated when he started describing to Emily how the department turned around the need to baby-sit Louie Brandon.

"I beg your pardon?" I said as icily as I could through a mouthful of toast.

"Hey," Adam said, raising greasy fingers in surrender, "the whole squad knows to look out for Louie." And the look he gave me was probably the same mask of innocence he had used to bedevil his real mother.

"The uniforms have *not* been told to let that boy skate," I huffed. Barney tucked his tail between his legs and slinked to Emily's side of the table.

"Don't have to be *told*," Adam said as he rolled a pancake around a sausage and lifted it to his mouth. "They *know*."

"If I recall," I reminded him, waving a syrupy fork over the table, "*you're* the one who called *me* about his accident."

"Like I had a choice," Adam said, and bit aggressively into his pancake.

Emily hunched over Barney, out of the line of fire.

Dave reluctantly lowered his newspaper and looked at Mother. "Am I missing something here?"

"Apparently," Mother said drily.

Adam snorted through his sausage. Barney automatically lifted his snout and caught a greasy morsel before it could land on Adam's uniform. The dog is very agile for his size.

Mother looked at me. "What has that poor Brandon boy done now?"

"Nothing," I said firmly. "He was an innocent victim of a car accident."

Adam gagged over the word "innocent."

Mother was horrified. "Was he hurt?"

"No – miraculously," I added for Adam's benefit.

Mother asked for details. Dave grew bored and went back to his newspaper. Emily bumped Adam's shoulder with a well-rounded hip as she rose from the table to pack his lunch and he was properly distracted. The conversation de-escalated to just Mother and me.

Mother shook her head as I described the destruction of Brandon's car and the shaky state of his job without reliable transportation. "What will his family do?" she muttered as she wandered to the counter for seconds on coffee.

I thought that ended the discussion and shoveled the rest of my pancake into my mouth. We had seventeen minutes to shift change and Adam was vacuuming his plate clean.

Two minutes later, I was packing my purse with gun and badge and Adam was surreptitiously wiping his hands on Emily's butt when Mother asked whether it would help if someone loaned Brandon a car.

"Someone?" I asked suspiciously.

"Well," Mother said, blushing slightly, "me, actually."

"Aw geez," Adam moaned into Emily's shoulder.

"It wouldn't be a long-term loan," Mother said. "He *will* be compensated by the insurance company, won't he?"

"Absolutely," I said. "He wasn't at fault."

"Well, we could get by for a couple of weeks without my car, couldn't we? I could ride to class with Dave or Emily, and you could run me on my errands, and we'd manage, wouldn't we?"

Dave and I exchanged quick looks, barely on this side of ecstatic. Since Mother had broken her hip the year before, her driving had slowly but surely deteriorated. She just wasn't as *flexible* anymore. But gentle hints that perhaps she should hang up her keys had been met with strident retorts that we should mind our own business. Mother was fiercely independent, and her car was a proud symbol of her ability to take care of herself.

So I gulped, afraid that if I responded too joyously, Mother would renege.

But Dave sighed with just the right measure of doubt. "Of course, we'd manage, Ruth, but do you really want to give your car to someone with his record?"

Behind Mother's back, Adam gave his father a thumbs-up.

But Mother's resolve was growing in the face of Dave's mild opposition. "If people had given the boy a hand sooner, maybe he wouldn't *have* such a record."

"For Christ's sake," Adam muttered.

Mother flashed her displeasure at Adam. "Not all young men have had the advantages you've enjoyed, Adam. It is our *responsibility* to help those in need."

"Yes, ma'am," Adam said. He always knows precisely when to back down from Mother.

"It's settled then," Mother said crisply. "Jo can inform Mr. Brandon. I'll clean out the car."

And that was how Mother lost her wheels.

CHAPTER NINE

Mother and I delivered her middle-aged Golf to Louie Brandon on my lunch break. She had defiantly turned down Emily's offer to drive, and for one last time (I hoped) got behind the wheel to follow me to Brandon's duplex. It was only six blocks from our house, but it felt like miles. I could just imagine Mother ramming through a parade of schoolchildren on her final joy ride.

But we made it to Brandon's street unscathed, and Mother pulled sedately into the driveway. I parked at the curb and escorted Mother to the front porch to hand over the keys.

The duplex was well-worn shingle that could have used a coat of paint. The porch was tiny, with a thin banister down the middle to separate the occupants. Brandon's side was clogged with scuffed toys; the neighbor's side featured a leaking garbage bag. Mother's lips tightened in disapproval.

I had expected Brandon to answer my knock. He had been insistent when I called to offer him the car that he needed it by two o'clock to get to work on time. He had also eventually remembered to thank me, but the tight time frame had dominated his half of the conversation, as though one more late arrival really would cost him his job.

So I was startled when the door was opened by a very young woman still padded by the weight of her last pregnancy. An infant only a few months old was burping half-heartedly on her shoulder and a toddler with jelly-smeared cheeks was hiding behind her legs, peering around them tentatively at Mother and me. A cartoon show squawked on the television behind them, and deeper in the house, there was a blast of Nirvana.

"Oh, gosh," she bubbled, just like Emily, "are you the ladies with the car?"

"We are," Mother said proudly. "I'm Ruth Ferris, and this is my daughter, Jo."

"Awesome," she said, shifting the baby to her other shoulder so she could shake Mother's hand. "Which one of you is the cop?"

I think my jaw dropped. I'm sure Mother's did. She cleans up nicely, and quite a few gentlemen of Medicare age think she's one hot dame, but for heaven's sake, mistaking Mother for a *cop*? In her dreams.

I officiously pointed to the ID hanging from my belt loop, just to set the record straight. The young woman giggled. "Oh, *duuuhhhh*," she said, and slapped her forehead. The baby jiggled precariously.

Mother sucked in her breath, but refrained from grabbing the child.

"Lou!" the woman called over her shoulder. "Louie, the car's here!"

There was a grumble from the back of the house. Or maybe it was just the band.

The woman rolled her eyes, then planted her hand on the toddler's head and steered him out the door. "Let's go look at our new car!"

Mother flinched slightly at her abrupt loss of ownership but bravely smiled.

We all trooped off the porch to the driveway.

"I'm Jenny," the woman said as we walked. "This is Tyler – " and she patted the baby's bottom – "and that's Jason and – oh, my God, what a beautiful car!"

Mother's car has always commanded prime parking space in the garage, so it didn't show the usual wear of Midwest winters. And, frankly, daily trips to campus don't rack up that many miles. So the Golf looked smashing as it sat in the sunny driveway, even if it was a little boxy for my tastes.

Jenny was circling it in growing excitement, trying every door and flipping open the hatchback. Jason put his sticky hands on the bumper and tried to crawl in. Jenny laughed, hauled him up by his training pants and hoisted him into the back. He rolled around and squealed in pleasure.

"I think they like the car," I said drily.

"I sincerely hope they understand the use of seat belts," Mother said as Jason somersaulted into the back seat. Jenny slipped into the front with the baby and began poking at the dials and latches.

"Having second thoughts?" I asked and nudged Mother with my elbow.

"Absolutely not," she huffed. "It's the right thing to do."

But the look she gave the Golf was wistful.

I swiftly hugged her while Jenny wasn't looking. "It's just for a couple weeks," I said, mentally crossing my fingers.

Mother just nodded.

"You got the keys?" Brandon asked abruptly behind us.

I jumped – startled, then irritated that a man half my age had crept up on us. I had obviously left my cop instincts parked on the street.

Brandon was grinning – like he knew exactly what he had done and was enjoying it.

But it looked as though he had put a little effort into his appearance to take possession of the car. His hair was still damp from the shower and neatly combed into place, the jeans and flannel had been replaced by khakis and a freshly laundered polo shirt, and a faint cloud of Listerine hung over his head.

Or maybe he just had a girlfriend on the side. He had those kind of eyes.

I introduced Mother, and she dangled the keys over Brandon's outstretched palm. "Are you familiar with Volkswagens?"

Brandon's devilish grin became a nostalgic smile. "My big brother had an old Beetle – it was the first car I ever drove."

"Really?" Mother said, warming up to him.

"Flaming orange," Brandon said, nodding at the memory. "Used to stick a little between second and third, but if you coaxed real nice, she'd pop right into gear. I loved that car."

"Well, then," Mother said as she closed his fingers around the keys, "I think you'll find the Golf quite *adequate*." And she launched into the car's maintenance history in such detail that all of our eyes glazed over.

But Brandon kept that smile carefully stitched in place as they inspected the car, Mother noting every ding and Brandon acknowledging it. If he thought he had a license to beat the hell out of Mother's car, he was sadly mistaken. Mother had two cops in the house to enforce her ownership rights, and one of them was just dying for an excuse to beat the crap out of Brandon.

Mother was assuring Brandon that the tank was full – minus the splash or two she had used up driving six blocks. Brandon looked ostentatiously at his watch and his eyes widened. "Oh, man, I really gotta go, Ms. Ferris. You know – my boss."

"I understand, dear," Mother said. "You're a working man. Go!"

Brandon hastily shooed Jenny and the kids out of the car, jiggled the rearview mirror and the seat till they were both to his liking, pumped the gas and shot out of the driveway.

Mother swallowed hard.

Brandon smiled broadly, honked the horn, making Jason and the baby squeal, and the Golf was gone.

"Well," Mother said stoically, "he appears to have the hang of it, don't you think?"

I snorted.

"Oh, gosh," Jenny said as she tried to quiet the baby, "he forgot to thank you, didn't he?" And she blushed prettily in embarrassment.

"I'm sure he meant to," Mother said generously.

"He just gets caught up in things," Jenny said, busily bouncing the baby on her shoulder, "he forgets his manners. But honest, he's so grateful to have the car – we all are – he'll take really good care of it."

Mother patted her arm. "Of course, he will."

I cleared my throat and tapped my own watch. I was still on the clock. Mother got the message and disengaged from Jenny, who continued to chatter her own thanks as we walked to the street and climbed into my car.

We were silent as I drove toward home to drop Mother off. I was relieved to have her out of the driver's seat, if only for a while, and she was adjusting to the view from the passenger's side. It had been extremely generous of Mother to give up her own car to help Brandon and his family out of a jam, and for my own selfish reasons, I hadn't uttered a word to dissuade her, so my conscience was nagging at me.

"You know," I finally said as I turned onto our street, "Louie Brandon is an only child."

Mother allowed herself a most unladylike grunt. "No big brother with a Beetle?"

"Not a chance," I admitted.

"Well," Mother said equably, "he tells a nice story."

"That he does," I agreed.

"His girlfriend," Mother observed as I signaled the turn into our driveway, "is a very pretty young woman. Too much makeup, but very pretty."

It was my turn to grunt.

"Odd, though," Mother said. "I thought green eye shadow was out of fashion."

I sighed. "That wasn't eye shadow."

Mother sighed with me. "I know."

CHAPTER TEN

The rest of my shift was flat-out boring, with nothing but paperwork to take my mind off Louie Brandon. In hindsight, Adam's position was making more sense. Brandon was a known troublemaker. He had a record. And he lied as easily as he breathed. From a police standpoint, the only thing in Brandon's favor was he hadn't caused the accident that totaled his car.

But I felt so bound by my promise to his mother that in the time it took me to wolf down breakfast, I had allowed *my* mother to hand over her most significant physical asset to an ungrateful hell-raiser who had only a tenuous grip on his job and perhaps too harsh a grip on his girlfriend. I had been so anxious to get Mother out of her car, I hadn't given her time to reconsider her offer, let alone talk it over with her insurance agent. What if Brandon totaled Mother's car, too? Just who would pay *that* expense? And what if he blew his insurance settlement on a really fine TV and video system with a whole library of porn tapes for himself and cartoons for the kids? Just how was I supposed to pry the car keys back out of his fingers?

Adam was right. Brandon wasn't a good risk. I had acted hastily just because his father had died in a fire.

I was munching in regret on a bag of chips when Ellen Graham checked in. We were sharing the day shift that month, but she had spent most of her time on the clock sitting at the courthouse while the grand jury considered two of her cases. Ellen is a meticulous investigator, and she usually has every single detail cemented in place before the grand jury even convenes, so I raised a curious eyebrow at her long day in court.

"The boys wanted to deal," she said, referring to a fraternity drug ring she had helped bust. "It backed everything up."

I made a face in sympathy, even though I secretly enjoyed it when she was tied up in court. It kept her out of my way.

Ellen and I aren't sisters in blue. Vague memories of motherhood usually prompt me to tilt the schedule in her favor when I'm juggling conflicting vacation requests, and I rarely bat an eye if she scoots out early to retrieve her two preschoolers from day care, because Ellen will scrupulously make up the time somewhere down the line. But it is that same scrupulous mind-set that separates us. Ellen is incapable of fudging, even if it means a really bad guy walks. Dave applauds her – frequently – but I lean toward Henry's way of doing things. Sometimes you have to trash the rules for the greater good.

Ellen signed onto her computer and began scanning the day's arrest reports. We didn't make small talk. There wasn't much new in the files and Ellen didn't need me to help her catch up.

I was scrolling through the municipal court docket, checking whether I had any cases of my own coming up, when I noticed an initial hearing for the guy who had wrecked Brandon's car. Which only rekindled the feeling that I had screwed up by allowing Mother to entrust her car to the boy.

So I switched over to the family court docket. (Berger had taught me a thing or two about prying into records) and checked back nearly two years for any references to Brandon and his girlfriend Jenny. Even though they weren't married, if there had been any incidents that put the kids at risk, they would show up in the family court files.

I relaxed marginally when I found no trace of Brandon's name. Of course, Berger would point out that might simply mean I didn't know what I was doing.

Ellen was staring at her computer screen and unconsciously rubbing a yellowing bruise at the corner of her eyebrow. She and her youngest had cracked heads while the baby protested her nightly bath. The baby had escaped unbruised. Ellen had reported to work the next morning with a black eye.

There had been some snickers from Henry and Jamal that her old man had finally punched her out. One look from Ellen had permanently squelched *that* talk. I had no doubt that if Ellen's husband ever did raise a hand to her, he'd be kicked out on his ass and *never* allowed to come home.

But the fading bruise irrationally eased my mind. Kids inadvertently beat up on their parents. Ellen's baby had given her a black eye. It was probable that baby Tyler had walloped his mother, too. A bruise on his girlfriend didn't prove Louie Brandon was abusive.

So I signed off my computer and scooted over to the county recorder's office to scratch an itch of a different sort.

*   *   *

The work day was winding down and so was business at the recorder's office. The two clerks were briskly dealing with their last customers in hopes of locking up on time and didn't even bother to spar with me over access to their records. They both knew I was a cop and was nearly as familiar with the filing system as they were. They simply waved me through the gate at the counter and I scurried back to the file room before members of the paying public could protest that I was jumping to the head of the line.

The recorder's office had recently won a federal grant to computerize its data, but so far that meant only current deaths were going digital. There had been no effort yet to convert older records from paper to disk, so the death certificate I wanted was still stored in a long row of filing cabinets labeled by the year. I lucked out by two years. The certificate for Louie Brandon's father was still in the main file room. Older files were unceremoniously stored in the courthouse basement, where they suffered from rats, burst water pipes and general neglect.

There was no logical reason to pull the Brandon file. But Dave thought I was letting my daughter's death color my decisions, and his perceptions are usually right on. So I needed to reassure myself that Louie was worthy of a few breaks.

I found the certificate in minutes and hunched over the file drawer to shield it from prying eyes should someone with more authority than the clerks wander into the file room. I wasn't doing anything illegal – death certificates are public records – but most members of the public aren't permitted to thumb through the files for free. They pay a fee for the clerks to do the rummaging for them. Those clerks were letting me skirt the red tape because of my badge, and I didn't want to abuse the privilege by being careless.

The light was bad and the type was fading, but I squinted through the pertinent information and decided that this time, Dave was dead wrong. The death of Brandon's father had been ruled accidental, due to smoke inhalation from a fire that had also been ruled accidental. No contributory health causes were listed – no heart attack, no stroke, no head injuries that could have knocked him out before the fire started. The death certificate reflected what the fire department report had said. Brandon's father had fallen asleep while smoking and died because of it.

Louie truly was a victim, a boy made fatherless through no fault of his own. Yes, I was treating him differently because of my dead daughter. But I also knew how a little extra consideration might blunt the trauma of a loss by fire. If Bradley hadn't treated *me* differently after my husband and daughter had died, I'd have never become a cop, and maybe a couple more bad guys would still be walking the streets. In my mind, the ends justified the means. (Well, okay, Bradley's wife probably wouldn't have approved of the sex that accompanied his extra special consideration, but since I wasn't planning to bed Brandon, I didn't see any flaws in my mental gymnastics. Brandon deserved help, and I was uniquely qualified to give it.)

So I slipped his father's death certificate back into the file and returned to the front office to thank the clerks profusely for letting me have my way.

The courthouse clock was chiming five and one clerk was already packing up her purse to leave. The other clerk was trying to hurry along her last customer.

It's strange how you can go thirty years without seeing people – like members of your old Girl Scout troop – and then bump into them again in quick succession. Just the afternoon before I'd passed Ginny Edgerton and part of her brood in the McDonald's parking lot, and now there was Sandra Porter at the public service counter.

I thought of ducking out without acknowledging her. She was deep in conversation with the clerk and she wasn't looking directly at me. I had a couple more errands to run before dinner, and my stomach didn't really want to delay the first forkful by taking another trip down memory lane. Besides, Sandra and I had never been buddies. Outside of Scouts, we had run with entirely different crowds. I didn't even remember sharing any classes with her. Everything we had to say to each other after thirty years had been covered at the reunion. So I wanted to escape.

But I could see the conversation with the clerk wasn't going well. She was drumming her fingers on the counter and looking pointedly at the clock on the wall.

Sandra was quietly but firmly explaining her position. "I don't want a *copy* of the death certificate. I just want to *see* it. I don't think I should have to pay a ten-dollar fee just to *see* it."

"It's the rules, ma'am," the clerk said impatiently.

"But it's a *public document*," Sandra countered.

"And no one's denying you access, ma'am," the clerk said. "You just gotta pay the fee."

I stepped up to the counter beside the clerk. "Can I help?" I asked – "help" meaning maybe the clerk would fudge a little on the regulations in deference to my badge.

The clerk thought "help" might mean strong-arming the public so she could go home. "This *lady*," the clerk said, though she certainly didn't mean it, "doesn't understand the rules."

"I understand the rules perfectly," Sandra said irritably to the clerk, then she focused on me and, as recognition clicked in her eyes, she did the damnedest thing.

She blushed.

Furiously.

"Ah, Jo," she managed. "So surprised to see you here."

"Me, too," I said as I leaned companionably on the counter. "What's up?"

"Ah – well – nothing really," Sandra said hastily as she snatched a scrap of paper back from the clerk and stuffed it into her purse. "A small insurance matter." She glanced at the clock and feigned surprise. "I didn't realize it was so late. I'll just come back another day."

"I'm sure it would take only a minute to pull the certificate," I said, just to be ornery.

The clerk glared at me.

"No, really, I don't want to be a bother," Sandra said as she backed away from the counter.

Acquiescence was so unlike the Sandra I used to know that, dinner be damned, I wanted to toy with her. It was quite the role reversal from our high school days. But Sandra simply spun away from the counter and, with her purse clutched to her chest, fled without so much as a goodbye. It was very un-Scout-like.

The clerk and I stared at her retreating butt until the door slammed shut.

"*That* was rude," the clerk fumed.

"And unproductive," I said. "Whose certificate did she want?"

The clerk shrugged. "I don't remember. Nicola Ho-something."

I thought I was hearing things. "Nikki Hocevar? But she's *dead.*"

The clerk gave me a look. "Well, *yeah*."

I felt myself blushing just like Sandra. "I mean dead a long *time*. Like almost thirty years."

"It's the name the lady asked for," the clerk sniffed. "I can't help it when the subject died." And she turned her back on me in a determined effort to clear off the counter and lock up.

I got the message and left. But I was mildly puzzled as I dashed through my errands. Why in the world would Sandra Porter lie to me about a death certificate? She certainly wasn't in the recorder's office over a "small insurance matter," not if the death certificate she wanted was for Nikki Hocevar. They hadn't been remotely related, so any estate Nikki had left behind couldn't have been destined for Sandra. In fact, I seriously doubted Nikki had any estate to bestow. She had been just sixteen – her driver's license barely twenty-four hours old – when she had slammed her car into a tree. Nikki had died instantly, and she had nearly taken three girlfriends with her. As far as I could recall, Sandra hadn't been one of them.

But puzzles being what they are, this one quickly faded from my consciousness as I wrangled with the dry cleaner over a torn blouse and fretted over what video to rent for the evening's entertainment – something hot enough to get Dave's attention but not so hot that Adam and Emily would tear the house down.

I forgot Sandra Porter.

I should have known better.

CHAPTER ELEVEN

The blond girl slouched in the passenger seat and pouted. She was three whole months older than Nikki, but because of one *stupid* orange cone, she had flunked her parking test and there was *Nikki*, gnawing most unattractively on her Dentyne and flaunting her driver's license. It wasn't *right*. The blond girl knew she was smarter (she topped the honor roll every six weeks) and much more popular (she'd run away with the junior class election for Student Council *and* had sat on both the football and basketball homecoming courts) and infinitely prettier than Nikki (after all, she was a real blonde and she nearly spilled out of her C cups). But Nikki was the one who got her license first, and now *she* was the one chauffeuring the girls on a shopping trip to a mall ten miles up the highway, and everyone was gushing over how *well* she was driving. It just wasn't fair.

Her mood didn't improve at the mall, where the sweater she really, *really* wanted wasn't available in her size, although flat-chested Nikki was able to snatch up a small that fit her like a sausage casing and actually looked sexy. But the blonde got back at her when they piled into a booth at the Sugar Bowl and she sort of whispered quite solicitously to Nikki that maybe she *shouldn't* order the chocolate shake because it was really quite bad for her complexion. Nikki gulped and hastily ordered a ginger ale instead. The blond girl purred her approval.

But she was still feeling quite out of the spotlight as the other girls giggled their way back into Nikki's car. The girls in back (who she had thought were *her* friends) were positively fawning over Nikki as she carefully backed out of the parking space, and when Nikki smoothly braked to a stop at the first intersection instead of dashing through the yellow light, their praise for her cautious approach to driving was nauseating. *Anyone* could stop for a traffic light, the blonde fumed in her head; the proof of a *real* driver was to beat the light.

So when Nikki dutifully signaled to make the turn onto the highway home, the blonde manipulatively piped up: “Oh, not that way! Let's take the old road down by the river.”

The old road was a narrow, two-lane country route that twisted in and out of the trees along the river. The highway was four straight lanes of wide berms across land so flat, you could almost see the courthouse clock tower sitting on the horizon miles and miles away.

Nikki shot the blond girl a nervous smile. “I promised my dad I'd take the highway.”

“But that's so *boring*,” the blonde said.

“But I promised,” Nikki repeated.

The girls in back suddenly shifted gears and started teasing Nikki for being such a Goody-Goody Two Shoes.

Nikki blushed.

“You're the driver,” the blonde said dismissively and turned purposely away from Nikki to stare in boredom out the side window.

Nikki chomped hard on her gum and abruptly pulled out of the turn lane without signaling her intentions. Horns honked angrily behind them. The blonde smiled at her reflection in the window.

Nikki was perspiring noticeably as she negotiated the three blocks to the old river road. She didn't *like* to disobey her parents and she was afraid of the old curving road. But she didn't want the girls to think she was a namby-pamby, either. So she gripped the steering wheel with both hands and kept her eyes on the pavement ahead.

It was a warm spring day and the girls had rolled all the windows down. The blonde had found a rock station on the radio, and everyone but Nikki was singing happily into the wind as she turned onto the old road. The speed limit was 45, but she doggedly kept the car well below 40. Within minutes they were out of suburbia and drifting past freshly plowed farm fields.

Nikki grit her teeth when a pickup truck roared past them on a curve and the juvenile delinquent in the passenger seat gave them the finger.

The blonde was incensed. “That son of a bitch!” she hissed.

The girls in back gasped at her language.

Nikki tried to keep focused on the road, and her speed slowed.

The blonde whirled on her, eyes narrowed and furious. “You've got to catch that truck,” she ordered.

Nikki cringed at the idea.

“Faster, Nikki,” the blonde insisted. “You can't let them get away with this.”

The girls in back were chiming their agreement.

“No,” Nikki said. “My dad'll get mad.”

“Your dad's not here,” the blonde snapped back, her voice rising stridently. “Speed up!”

Nikki shook her head, but the car was listening to the blonde instead. The speedometer crept up over 45.

They were on serious curves now as the road twisted with the river. The girls in back rolled with the car around a particularly sharp bend and giggled to mask their nervousness. Nikki gulped and eased her foot back from the accelerator.

But then the blonde caught sight of the back end of the pickup zipping around the next curve and she shrieked: “Get them!”

Nikki's attention jerked to the blonde and the car swerved briefly from hard pavement to the soft gravel shoulder.

"For God's sake," the blonde yelled at her, "watch the road!" And she grabbed the wheel herself and turned the car back to the road.

"Let go!" Nikki shouted, and slapped the blonde's hand away. The car wobbled but kept to the pavement. Only Nikki must have pressed down on the accelerator as she tussled with the blonde, because suddenly the needle on the speedometer was shivering around 60.

And there were so many curves.

The giggles in back ramped up to screams as a blur of trees and riverbank swept past them. Nikki clung to the steering wheel and tried to keep to the center of the road, but she didn't have a delicate touch and the car zigzagged viciously right and left.

The madness was sucked out of the blond girl's eyes as she suddenly realized Nikki really was losing control of the car. And the muddy brown river was only feet from her window.

"Nikki," she said, her voice suddenly calm, "stop the car."

"I can't!" Nikki cried, and her face was red and contorted with terror. "I don't know how!"

"Step on the brake, Nikki," the blonde instructed, her voice quivering only slightly.

"I'm trying!" Nikki wailed, and she squeezed her eyes shut as she stomped hard on the pedal.

Except it was the accelerator.

Even the blond girl screamed as Nikki missed the curve and the car sped straight across the road and slammed into a giant oak tree.

And then there was only silence.

* * *

Nikki died on impact.

The other girls escaped with cuts and bruises. In a freakish twist of good fortune, only the front end on the driver's side hit the tree, crushing steel, glass and the steering wheel into Nikki's chest. The other girls were able to pull themselves from the wreckage, and the first driver to stop on the scene found them on the berm, hugging and crying and bleeding onto each other.

When deputies questioned them at the hospital, the blond girl fretted that the others would reveal how she had goaded Nikki into driving too fast. She had no intention of taking the blame for the accident when it was Nikki's bad driving that had nearly killed them all. So she was prepared to lie.

But the two other girls were so rattled, they could barely remember the horrific moments leading up to the crash. They babbled and whined through their statements – although one girl remembered the blonde telling Nikki to stop the car.

"Is that true?" the deputy asked the blonde.

She slowly shook her head, as though befuddled. "I might have," she admitted.

The deputy patted her shoulder. "You saved those other girls," he declared.

The blonde smiled at him shyly from beneath her lashes.

And when her mother finally let her return to school, everyone called her a hero.

CHAPTER TWELVE

The following Monday afternoon, I was trailing an ambulance into the hospital parking lot because a burglary suspect had managed to shoot himself in the leg and I wasn't particularly happy because the inept perp was going to cost me a lot of time on paperwork. Then I spotted a familiar car outside the emergency room and my mood took a real nosedive.

But I waited until my suspect was safely under the supervision of a beefy intern and an armed and dangerous hospital cop before I went searching for Louie Brandon.

He was leaning against the doorjamb of an examination room, his hands stuffed into his jeans pockets as he scowled at the patients trundling by. I could smell the beer wafting off him long before he could smell the irritation simmering in me.

"Louie," I said sternly, "what are you doing here?"

He transferred his scowl from the elderly man groaning on a passing gurney to my chest and his nostrils flared in either anger or sheer ecstasy over meeting up with me. "I'm *here*," he said, "because they won't let me in *there*." And he jerked his thumb to the room behind him.

I peered around his shoulder and saw the boy Jason huddling on a bed and his mother Jenny squeezing up next to him. There was no blood on either one, but the boy was cradling his left wrist and his eyes were big and scared.

A young woman in a white coat and clipboard was talking to Jenny while a nurse in a uniform straight out of *Sesame Street* was cheerfully fussing with a tray of ominously sharp instruments. Jason's eyes rolled between the doctor and the nurse and just got bigger.

"What's wrong?" I snapped at Louie.

"Hey, I didn't do *nothing*," he snapped back.

And the fact that he felt the need to defend himself before he was even asked set all my child abuse antennae quivering.

Louie saw the suspicion in my eyes and raised his hands defensively. "The kid fell down the stairs and landed on his arm. It might be busted." And right on cue, the boy whimpered as the doctor fingered his wrist.

Louie winced. "Aw, geez, I don't need this shit. This is gonna take *forever* and it's my day *off*."

"How nice you were available to bring the boy to the hospital," I said as I wedged myself between the door and Louie, nicely blocking his view of the proceedings in the examination room and forcing him to focus on me. "How'd he fall?"

Louie's eyes danced around – maybe from nerves, maybe from the beer still sloshing around his stomach. "How the hell should I know? He's a kid. Kids fall."

"Down the stairs?"

"Half the stairs," Louie amended. "Just to the landing. Six steps, tops." And he nodded as though six steps proved it wasn't a *bad* fall. The boy just landed wrong.

"And the doctor won't let you in because – ?" I prodded.

Louie's temper boiled over again. "Well, I'm not his *dad*, am I?" he said acidly. "I pay the rent and I buy the goddamned groceries and I'm gonna end up paying for that doctor in there, but the bitch ordered me out because *I'm not family*!" And he punched the air with his fist and his face reddened in indignation.

I could feel the sudden silence in the room behind me, as though everyone was calculating where to run if Louie decided to punch something a little more substantial. So I captured his arm on the downswing, spun him around and marched him to the waiting room down the hall.

Louie squawked – mostly in surprise that a lady cop nearly twice his age could manhandle him. But Dave keeps me in tip-top shape and I've been dealing with inebriated young men for too many years to count. All it takes is momentum and the right pressure points. So I easily steered him to a chair and he allowed himself to be seated.

I sat across from him and leaned into his beer fumes. "You drink too much."

"It's my day off," he repeated sullenly.

"It's midafternoon and you're barely tracking."

"I'm worried," he countered. "The kid really hurt himself."

"It doesn't look fatal," I pointed out.

"Fatal for my wallet," he corrected. "You know how much this is gonna cost?"

"Too much for you to be drinking your paycheck away," I agreed.

Louie sucked in his breath. "Jesus, you're as big a bitch as that fat-assed doctor." And he purposely turned away from me to chew on his thumbnail.

I slouched back in my chair and puffed the bangs off my forehead in frustration. I'd had visions of a lazy dinner and drinks on the deck with Dave. Now I was looking at serious overtime just to clear up the burglary that had brought me to the hospital in the first place. I didn't need Louie Brandon's problems complicating my life even more.

But as he was now the custodian of Mother's car, not to mention the passport to my future dental happiness, I felt an obligation to meddle in his affairs. So I dialed down the irritation in my voice and asked what was *really* bugging him.

Louie snorted. "Like you give a shit."

"I'm *asking*," I said.

“Screw you,” he said, and transferred his attention to his other thumb.

But he was still sitting in his incredibly uncomfortable plastic chair, so I crossed my legs and patiently waited. Maybe the remnants of his polite upbringing would gnaw on his conscience as he gnawed on his nails.

I was mentally composing my report to Bradley on my burglary suspect – looking for just the right tone to convey that it wasn't my fault that the guy had shot himself without actually saying so – when Louie sighed.

I quickly leaned back into his face. “I beg your pardon?”

Louie was irritated that I hadn't been paying attention. “I said, Blockbuster. Can't you hear?”

“Not when you're talking through your thumb,” I sniped.

Louie ungraciously removed his hand from his face and said with greatly exaggerated enunciation, “Block-bust-er. Got it now?”

“Loud and clear,” I assured him, “but what does a blockbuster have to do with anything?”

“Not *a* blockbuster,” he corrected. “*The* Blockbuster. And it's got everything to do with *this*.” And he waved an arm to take in the waiting room, the hospital, the universe.

“Perhaps you could explain,” I suggested.

He sighed again – it had been a while since his last beer and the buzz was fading – but he leaned forward to meet me across the aisle. “Blockbuster – the video chain, ya know? – is gonna open a big store across from campus. There was a story about it in the paper. Don't you read?”

“I must have missed it,” I said solemnly. “Is this bad news?”

“Well, *yeah*,” he said. “It's gonna be just down the street from *my* store. My boss says it's gonna put us outta business. We can't compete with their prices, and the selection of movies – man, there's no comparison.”

"Oh, my," I said, "that *is* bad."

"Damn straight," Louie said, nodding vigorously. "I'm gonna lose my job, and Jenny and me can hardly keep up with the bills as it is. What are we gonna do when she's the only one working?" And his eyes raked me with the fears that haunt all parents, even when they're sober.

"Well – maybe you can get a job at this Blockbuster instead," I said. "They'll need people familiar with the business."

"They'll need *me* for sure," Louie agreed. "I know video rentals inside 'n' out. But, Christ, there's no *future* in it. I can't make a career outta renting movies." He slumped back in his chair. "And I got these *kids* to feed."

And we both pondered the impossibility of raising kids on minimum wage.

Louie stared at the ceiling and groaned. "I need to get into computers."

That caught me by surprise. Louie hadn't struck me as a technological wizard – I had uncharitably assumed that if a guy his age was following a career path in video rentals, then riding a cash register was the upper end of his technical range. But hell, I admonished myself, what did I really know about the guy's capabilities? If he was savvy enough to recognize that computers would be much more lucrative than VCRs, maybe there was a bit more intelligence under that mop of hair than I had suspected.

"You know computers?" I asked.

"Enough to know that's where the good jobs are gonna be." And the look he darted my way was more animated than anything I'd seen since the day he tried to shove a clipboard into the back of Adam's head.

My own expression must not have been appropriately enthusiastic, because he immediately challenged me. "You got computers at work?"

I reluctantly nodded, thinking of all the evils Berger had introduced to my life by dragging the police department into the computer age.

"Of course, you do," he said, nodding along with me. "*Everyone's* getting into computers – the government, the military, business. Someday, there's gonna be a computer in every home. They'll make your telephones and televisions and maybe even your *books* obsolete."

I shuddered at the thought. Working with computers was bad enough. Living with them was too outrageous to contemplate. Bradley would *never* let me off the clock.

"Computers," Louie repeated, almost like a soothing mantra. I could even see his muscles relax as he said it and his eyes half closed as he imagined tapping on a keyboard rather than bagging video tapes and making change for his customers.

"So why not study computers?" I asked. "Go back to school?"

"I'd like that," he said, still dreaming. But then he really *heard* the question and shook himself back to the here and now. "But how do I pay for *that* if I don't have a job?"

"Scholarships?" I stupidly suggested.

Louie snorted. "Lady, I barely graduated high school."

"So scratch scholarships," I agreed.

"Scratch the whole damn thing," he said bitterly as he caught sight of his future over my shoulder.

I twisted around and saw the nurse pushing the boy Jason in a wheelchair out of the examination room. His mother was scurrying close behind, jabbering at Jason around the nurse's shoulders.

"Fuck," Louie said, and he bolted from the chair after them.

I should have disengaged then – Louie Brandon wasn't even officially on my dance card – but cops are a notoriously nosy bunch, so I trailed him down the hall. The wheelchair and its entourage were heading into the bowels of the hospital and my jurisdiction outside the emergency room was questionable, so I ducked instead into the examination room, where the doctor was still scribbling in her charts.

The doctor looked up at me and her eyes were too tired for someone her age. I wondered how long she'd been on duty. "Yes?" she said, and her attention locked reluctantly on the badge clipped to my belt.

I introduced myself, stressing the detective part of the title. I'm not above using my job to get what I want. "Is the boy being admitted?" I asked.

"Is that an official question?" she hedged.

I just smiled.

She sighed. "He's going to X-ray. The wrist may be broken. If it is, we'll set it. If it's just sprained, we may still immobilize it for a day or two. Either way, we'll be sending him home tonight."

"And does that concern you?" I asked.

"Should it?" she countered.

"You wouldn't allow Mr. Brandon in the room," I pointed out.

She bristled. "He was *drunk* and *loud* and *interfering* with the examination. I was perfectly within my rights to bar him from the room."

"And he isn't the boy's father."

"Even if he *had* been his father, I'd have barred him," she insisted.

"So you could question the boy away from Mr. Brandon?"

She began to protest her innocence, then abruptly decided to come clean, perhaps hoping to share any guilt down the road. "This is the second time the boy's been brought to the emergency room in four months. It raises flags."

"And?" I prodded. I did not like the way this was headed at all.

"The boy remembers falling down the stairs. He doesn't remember *why*. His mother says he might have tripped on a toy truck on the staircase."

"That's plausible," I said.

"He came to the emergency room the first time for a bump on the head. His mother says he ran into a door. That's plausible, too."

"But?"

The doctor irritably flipped the chart shut. "No buts. The boy and his mother were both convincing. The injuries were accidental. Kids are clumsy. They get hurt."

"And you're comfortable with that?" I pressed.

"I wouldn't let him go home if I weren't," she said firmly.

"Okay," I said, allowing myself to breathe in a little relief. "Just another chapter in the misadventures of childhood."

"Right," the doctor said and stepped purposefully around me toward the door. But at the threshold, she hesitated and shot me a defiant look.

"I still don't *trust* that man," she said.

I sighed. "Neither do I."

* * *

My burglary suspect was wheeled off to surgery – he would live, the intern assured me, but there were some messy bone splinters to clean out of his leg – so I parked a young cop named Perry outside the surgery suite to keep tabs on the proceedings and headed for the parking lot. If I really hurried, I might still get home in time for cocktails with Dave on a chilly, damp deck. And maybe he'd come up with some provocative ways to keep me warm.

I irresponsibly ducked out a door marked "Employees only" and was immediately wrapped in a fog of cigarette smoke.

"Oh, sorry," a female voice said as I gagged.

"No problem," I sputtered as I waved the smoke out of my face. "I remember the habit."

"I imagine you do," the woman laughed, "since I gave you your first cigarette."

I peered through watering eyes and recognized my old Girl Scout nemesis, Patty. She was smartly turned out in a business suit – the director of physical therapy apparently was unencumbered by the need to wear a silly uniform – and the frosty highlights in her hair had been recently burnished, but sharp lines poked through her expertly applied makeup as she inhaled, and I tried not to smirk.

We were standing on a neglected piece of the parking lot around the corner from the emergency room, and it apparently was a favorite haunt of hospital smokers. Dozens of cigarette butts in various stages of disintegration littered the blacktop, and an empty Marlboro pack fluttered in an April breeze that promised rain.

My hopes for the deck floated away with the smoke.

Patty exhaled from the side of her mouth, politely blowing the fumes away from my face. "So you've kicked the habit?" she asked.

"You never kick it," I said as I zipped my jacket against the wind. "You just don't *do* it."

Patty grunted and glanced at her watch. "Well, I have two more minutes to *do* it, and I'm going to enjoy it." And the end of her cigarette glowed as she sucked in more smoke.

I resisted the urge to snatch her cigarette and finish it myself. Mother would not approve of a relapse.

Patty savored her last lungful, then unattractively let the remnants dribble out her nose. I greedily inhaled her secondhand dregs.

"Should have known I'd run into you," Patty sort of grouched as she poked around the pockets of her jacket. What that did to the finely pressed lines of her ensemble was criminal.

"Me?" I said, startled. "Have you been looking for *me*?" And I fervently prayed that didn't come out as hopeful as it sounded to me, like it had back in junior high. No matter how old I was, being around Patty – or her equally sophisticated cohort Marilyn – could reduce my self-image to awkward and pimply-faced in five seconds flat.

"Well, not you per se," Patty said as she fished a peppermint out of a pocket, "just one of the girls."

And given our recent reunion, I knew immediately she was referring to our Scout troop.

"I'm seeing Scouts everywhere," Patty complained. "I ran into Ginny Edgerton at the gas station just last weekend. Did you know she's a *grandmother*?" Patty shuddered as she popped the peppermint into her mouth.

"We're not old enough to be grandmothers," I said gravely.

"I should think *not*," Patty said, and she automatically sucked in her tummy in case anyone male should be watching.

"And then yesterday I was accosted at the drugstore by Sandra Porter."

I had been losing interest in the conversation ever since Patty had extinguished her cigarette, but Sandra's name brought me back to attention. The fact that both of us had recently crossed paths with Sandra aroused my curiosity.

"She accosted you?" I asked like a cop.

"Well, not physically accosted," Patty hastily amended. "She just kept talking about the troop. All I wanted was to pick up a prescription and go home, but she had me blocked in the shampoo aisle, and she wouldn't stop babbling about those other girls."

"From the reunion?" I asked.

Patty grimaced slightly around her peppermint. "No, not *them*. She was fixated on the ones who *weren't* there – you know, the dead ones."

I sucked in my breath just a little. I remembered how Sandra had made us all uncomfortable at the reunion by ticking off the names of our dead alumni, and then how she had irritated the clerk at the courthouse by balking at the fee for a death certificate. Now it appeared she was pestering Patty about the dead, too.

"Did she mention Nikki Hocevar?" I asked.

"She did, and I did *not* appreciate it," Patty huffed. "Marilyn and I were in that car, too, and we could have both been killed, just like Nikki."

"I'd forgotten that," I admitted. Well, of course, you remember the dead. That's spectacular. But the survivors tend to fade from your memory banks.

"I'll *never* forget it," Patty said. "Nikki died right in front of my eyes. It was the most horrifying thing I'd ever seen."

I made sympathetic noises. After so many years as a cop, I've built a wall between myself and the bodies I occasionally see, but I could still imagine how awful it must have been for Patty, crawling out of the wreckage as Nikki died.

"And then she had to bring up Debbie Gauer," Patty said, her irritation building as she relived the conversation with Sandra.

"Was she in Nikki's car, too?" I asked.

"No," Patty snapped. "She overdosed. Don't you remember?"

"I thought it was a reaction to anesthesia."

"Same difference. And at *my* college," Patty said angrily. "Not that her death had anything to do with *me*. Lots of kids from our class went to State. Marilyn was there, too. But Sandra was questioning *me* like somehow *I* would know something about it. Where would she get an idea like that?"

"Well, what was she asking?" I countered.

Patty shrugged dismissively. "Why was Debbie having surgery? Why didn't she come home for it instead of staying at school? Did I see her before she died? Stupid, stupid questions. Debbie and I did not run in the same crowd, you know. I have no idea why she died, and I certainly don't appreciate the likes of Sandra Porter interrogating me as though I *should* know."

“Perhaps,” I mused, more to myself than to Patty, “Sandra is just trying to come to grips with the death of girls we used to know. They died awfully young.”

“I don't care *what* she's grappling with. She can leave me out of her sordid memories.” And Patty crunched firmly on her peppermint.

I winced for her molars.

Patty glanced again at her watch. “And now this nasty trip down memory lane has made me late for a meeting. You'll excuse me if I don't say how nice it was to see you again.”

“The feeling is mutual,” I assured her.

She hesitated with her hand on the doorknob, and the smile she bestowed on me was frosty. “You've grown a backbone, Jo Ferris. It's about time.”

She ducked inside before I could rake my fingernails across her face.

CHAPTER THIRTEEN

When I got to the station, there was a message from Dave that he'd been invited to an impromptu dinner with a visiting lecturer, so my hopes of cuddling on the deck fizzled. I didn't mind *too* much. A cold drizzle had started to fall as I scurried through the back door of the station. Cold rain and slippery decks weren't a good combination for sex at our age.

But it left me with no reason to wrap up my burglary report and hurry home. Mother was studying for midterms and had announced at breakfast that she had neither the time nor the inclination to cook dinner. Adam was using his day off to introduce Emily to the firing range, which undoubtedly would lead to activities that would only make me envious, April showers notwithstanding. The only creatures waiting anxiously for me at home were Barney and the cats, and they loved me only for my treats.

So I dawdled over my report, drank way too much coffee and then was too wired to even think of going home. I toyed with the idea of returning to the hospital to brace my suspect, but when I checked in with Perry, he said the perp was zonked out on painkillers. It would be morning before he was coherent.

I sighed and gave in to the itch that had been growing at the back of my brain.

I went to the newspaper to resurrect Debbie Gauer.

*   *   *

Gene Emery was on his way out as I was on my way in. His family owned the paper and Gene was the latest in a long line of Emerys to be its editor. So far, the family had resisted the urge to sell out to a media chain, but Gene candidly admitted that it was only the commercial printing side of the business that was keeping the newspaper afloat. Gene was a little older than Bradley and, though he still enjoyed bullying the town fathers from his editorial page, someday he would tire of the hassles, negotiate a handsome deal with an out-of-town conglomerate, and retire very handsomely to his "cabin" in Colorado.

But this evening he was late for the monthly Chamber of Commerce dinner and had little time to chat as we passed at the door. He barely sniffed at the bait when I said I wanted to dig through the clippings in the newspaper's morgue.

"Should I be interested?" he asked with only a hint of his normal suspicion.

"Just an old obituary," I assured him. "Of a friend. Nothing official."

Gene snorted like he knew better, but he really didn't have the time. "Tell the librarian I gave you a free pass – but only for *obituaries*." And he dashed out into the rain with a copy of the afternoon paper shielding his well-barbered head.

The library – or morgue – was hidden in a windowless room in the basement, next to the rumbling presses. Like the county recorder's office, the newspaper had begun to computerize its records, but only stories from the past five years were accessible electronically. The older stories, dating from the newspaper's founding after the Civil War, were still saved as clippings, filed in envelopes according to subject and date. Newer envelopes were kept in easy-to-reach filing cabinets. Older envelopes were packed into cardboard boxes stacked to the ceiling. In between the stacks, there was room for two small tables, and they had to share the desk lamp.

Like many of Gene's employees, the night librarian was a university student, policing the stacks of clippings for minimum wage. I had to resort to dropping Gene's name before he would disengage from his geology textbook, and when I told him I was looking for newspaper clippings for a girl who had been dead for twenty-three years, his mouth puckered in distaste. "That's so old, it'll be up in the boxes, and I've got asthma." And he looked mournfully at the stacks and nearly sneezed thinking about them.

I apologized most sincerely for troubling him, then dropped my voice conspiratorially. "It's police business, you see, and it's *vital* that I read those clippings."

"Well," he huffed, "if it's *important*." And he reluctantly carried a stepladder into the rows of cardboard boxes.

I claimed the table across from his and surreptitiously angled the desk lamp in my direction. Then I waited an inordinately long time for the librarian to retrieve the appropriate envelope – so long that I began to wonder about his mastery of the alphabet. But eventually he wheezed down to me from the cobwebs along the ceiling, "Sorry, no Debbie Gauer."

I found that hard to believe and sternly told him so.

"Hey," he protested, "no Debbie. Just a Deborah."

I rolled my eyes. "You think that might be it?" I asked. "Debbie – Deborah?"

There was a grouchy sigh from the stacks. "If you wanted Deborah, you should have *asked* for Deborah."

He carefully made his way down the ladder and deposited a distressingly thin envelope on the table in front of me. "That's it?" I asked as I weighed the yellowed envelope in my hand.

"Hey, you said she was dead," he said defensively. "Dead people don't produce clippings."

I declined to debate his logic and leaned into the desk lamp to explore my finds. He harrumphed at the loss of the lamp and made a great show of squinting in the dim light as he returned to his textbook. I ignored him.

And discovered that the newspaper world had pretty much ignored the life of Debbie Gauer as well.

There were a few clippings from the days when the newspaper still printed the junior high school honor roll – very *few* clippings, because Debbie hadn't been a star student. I could still remember her trying to copy my answers on a biology test, when alphabetical seating put us side by side in lab. (Fortunately, I shared more classes with Joey Franklin, and sitting alphabetically was much more fun when he was around because *he* was a hunk.)

There was also a small grainy photograph of Debbie and three other girls singing in the chorus to promote the choir's production of *South Pacific* our sophomore year in high school. I could barely read music, so choir wasn't one of my extracurriculars, but I could vaguely remember Debbie singing from time to time in Scouts or at patriotic school assemblies. Her pitch was good, but she sang through her nose – *not* appealing.

The biggest clipping by far was her obituary, and since she had died young under "mysterious circumstances," the newspaper had written a rather long article. Unfortunately, the extra verbiage was not enlightening. The first paragraph said a 20-year-old hometown girl had died unexpectedly at a university downstate. The second paragraph said the county coroner in that jurisdiction was investigating. The rest was standard obituary fare – her memberships in various school and church organizations (the Scout troop was given prominent mention), her educational achievements (she had been majoring in elementary education), a long list of surviving family members, and the standard announcement of calling hours and funeral services. The obituary didn't tell me anything I didn't already know about Debbie Gauer.

The final clipping, dated two weeks after the obituary, was a two-paragraph acknowledgment that the coroner had ruled

Debbie's death accidental. There were no details describing the "accident."

I slouched in the chair and stared in frustration at the studio photo accompanying the obituary. A young woman I barely remembered stared back at me. The photo must have been Debbie's senior class picture, and it was typical of the era: long, straight hair a la Cher, carefully sculpted eyebrows and heavy mascara, pancake makeup covering the acne, and a slight squint because no self-respecting girl wore glasses in her senior photo. I squinted myself and tried to make a connection over the decades to the girl I had known in Scouts and the occasional class, but there was nothing. Debbie Gauer had lived and died without making any impression on me.

But something about her had impressed Sandra Porter.

For the life of me, I couldn't imagine what.

* * *

Berger was directing a symphony on his computer keyboard when I got back to the station. That was normal – Berger was *always* playing with his computer when mundane small-town crime didn't get in his way – but this was his day off, and he blushed noticeably when he caught sight of me stalking into the squad room with a folder holding photocopies of Debbie Gauer's clippings.

So I made a point of passing behind his desk on my way to the coffeepot and smirked to myself when I saw what was propped open on his keyboard: an old-fashioned grade book.

Berger was teaching an adult vocational class in computers three nights a week at the high school. He was supposed to be doing it strictly on his own time – he had brashly assured Bradley that with a little creative scheduling, we wouldn't even notice his absence from the station – and mostly that had been the case. No great crimes against humanity had gone undetected while Berger was in the classroom.

But here he was, fussing with his grade book while on the station's computer, and even though he wasn't technically on duty, I figured Berger would owe me to keep my mouth shut.

And Berger knew it. He didn't stop what he was doing – I could see different computer pages reflected in his glasses, and none of them shouted police department business – but that uncharacteristic blush was steadily creeping up to his hairline.

"Catching up on your caseload?" I asked innocently as I settled back at my desk and cradled my mug in both hands, ostensibly to let the aroma of day-old coffee delicately tickle my nose buds.

Berger steadfastly ignored me, but he didn't dislodge the grade book.

I was getting a hare-brained idea, and wondered whether it was worth using my leverage over Berger to chase it.

Berger was wondering whether I would ever sign onto my own computer and stop staring at him.

I sipped coffee and patiently waited.

Berger's blush was turning purple.

And since his computer kingdom was at stake, he cracked first, as I knew he would.

"What do you want?" he asked in bitter defeat.

"To add a student to your class," I said and smiled serenely.

Berger shook his head vigorously. "Can't be done. We're six weeks into the course. Too late. Your student would never catch up." And he turned back in relief to his computer screen. The integrity of his teaching career was intact. I couldn't squeeze him to do the impossible.

But I was resilient. "Aren't you teaching again this summer?"

Berger stiffened. "It has been discussed," he admitted.

"And as the teacher, you could hold one of the slots for my student, couldn't you?"

"Why would I?" he asked levelly.

"So I don't bitch to Bradley that it's been damned difficult juggling the schedule around your classes," I said brightly.

"That would be a blatant lie," Berger pointed out.

"Not when summer vacations kick in," I countered.

Berger regarded me coldly. Now that we were in bargaining mode, he was automatically reverting to his true calculating self. "Not good enough. You want me to bend the rules to admit a pet student, I should get more than a break on the schedule."

I rolled my eyes. "Oh, puh-leeze. You are hardly in a position to make demands."

"Meaning?"

"Meaning, take my student and I don't rat on you for using police resources for personal business."

Berger looked at his grade book and sighed. "Does this student have a name?"

I did not cheer in triumph, but I was simpering just a little as I spelled out Louie Brandon's name for him.

Berger, of course, had to put conditions on the deal. "I hold the spot only until the first class. He doesn't show up, he's out."

"That's reasonable," I agreed.

"And he has to pay the fee in full the first night."

I gulped just a little. "Fee?"

"One hundred bucks," Berger said forcefully. "This isn't some fly-by-night mail-order course. It's a fully certified adult vocational program, administered by the city school board. And that costs one hundred bucks."

"He'll pay it," I said with much more confidence than I felt.

"He doesn't, he's out," Berger warned.

"It won't be a problem."

Berger just grunted, but he carefully slipped a piece of paper with Louie's name on it into his grade book. The deal was done.

Now all I had to do was persuade his mother to pay for it.

CHAPTER FOURTEEN

I detoured to a popular pizza joint on the way home, and as I waited for the kids behind the counter to bake Mother's favorite (pepperoni, green peppers and mushrooms with extra cheese) I was irritated by unsolicited flashbacks of Debbie Gauer – Debbie howling and bleeding in the grade school playground after she was smashed in the face with a dodgeball, tottering on improbably high heels at the eighth-grade dance, scrambling on hands and knees for her notes after a jock purposely ran into her in the main hall of the high school. The longer I waited for the pizza, the more the remnants of Debbie Gauer swirled into a sharper picture of the girl, yet I couldn't pick up on the *thing* that was making her so intriguing to Sandra.

So I took the pizza and my irritation home to Mother.

She was propped up on a mound of pillows on her bed, surrounded by textbooks and cats – a sure sign that she was into serious studying. Usually, she enthroned herself at the kitchen table, where she could keep tabs on her family while thumbing through her meticulous lecture notes. This particular midterm must be critical to send her into the relative solitude of her bedroom, and I fretted that she would brusquely turn me away.

But the smell of pizza was seductive, and after one guilty look at her textbooks, she uncharacteristically swept them onto the floor and we had a picnic on her bed.

It wasn't until most of the pizza had been demolished that either of us bothered to speak. By then, the cats were delicately licking cheese off their paws as they lounged on the pillows and Barney had planted his snout longingly on the top of the pizza box. Mother sighed and gave him her crust. He rolled with it ecstatically on the carpet.

"So," Mother said as she picked a mushroom off her bedspread, "to what do I owe the honor?"

"I was hungry?" I said as I scraped at the grease under my fingernails with a napkin.

"Oh, pshaw," Mother said. "If you were merely hungry, you could have gone to the Farmhouse to cavort with the boys from the station."

"The boys at the station don't often invite me anymore," I sadly admitted.

"It sucks getting old," Mother agreed. "But that isn't exactly news. Why are you *really* interrupting my studies to ply me with pizza?"

"Because I wanted to spend quality time with my mother," I said.

She rolled her eyes so vigorously, she nearly dislodged her wig.

"Would you believe I'm haunted by ghosts?"

Mother brightened. "Now *that* has possibilities. Tell me *everything*."

So I told her about Sandra Porter and her bizarre interest in Nikki Hocevar and Debbie Gauer. Mother hadn't been the type to bulldoze her way into the lives of her daughters as we were growing up – she had preferred to spend her free time with adults, thank you – but as an assistant Scout leader, she had known both Nikki and Debbie fairly well. So I didn't have to remind her who they were. But she wasn't quite sure what I wanted from her.

Neither was I.

"Everyone says Debbie died from some kind of allergic reaction to an anesthetic, but her obituary refers only to an accidental death," I said. "If it was some kind of malpractice, wouldn't the coroner have said so? Wouldn't the newspaper have reported it? Wouldn't the family have *sued*?"

Mother grew unusually silent as I peppered her with the questions that had been swirling in my head, and her gaze was fixed on the well-worn pattern of her bedspread. When I finally shut up, she didn't jump in for a good gossip, as I had hoped. Instead, the human silence in the room became so complete, I could clearly hear the rasp of cat tongues on fur.

And the tension was suddenly palpable.

"Come *on*," I said, gently slapping her knee, "what's the story?"

Mother's face was pinched. "It wasn't malpractice," she admitted. Then she shook herself as though coming to a decision and declared, "But it *certainly* was malfeasance."

I sat up straight. "Explain yourself, woman."

"Oh, use your head, Jo," Mother snapped. "It *was* an accidental drug death, but the drug wasn't an anesthetic."

My eyes widened. "No way."

Mother said nothing.

"Debbie Gauer *overdosed*?" I asked. "On hard drugs? Our wishy-washy white bread *Girl Scout*?"

Mother solemnly nodded.

I fell back onto the pillows. "I don't believe it."

"It is the sorrowful truth," Mother said as she slowly began depositing napkins and other debris in the pizza box. There was a tiny tremor in her left hand, and I stared at it in fascination as the cop part of my brain began adding up the pieces: young woman away from home, alone at college; hippies and the social upheaval of the early '70s; an unexpected "reaction" to an unnamed anesthetic under unexplained circumstances. Of course, it was an overdose.

But *Debbie Gauer*?

"But nobody said anything," I protested weakly. "Not a *word*."

"Of course not," Mother said, her voice almost its old crisp self. "We made sure of it."

"*We*?" I asked, befuddled.

"We parents."

I transferred my stare from her hand to her eyes. "But *why*?"

"Well, to shield the family, for one thing. *Good* girls didn't die from drug overdoses. Good *families* didn't raise *children* who died from drug overdoses. It was tragic enough that Debbie died. The family didn't deserve to suffer from malicious gossip as well."

"The entire town kept its mouth shut out of deference to Debbie's family?" I snorted. "*That's* hard to believe."

"The entire town didn't know," Mother said primly. "Thanks to Gene Emery."

"Gene Emery sat on a story?" I rattled my head to clear it of the bizarre images buzzing my brain. Debbie Gauer overdosing. The town fathers – and mothers – keeping it secret. And Gene Emery declining to publicize it. What planet had I been living on when this was happening?

"Mr. Emery agreed there was nothing to be gained by smearing Debbie and her family in the newspaper," Mother said.

"There had to be more to it than that," I persisted. "Dozens of people had to know. They wouldn't all keep quiet just to help the Gauers save face."

"Of course, there was more," Mother chided me. "We – the parents – were also terrified."

"Of gossip?"

"Don't be an ass. *Gossip* wouldn't kill our children, but *drugs* could. You aren't remembering the times very clearly, Jo. Debbie wasn't the only victim. Celebrities – people you and your sister admired – people like those musicians Janis Joplin and Jimi

– what was his name? – they were all dying the same way. They'd pass out on drugs and then choke to death on their own vomit. It frightened us. We didn't want to publicize it. We didn't want to give our own children ideas."

"So you – all of you – said nothing." There was a hint of awe in my voice – not over the morals of the drug debate, but over the fact that a generation of parents in my town had been able to keep the truth of one girl's death a secret for so long.

"Is it such a crime to try to protect our children?" Mother asked.

The eyes blinking behind her trifocals were suddenly vulnerable, and the sight wrenched my gut. I would have done anything to protect my daughter if I'd been given the chance. Could I chastise my mother and her friends for their misguided efforts to protect their kids?

So I swiftly hugged her and said, "You've always done right by me and Maureen."

Mother shook me off in embarrassment and reached purposefully for her textbooks. I took the hint – we never had extended moments of tenderness, Mother and I – and hopped off the bed with the pizza box.

But Sandra Porter's behavior was still bothering me.

"Why?" Mother asked in barely concealed irritation. She *really* wanted to get back to her studies.

"Debbie Gauer's death was a run-of-the-mill overdose. Seriously – " I said as Mother attempted to protest – "hundreds of people die that way every day. It isn't even news anymore. So why does Sandra Porter care?"

"Jo," Mother sighed in exasperation, "why don't you simply ask her?"

And she shooed me out the door.

CHAPTER FIFTEEN

The blonde lay back on the bunk, counted seconds for as long as she could stand it, exhaled in a burst toward the ceiling and waited for the rush.

It didn't come.

It never did.

Not with grass. Not with sex. She was beginning to think they were both highly overrated.

Debbie hunched over her knees on a beanbag chair and puffed nervously on her own joint. She'd packed on the dreaded freshman ten and had added ten more pounds as a sophomore. Her complexion was as greasy as the pizza boxes and hamburger wrappers spilling out of the waste basket and her hair was tied back in a ragged knot at the base of her sweaty neck. Two unclipped toes poked out of the holes in her grimy gym socks, but she didn't seem to care. All she could focus on was the joint and her damned biology class.

"I gotta get at least a B on the midterm," she moaned around the joint. "If my GPA drops anymore, I'm gonna lose *this*." And she waved the hand that wasn't hogging the joint at the cramped dorm room that was her world.

Debbie was a resident adviser, or RA, in a freshman women's dorm. In return for keeping an eye on the younger girls on her floor, she got a room of her own and a discounted meal ticket. But she had to keep her grades up or she'd be booted out of the RA corps, and her biology course was killing her.

The blonde couldn't see why Debbie even wanted to stay in her dumpy dorm room. The blonde and her old friend from high school had rushed one of the choicest sororities on campus in the spring and were now living in the sorority house. Granted, they were bunking in the attic, where they had to share a bathroom with six other girls, but next year they'd be in line for the double rooms on the second floor – *and* their own bathroom – and in the meantime, they had a house mother who looked after their laundry, took telephone messages from their boyfriends, baked sinful cookies and conveniently snored through curfew. Why in God's name would Debbie prefer this dismal dorm room?

"I just gotta get a B," Debbie repeated desperately, and sucked the burning joint down to her fingertips.

"Then get a tutor," the blonde said irritably. She was not feeling mellow at all, and was beginning to regret accepting Debbie's invitation to smoke some dope in her dorm room. The blonde had just wanted to mooch a joint. She wasn't in the mood to offer career counseling.

Debbie gagged and coughed out a choking cloud of smoke. "I can't afford a tutor!" she sputtered. "I can't even afford socks!" And she stared in horror at her unmanicured toes.

You *can* afford a shower, the blonde thought as she batted the smoke out of her face.

"*You* took biology," Debbie said. "What'd you get?"

The blonde shrugged. "I aced it," she said blithely. That wasn't technically true. She'd aced the *midterm*, but then had become distracted by Rush Week and had barely managed a B at the end. But she wouldn't tell Debbie that.

Debbie momentarily brightened. "Can I have your notes?"

"I threw them out," the blonde lied.

Debbie's smile melted. "Honest?" she squeaked.

"Really," the blonde said swiftly, pleased to crush Debbie's hopes. Now she understood why Debbie had asked her up to her room. She wanted the blonde to bail her out.

Like she could be bothered.

"Shit, shit, shit!" Debbie erupted, and she scrambled out of the beanbag – *not* a graceful maneuver – and pawed frantically through the mess on her desk. Papers, notebooks and pens clattered to the floor as she dug and – dear God – she might have been drooling. The blonde thought it might be a good time to leave – in fact, she could *see* herself striding purposefully to the door – but she was feeling vaguely disinclined to stir from the bed.

"Yes!" Debbie hissed as she wrapped her fingers around several little white pills on the desk top. She popped them into her mouth and washed them down with a day-old can of Coke.

The blonde roused herself enough to ask Debbie what in hell she was doing.

"I gotta get these bad thoughts outta my head," Debbie chattered. "I gotta come *down*."

"But are those pills *safe*?" the blonde asked, more out of curiosity than concern. Although she was a sophisticated sophomore, she had no firsthand knowledge of pharmaceuticals.

"Everybody takes them," Debbie assured her as she began pacing in front of the bunk. "They're *perfectly* safe."

"How many did you take?" the blonde asked.

"Enough," Debbie huffed. And she continued pacing, five steps to the door, five back to the bunk, to and fro, to and fro. It was making the blonde dizzy, so she focused instead on the drab curtains and planned her wardrobe for her date Friday night. The new gold sweater would complement her hair, but her tan had faded with the first frost. Would gold make her look sallow?

"Not enough," Debbie decided, and while the blonde was still contemplating her sweater chest, she gulped down another four or five pills.

But before the blonde could question her impulsive behavior, she lit another joint, and since it would have been rude to turn her down, the blonde obligingly took a hit.

And another.

Time passed.

* * *

The blonde slowly drifted back to the here and now and realized it was getting late. Debbie's room had grown shadows, and the blonde sensed if she didn't leave *now*, the cafeteria would be closed for dinner. She yawned and rolled off the bunk.

Debbie was sprawled on the floor, her head lolling on the edge of the beanbag.

"I have to go," the blonde said as she fumbled around the floor for her purse.

Debbie said nothing.

"Did you hear me?" the blonde asked irritably. "I'm *leaving*." She swept her hands through the trash on the floor, feeling for her purse, and grazed Debbie's cheek instead.

It was clammy.

The blonde snatched back her hand and squinted at Debbie through the gloom. The girl didn't move. Didn't make a sound.

The blonde gingerly shook her shoulder. "Deb? Can you hear me?"

Nothing. Not even a snore.

"Oh, God," the blonde groaned. But she forced herself to lean in close to Debbie's face and eventually detected a tiny puff of rancid breath.

"Deb, wake up!" the blonde ordered, and she shook the girl's shoulder even harder. When that didn't work, she slapped Debbie's cheeks a couple of times, and her voice rose harshly.

Debbie didn't respond.

The blonde sat back on her heels. Okay, she thought, she needed to get help. Debbie had obviously taken too many pills and she probably needed to get her stomach pumped.

But as the blonde scratched her own head, pondering her options, she could smell the marijuana smoke clinging to her hair and hands. If she ran for help, the firemen or the police would smell the dope, too, and she'd be busted.

Well, she thought, she could make an anonymous phone call and just leave before help arrived.

But where, she asked herself, was the glory in that?

And then she got an idea.

* * *

The blonde ran across campus to her sorority house, charged up the stairs to the attic and stripped. She loved that particular skirt and sweater vest, but they reeked, so she stuffed every piece of clothing she'd been wearing into a shopping bag, then scrubbed herself down in a scalding shower, slipped into a fresh shirt and jeans, slapped a woolly cap onto her wet curls, then slithered back downstairs to dispose of the bag full of clothes in the garbage cans behind the sorority house.

Then she dragged her roommate out of the lounge. “We have to go save Debbie,” she announced.

Her friend looked at her in some consternation. She had been engrossed in the television with some of her sorority sisters and wasn't tracking. “Debbie who? Save her from what?”

“She's threatening to take pills,” the blonde said. “She called me. We've got to stop her.”

And before her friend could suggest something practical, like calling the cops, the blonde was marching purposefully out the door. The friend shrugged helplessly, grabbed a jacket and chased after the blonde.

The blonde rapidly recalculated the glory quotient for her efforts. Normally, she didn't care to share the limelight. Saving a drugged-out student in her own dorm room would be a very big deal. The university president might even issue a proclamation and congratulate her at the homecoming game. On the other hand, drugs were illegal. The blonde figured it would be best to have a witness when she crashed Debbie's room to save her.

As they huffed up the staircase in the dorm, the blonde guessed it had been twenty to twenty-five minutes since she'd found Debbie passed out on the floor. No problem, she chattered to herself. Debbie was a big, strong girl. She'd be fine.

They ran down the hallway and slammed through Debbie's door (the blonde had conveniently left it unlocked). Debbie was still lying on the floor.

She was blue and most definitely dead.

"Oh, sweet Jesus," the friend moaned.

The blonde's dreams crumbled. "You stupid *ass*!" she hissed at the body.

But she dutifully dialed the desk for help.

* * *

The president did not issue a proclamation. The university public relations machine revved up and effectively put a lid on the details of the unfortunate death in one of its dorms. The blonde, her friend and any other student or employee who had happened to glimpse the body or the mortuary van was strongly urged to refrain from talking to anyone – for the sake of the school. The blonde grudgingly acquiesced, figuring that at least she could get some well-deserved credit back home.

But at the funeral home, before the blonde could even begin to insinuate herself in the proceedings, Debbie's mother tearfully cornered her and her best friend and begged them – in front of their parents, which was really playing unfair – not to breathe a word to anyone about the overdose. For Debbie's sake, she pleaded. For the family's peace of mind. And she looked at them with ravaged eyes.

The blonde almost rebelled. She deserved *something* for her trouble.

But her own mother stepped in and pledged the blonde's silence for her.

The blonde silently fumed.

But she learned a good lesson.

Always plan ahead.

CHAPTER SIXTEEN

"Shit," Adam growled when he heard I was once again helping Louie Brandon, and he stomped from the breakfast table to drive himself to the station.

Emily glared at me and ran after him to the garage, jiggling provocatively in her shorty pajamas.

I looked at Dave for backup.

He just shrugged and hid behind the newspaper.

Mother sighed and collected Emily's and Adam's plates. "I think the boy might be a tad jealous," she observed.

"Of Louie Brandon?" I scoffed. "That's absurd!"

But Adam had been in a fairly pleasant mood – well, bacon does bring out the best in any man – until I'd informed the table that I'd coerced Berger into saving a slot for Louie in his summer computer class. Mother had nodded her approval, Dave had acted like he hadn't heard a word I'd said (I knew better), Emily had been clueless, but Adam's face had darkened, and it was all he could do to swallow his last mouthful of toast before bolting out the back door.

Mother squirted soap into the sink and began sliding dishes into the suds. "It's isn't absurd in the least. You're focusing a good deal of attention on Louie – of which I *approve* – but I imagine Adam feels slighted."

"Oh, for God's sake," I groaned, "all I did was squeeze Berger for a favor. How does that slight *Adam*?"

"Whom have you squeezed lately for Adam's benefit?" Mother countered.

I did *not* look at Dave, but I heard him snickering behind the paper.

"I don't squeeze anyone for Adam's benefit," I said stoutly. "That would be nepotism."

"Well, perhaps you should practice a little more of it," Mother said as she slapped the dish rag over the plates.

"And just what does that mean?" I demanded, bristling at the suggestion.

"It means," Mother said as she tossed some bacon scraps Barney's way, "Adam's feeling insecure. He's in a new job, he's still trying to prove himself, and the one person whose approval he desperately needs appears to care more about Louie Brandon's success than his."

"That is not true," I said hotly.

"Of course it isn't," Mother agreed. "But Adam apparently thinks so. You overruled him on Louie's drunk and disorderly arrest, you chastised him for the way he handled Louie's traffic accident, you persuaded *me* to loan Louie my car, and now you're browbeating Detective Berger into enrolling Louie in his class. How do you think that looks to Adam?"

"Like I'm doing my job," I said obstinately.

"Jo," Mother sighed as the phone began ringing in the dining room, "Adam sees you as his mother."

Audible gulp from Dave.

"Start acting like it."

And she wrung her hands dry on her apron as she trotted to the dining room to answer the phone.

There was a belated pregnant silence behind the newspaper.

"His *mother*?" I finally said.

"You are much younger than Molly," Dave said hastily.

I batted the newspaper from his face.

"And sexier," he added in self-defense.

"Your ex-wife has bigger tits," I reminded him.

"More than offset by your splendid ass," he said chivalrously.

I peered over my shoulder at my back side. "It *is* rather nice," I agreed. But I wasn't yet mollified. "Do you really think Adam looks at me as his mother?"

"I *am* his father," Dave said logically. "And you *are* my honey."

I bit my lip. "I was never a good mother," I said shakily.

Dave's eyes softened. "Babe, you never had the chance."

And we sat at the table for a moment, gripping hands and staring into each other's soul.

But eventually, I had to collect my badge and gun and go to work. Heartfelt moments are fleeting.

Dave did stop me before I could slip out the door.

"You aren't planning to pay this Brandon guy's tuition, are you?"

"A hundred bucks?" I scoffed. "When pigs fly."

Dave beamed. "That's my girl!"

CHAPTER SEVENTEEN

I didn't catch up with Adam at all during my shift. The perp who'd shot himself was awake and scared shitless, so against the advice of his attorney, he was spilling his guts about all sorts of interesting unrelated drug connections at the university, hoping that the more names he named, the less inclined the cops would be to nail him for burglary. I wasn't promising him anything, but since Bradley really likes to keep the lid on drugs, Jamal and I spent the morning at the hospital questioning the suspect and the afternoon closeted with Sarah Tate, the university security chief, plotting how to run with this new information.

Well, Jamal and Sarah plotted. Even though the tattletale was originally my collar, Jamal can sniff out a high-profile investigation in his sleep. Jamal has great expectations for his future, and isn't above shoving other detectives aside. I didn't really need to impress Bradley anymore, so I was okay with taking the occasional note and letting Jamal and Sarah sink their teeth into it. Besides, Bradley says I need to learn how to delegate.

So when it came time to clock out, I looked purposefully at my watch, politely excused myself (Jamal and Sarah barely noticed my departure) and drove to Louie Brandon's place to stoke his fires over computer school.

Of course, he wasn't home. As his girlfriend Jenny breathlessly reminded me, Louie worked the three-to-eleven shift at the video store.

Jenny was breathless because she was trying to cook dinner and catch up on the laundry while baby Tyler howled with colic and Jason tore through the duplex with two other preschoolers Jenny was watching.

"Gosh, can you take Tyler?" she asked as she thrust a kicking bundle of baby into my arms. "I gotta start the macaroni."

I squawked in protest – it is a fallacy that once a mother, always a mother; I was way out of practice when it came to safely hoisting a squirming four-month-old onto my shoulder – but Jenny blithely turned her back on me and whipped spoons around the pots on the stove. Her face was flushed from the heat of the kitchen and damp wisps of hair clung to her forehead. She was wearing a tank top and cutoffs – not nearly enough clothing for April, to my way of thinking, but her outfit did expose lots of post-pregnancy flesh, and my suspicious cop's eye could spot no evidence of fresh bruising. I relaxed as much as Baby Tyler would let me.

"I gotta admit," Jenny babbled as she emptied a box of macaroni and biliously orange cheese powder into a pot of boiling water, "I got scared when I saw you at the door. I thought something musta happened to Louie."

"I'm sorry," I said around the baby's bobbing head, "we sometimes forget people see cops as bad news."

"Oh, *you're* not bad news," Jenny said hastily. "You've been nothing but *nice* to us."

"But?" I prodded. The baby had burrowed into the crook of my neck and seemed temporarily secure.

"Well, geez," Jenny said as she pulled a nutritious package of hot dogs out of the fridge, "all I could think was he'd had another accident or something."

"Does that happen often? Accidents or something?"

"Not really," Jenny said – too swiftly. "I mean – he *can* get kinda out of line if he's drinking – as you know." And she giggled nervously, like we were some kind of comrades in arms. "But he's at work now – so *that's* not a problem."

"It's good to be working," I agreed, and ventured a mild pat to the baby's back. He might have cooed.

"And when you *didn't* tell me Louie was dead, well, I still kinda panicked at the thought maybe you'd come to take back the car." The look she flashed at me over the steam rising from the stove was suddenly desperate.

"I'm not here for the car," I assured her.

"Oh, thank God," she said, with such relief, it was almost embarrassing. "I mean, I know it's not really our car and we gotta give it back as soon as the insurance money comes through, but gosh, Miz Ferris, you have no idea what a godsend that car is. I don't know how we'd manage without it."

Well, they'd walk, or take a taxi, or borrow someone else's car, but only a crabby middle-aged woman with a short memory of young parenthood would crassly point out something so obvious, so I just smiled and continued to pat the baby's back.

There was an eruption from the living room, then Jason and his cohorts stampeded into the kitchen, stomped over my toes and crashed to the back door.

"Jason!" his mother scolded from the stove. "No running! *Walk*!"

Jason grinned impishly at his mother over his shoulder and flew outside. His companions slowed only fractionally and whipped out after him.

"God, boys!" Jenny said in exasperation, and dumped a handful of slimy hot dogs into a pot. My taste buds curdled.

"Jason looks good," I volunteered. I had noted the ace bandage still wrapped around his wrist and gritty with dirt and food stains.

"Oh, yeah," Jenny said breezily. "He heals fast. You know, being just a kid and all."

I nodded sagely. Tyler rewarded me with a wet burp.

Jenny tossed me a kitchen towel as though baby barf was no big deal. I grimaced and tried to sop up milky residue without dislodging the child.

"So," Jenny said as she yanked plates out of a cupboard, "if Louie's okay and you don't want the car back, why *are* you here?"

The girl acted like a gushing teenager, but she wasn't dumb. She knew cops didn't drop by just to burp the baby.

So I told her about Berger's computer class and how he was holding a spot for Louie if the Brandons could scrape up the tuition. Strictly speaking, I should have told Louie first. After all, if for some reason he didn't like the idea, he should be allowed to take a pass without Jenny nagging him. But I had scared her unnecessarily with my unannounced arrival, so it seemed only fair to give her some semi-good news.

And she was suddenly bubbling as much as her pots. "Oh, my God, that's so *neat*. Louie *loves* computers. And he's really, *really* smart. I can't believe you'd do this for us."

"*I* haven't done anything," I cautioned her. "*Louie* has to make the class work – *and* pay the tuition."

"We can do that," Jenny said, even though I could see her squinting hard as she tried to figure out just how they'd come up with a hundred bucks. "I mean, I can work some extra shifts, and we got friends who might give us a loan. Oh, gosh, Louie just *has* to get into that class." And she stirred the macaroni with fierce determination.

I'd let my attention on Baby Tyler wander, and I felt him sliding headfirst over my shoulder. I quickly grabbed him by the thighs and yanked him back from the brink, but I must have squeezed too hard, because suddenly he was shrieking.

Much more than a little tug on chubby baby legs warranted.

Jenny and I locked eyes over the stove as the baby screamed. Jenny licked dry lips. "I think I gotta change him," she said, and she started across the kitchen to retrieve him.

But I turned my back on her and took the squalling baby into the living room. I carefully placed him on the couch and, as his little arms thrashed and his face turned nearly purple with the effort of screeching, unwrapped the thin blanket that had swaddled him. His feet abruptly shot free and nearly clubbed me on the jaw. He was writhing in agony.

It was easy to see why. A violent purple bruise ringed his right thigh. It was so deep, it was stone hard to the touch. I must have inadvertently dug my fingers into it when I grabbed him as he slipped over my shoulder. I felt a hot flush of guilt for hurting him.

And a hotter wave of anger at his parents. "How did this happen?" I hissed at Jenny.

She was hanging back in fear in the doorway to the kitchen. "It's not what you're thinking, Miz Ferris," she protested weakly. "It was an accident."

"An *accident*?" I spat at her.

"Honest," she jabbered, "Louie was changing him and he started to roll off the table and Louie grabbed him – just like *you* did," she added, rallying briefly.

"No," I said, gently rewrapping Tyler in the blanket, "*not* like I did. I couldn't have caused bruising like this."

"Well, Louie's a man, isn't he?" Jenny said defensively.

I just shook my head and lifted the baby to cradle him. He was having no part of me. I didn't feel or smell right. So I wordlessly passed him to his mother.

Jenny clutched the baby desperately to her chest.

Outside, the boys squealed in play.

In the kitchen, the macaroni boiled over.

The baby gulped for air.

"Jenny," I said, "I have to report this."

Tears spilled onto Jenny's cheeks. "Oh, no, you *can't*. It was an *accident*. If you call in children's services, Louie'll freak out. You can't *do* this!"

Her eyes pleaded with me over the baby.

I sighed.
"I must."
Mother and baby howled.

CHAPTER EIGHTEEN

It was after business hours, and it took a while for the social worker on call to respond to my message. I was no longer welcome in the Brandon home, so I spent an uncomfortable hour in my car, parked at the curb, working a crossword puzzle and fretting that I might have jumped to too many conclusions too fast. But the children's services worker finally showed up, and together we confronted Jenny.

She was definitely hostile toward me – I was no longer the nice cop who had saved her family with a car – but the social worker was a low-key older woman who efficiently cut through Jenny's protests of innocence and persuaded her that the smart thing to do – and the quickest way to dispose of such ludicrous allegations – was to take Baby Tyler to the emergency room for an evaluation. Jenny reluctantly acquiesced.

I thought Louie should be apprised of the proceedings. The social worker shot me a disappointed look and agreed with Jenny that Louie's presence wasn't necessary.

Jenny balked at the thought of yet another emergency room bill. The social worker assured her that the visit would be on the house. And we all trooped off to the hospital.

The same doctor who had been on duty when Jason hurt his wrist was haunting the emergency room when we rolled in. I thought that was a plus for the cause of truth and justice; she was predisposed to suspect the worst. But after an hour of X-rays and carefully examining the baby, she could conclude only that the bruising was consistent with the injuries that could have occurred if a grown man had forcefully grabbed a baby while he was sliding headfirst for the floor.

Jenny was allowed to take the baby home.

But only after she told me to go fuck myself.

The social worker patted my arm as she and I watched Jenny stomp out. The doctor was skulking wordlessly behind us.

“They're on our radar now,” the social worker assured me. “We'll keep an eye on the kids.”

I turned in frustration to the doctor. “Am I wrong? Is this just another accident?”

The doctor gave me a pained look. “The baby's injuries are consistent with the mother's story. I can't prove otherwise.”

“But what do you *think*?” I pressed.

“You *know* what I think,” the doctor said, and excused herself to tend to the victims of a traffic accident.

“*Shit*!” I hissed.

“Jo,” the social worker intoned as she packed up her briefcase, “you know how these things go. We can't act without proof.”

“Meantime, if Louie *is* an abuser, I've just pissed him off big time,” I seethed. “He'll take it out on Jenny.”

“She's an adult,” the social worker said. “She knows who to call for help.”

“But she won't,” I said unhappily.

“Not yet,” the social worker agreed. “But he knows we're watching. He'll behave.”

I wasn't reassured.

But the social worker felt confident enough to call it a day.

I went home to break the news to Mother.

* * *

I had missed dinner – it was nearly ten o'clock when I plodded through the back door into the kitchen – but Mother took one look at my dejected face and immediately volunteered to reheat the leftovers. Dave gauged the depths of my scowl and wordlessly pulled two beers out of the refrigerator. Adam and Emily were curled up on the couch, intertwined as they watched *Coach* reruns, and no one was inclined to invite them to the kitchen to join us for a late-night snack. This was a war council for the adults.

"So explain yourself," Mother said as she shoved a plate of meat loaf and mashed potatoes under my nose.

I took a swig of beer and wiped the foam off my lips with the sleeve of my blouse. "It's bad," I said.

"We know *that*," Dave said. "You look like you've been run over by a bulldozer."

"I really fucked up," I admitted.

Dave looked at Mother. "I think this is the end of the world. Maybe you ought to get a drink yourself."

Mother nodded, and as she uncorked a bottle of wine, I described the unfortunate developments in the Brandon household and my own role in casting official suspicion on Louie. I was halfway through my dinner and Dave was reaching for another beer by the time I finished my report.

Mother's eyes were fixed on her wine glass. "This is distressing news," she said.

I poked forlornly at my meat loaf. "I feel like an ass," I said.

"Because you tried to help some misguided kid?" Dave asked. He firmly believed that a man was innocent until proven guilty, so "misguided kid" was as far as he was willing to go in condemning Louie. But Mother and I looked at each other and knew better.

"I ignored Jenny's black eye," I said doggedly. "I ignored the boy's sprained wrist. I ignored Louie's blatant hostility. All because his dad died in a fire, and fire has damaged my ability to think clearly."

Mother automatically came to my defense. "You were aided and abetted by me. You didn't act alone."

"He abused a *baby*!" I hissed.

"Allegedly," Dave said.

"For *sure*," I shot back. "I left those *children* in danger because of a half-assed connection between Louie and my dead daughter."

"It was *not* half-assed," Mother said stoutly. "You have certain *insights* because of Elizabeth's death. You *shouldn't* ignore them."

"But she shouldn't let them overrule her common sense either," Dave said grimly.

Mother's eyes flared, but I couldn't object as I slipped the last of my meat loaf to Barney. I deal daily with the Louies of the world. I should have known better.

"There *is* the question of my car," Mother said as she took my plate and silverware to the sink.

"We get it back tomorrow," Dave said firmly.

But Mother shook her head. "Who are we really hurting if we take back the car? Louie or Jenny and the children?"

"You really can't allow him to keep your car, Ruth," Dave protested. Despite his inclination to defend the downtrodden, he had a much more realistic grasp on our finances than either Mother or I. The car was an expensive investment. Leaving it in Louie's hands was risky. Therefore, the car had to come home.

"If we take back the car," Mother said reasonably, "it could destabilize Louie to the point where he takes it out on Jenny and the children."

"If we let him keep the car," Dave countered, "we just reinforce his bad behavior. He needs to know there are consequences to abusing the generosity of others."

I dreaded the thought of Mother back behind the wheel of a car, so it was probably convenient for me to agree with her. “I don't think it's wise to aggravate Louie at this point. He has too many problems to deal with as it is.”

Dave rolled his eyes as he unearthed another beer from the fridge. “Jo, it's time to cut your losses.”

This from a man who had nearly lost everything to a mine in Vietnam.

But as it turned out, the question of the car was taken out of our hands.

As Dave pried the cap off his beer, there was a distinct thump from the street. Barney lifted his ears and shot out of the kitchen, growling in a most ungentlemanly fashion. There was a grunt from the living room as Adam disengaged from Emily, and then the sound of Adam tracking Barney to the front door.

There was a grinding rasp from the street, then Barney was pawing ferociously at the front door.

“What the hell?” Dave said, beer bottle dangling from his hand.

We heard Adam unlatching the front door, then Barney crashing through the screen onto the porch.

“Adam!” Emily shouted from the hall.

We bolted from the kitchen.

We landed on the porch with Emily. Barney was barking loudly and racing furiously around Mother's car, which was hung up on the boulder that marks the foot of our driveway. The headlights were cutting at an odd angle into the night sky, but there was enough light to see Adam and Louie Brandon grappling in the street, just beyond the driver's door, which was hanging open.

“Adam!” Emily screamed again, and she tried to leap from the porch.

Dave grabbed her and shoved her back against Mother. Mother obediently wrapped her scrawny arms around Emily as

Dave and I jumped from the porch and zeroed in on Adam and Louie.

"Adam!" I shouted. "Back off!"

He ignored me. Big surprise.

Dave, who has never been a physical guy outside the bedroom, wedged himself between Adam and Louie. Louie, irritated by the interruption, took a swing at Dave. Adam, enraged at the attack on his dad, lowered his head and butted Louie in the chest. Louie fell back against Mother's car, and Adam sprawled on top of him, pinning Louie to the hood.

"Enough!" Dave hollered.

Dave never yells. He rules with reasoned argument and devastating logic. He *never* raises his voice.

So I froze in astonishment, and Adam lowered the fist raised to smash into Louie's jaw.

Louie stared wildly at all of us and squirmed beneath Adam's weight.

"This stops *now*," Dave said firmly. "Let him go, Adam."

"He smashed Ma's car," Adam protested breathlessly.

"It's a dented fender," Dave said. "Let him go."

Adam glared at his father. Years of abandonment flashed between them. Adam had grown up for the most part without a dad. Only his own initiative had brought him back into his father's life. So maybe his father had no right to tell him what to do.

Then he glanced at Mother huddling on the porch with Emily, and she slowly nodded at him. Adam huffed and lifted himself off Louie.

"You," Dave said, pointing a rigid finger at Louie, "get the hell off my property."

Well, that was a bit of bombast, too, since technically the house was in my name, but Louie didn't have a clue of our domestic finances as he scrambled away from Adam.

He dangled the car keys in front of us in a final show of bravado. “Take your goddamn car and shove it,” he said, most unimaginatively. “You called the county down on my *house*.”

“You hurt your kids,” I said.

“You're a fucking bitch,” Louie spat back.

Adam moved menacingly toward him.

Dave stilled him with one look.

Louie snorted as he straightened his jacket. “Fucking bitches think they run the world. Well, they don't run *me*.” And he threw the car keys onto the hood of the car.

Adam twitched.

Dave held him back with a palm to his chest.

Emily whimpered in Mother's arms.

I squeezed my eyes shut and wished I'd made many other choices.

Louie disappeared into the darkness up the street. Neighbors who had gathered on their porches because of the noise slithered back indoors. Dave scooped the keys off the hood and tossed them at Adam.

Adam caught them in midair. “I *told* you Louie Brandon was bad news,” he said as he slid into Mother's car to rock it off the boulder.

I gulped but forced myself to say it anyway. “You were right.”

Adam grunted.

Dave looked from me to Adam. “She's never *ever* said that to me.”

Adam shrugged dismissively. “Must be my lucky day.”

“Cherish it,” Dave said as he ushered the rest of us indoors. “It'll *never* happen again.”

CHAPTER NINETEEN

The blonde sighed with impatience. Becky Freeman, bathed in the yellow glow from a spotlight in the ceiling, moaned softly and twitched her shoulders in pain. She no longer had a clue where she was or who was sitting at her bedside. The cancer that had first been detected in her breast and prompted a double mastectomy was now running rampant in her lungs and her liver and her spine. She was twenty-four years old. She wouldn't see twenty-five.

The blonde was exceedingly healthy and regretting that she had allowed herself to be trapped into this useless vigil. It had seemed like a good idea a month ago. Back then, she had studied Becky's charts and couldn't imagine her lasting more than a week.

So she had blithely offered to sit with Becky at night so her exhausted parents could go home and catch a few hours of sleep. The blonde's newly acquired husband was not at all pleased with her absence – he had become accustomed to vigorous sex on a nightly basis, and the blonde had learned from her medical training how to make it quite worth his while – but she also knew that the longer she sacrificed her home life to keep watch on Becky, the more praise Becky's family would loudly heap onto her shoulders.

It had seemed like such a *small* effort to make then. The blonde and her husband had moved back to her hometown so they both could enroll in graduate school in the fall. He was going for an MBA, with hopes of parlaying the degree into a job offer from a

Fortune 500 company. She was going for a master's in hopes of turning her $25,000-a-year job into something a little more lucrative. Meanwhile, having established themselves in a smart ranch on the edge of town with some mortgage help from her in-laws, they had an entire summer to fritter away until classes started in the fall.

Her husband had taken up tennis and golf, to prepare himself for future clients. She was already proficient at tennis and disdained golf, so she lounged aimlessly under the hot July sun on her patio and wondered just what she could do with herself. And then Becky's mother had mournfully confided to the blonde's mother that treatment was no longer a viable option for her daughter, and a window of opportunity opened wide for the blonde. She could volunteer to sit with Becky, and her parents would be forever in her debt. It seemed a small inconvenience compared to the rewards down the road. Becky's father was a judge; her mother sat on the city's planning commission. Someday, their heartfelt references could make a difference.

Besides, how long could a woman battling such an aggressive cancer last?

Well, a long time, apparently.

The blonde had been sitting at Becky's beside for weeks, sometimes holding out until dawn before creeping home. At first, it had been mildly interesting. Becky was still lucid then, and she was quite frank in answering the blonde's questions about life and imminent death. The blonde thought such insight might be useful in her career. But Becky's communication skills had dropped with her increased reliance on painkillers, and it had been more than a week since she'd said anything coherent. The blonde had resolutely kept her vigil, doggedly reading the textbooks for her fall classes as Becky moaned and drooled through the night. But it was becoming a tedious commitment.

The blonde had planned to stick it out to the end. Her husband was complaining bitterly, but a few strategic morning wakeup calls were keeping him in line. And Becky's parents were already promising to do *everything* possible in return for the blonde's generosity. She modestly deflected such offers, but already had their names in her resume. All she had to do was maintain her sanity until Becky had the good grace to die.

Only that morning, the doctor's office had called with her own test results, and suddenly keeping herself in the limelight by inconveniencing herself with good deeds performed on Becky's behalf no longer seemed imperative. She had found a way to make *herself* the undisputed center of attention. She was pregnant.

The blonde closed her textbook and folded her hands as she watched Becky shudder through another wave of pain. If she didn't have a hit of morphine soon, the agony would awaken her and she would begin to wail. That would be most upsetting. The blonde really disliked it when patients wailed.

But Becky's IV was calibrated to release the drug at specific intervals. Even if she howled, she could get no more morphine than the drip allowed.

The blonde sat back in irritation, her finger marking her spot in the textbook, as Becky mewled into her pillow. Well, yes, it hurt, but what did anyone expect with cancer? Bliss?

She ought to just die, the blonde thought.

And then she unexpectedly burped. The fast-food burger she had wolfed down for dinner was not sitting well.

That was to be expected in the early stages of pregnancy, she reasoned.

But as a sour taste rose in her throat, she admitted that the nausea of pregnancy would be much easier to tolerate if someone *else* would witness how stoically she was withstanding it.

Becky groaned again into her pillow. It would be at least another hour before her IV would allow her another shot of relief.

The blonde stared, perplexed, at the many tubes running into Becky's veins and the many monitors recording her vital signs. They really seemed to be a waste of time – hers and Becky's. Her one-time friend was doomed to die. Cancer was eating her alive, and at this stage, there was no stopping it. The morphine in its allowed dosages would go only so far. It would keep Becky from screaming her lungs out, but it wouldn't save her.

Nothing would save her. At the most, she would last a few more weeks.

Meanwhile, her hospital bills would mount – were her parents even *thinking* about that? The blonde doubted it – and everything the blonde did at these vigils would be minimalized by Becky's death. The time she was spending at Becky's bedside could really be put to much better use by milking her own relatives for sympathy over her pregnancy.

The blonde stared at the IV. There was *so* much to do. Whipping her husband into line so he was catering to *her* instead of his job prospects. Manipulating her parents into fawning over *her* condition instead of obsessing over their retirement options. Perhaps injecting a little *danger* into her condition instead of bravely enduring the mediocre discomforts of pregnancy. She just didn't have time anymore for Becky.

But prudence told her she couldn't simply walk out. She had promised Becky's parents she would be here for them. Leaving now would appear *much* too selfish.

The blonde couldn't afford to look selfish. It was a violation of her game plan.

But her career had taught her a thing or two about IVs.

Wouldn't it really be in everyone's best interests if Becky's agony ended now?

The blonde glanced at the doorway. No one was watching. So she carefully fiddled with the IV.

And the next time Becky moaned, she told her most solicitously that it was okay, it was time to push the button for another hit of morphine. The blonde would have done it herself, but there was the troubling matter of fingerprints. So she waited in exasperation for Becky's traumatized brain to process the message.

Becky rolled her eyes, but the pain was strong, and she greedily pumped more morphine into her veins.

The blonde watched the monitors. Becky's breathing slowed as the pain abated, but the whimpering didn't stop. She was at the stage where the whimpering would *never* stop.

Oh, well, the blonde thought, and she fiddled with the IV again.

She huddled over Becky's head. “It's all right, dear,” she whispered. “Push the button for the meds. You'll feel *so* much better.”

Becky's eyelids fluttered, and her hand twitched as though reaching for the pump. But then she sighed and her hand fell to her chest. She breathed deeply. Strongly.

Well, *fuck*, the blonde thought. On the one hand, she pictured days of sitting at Becky's side, trapped by her own promise to Becky's mother. On the other, she pictured her own family, catering to all the demands of her morning sickness.

Was there really a choice?

“Becky,” she whispered, “push the button.”

But Becky was floating on the high of her last injection.

“God,” the blonde sighed, “this is your *own* fault. You're *making* me do this.”

Then she wrapped her hand around Becky's and forced her thumb down on the button.

She watched as another dose of morphine dripped into Becky's veins. She held her breath. She wasn't a pharmacology student. She wasn't positive that her manipulations with the IV would be enough. Maybe, just maybe, she'd have to fiddle with the IV again.

But Becky's breathing suddenly slowed.

Her fingers twitched and her eyes rolled up under her eyelids.

Her moans died as her heart slowly petered out.

The blonde patiently counted the seconds.

Then she went to the nurses' station and dabbed at her eyes with a Kleenex.

"I think we have a problem," she sniffed.

CHAPTER TWENTY

Louie's mother caught up with me by phone the next morning. I didn't get a chance to say much of anything as she screamed at me for persecuting her son. I eventually told her to have a nice day and hung up on her in mid-rant.

Henry grinned at me over his coffee. “Got a problem?” he asked.

I shrugged elaborately. “Can you recommend a dentist? I think I need a new one.”

Henry chortled maliciously.

There are *no* secrets in our squad room.

*   *   *

Bradley was taking a spring vacation to New Mexico, and I spent most of the morning with him, going over our budget and getting instructions from him for a city council meeting that would convene in his absence. There was nothing seriously affecting the police department on the agenda, but a general council tendency to tighten the belt had Bradley mildly concerned.

“You just need to be there to keep them from doing anything stupid,” he lectured me.

“Stupid, like what?” I demanded. I *hated* council meetings. Politicians give me hives.

"Like reducing the equipment budget," Bradley said. "We really need new cruisers."

"They're threatening our new *cruisers*?" I asked, appalled. Our fleet was ailing. The thought of Adam spending most of his shift in one of our aging patrol cars often gave me heartburn. I couldn't *imagine* losing the three new cruisers we had been promised.

"Or maybe the overtime budget," Bradley said absently. His heart was already in the desert.

"*Overtime*?" I hissed. "Good God, without overtime, half our weekend shifts would go uncovered."

"It's just a possibility," Bradley said as he steered me to the door. "You just need to be prepared."

I stonewalled in the doorway. "Maybe you need to send someone else to council – someone with more diplomatic skills."

"I already asked Jamal," Bradley said. "He has a prior commitment."

"You asked *Jamal*?" I sputtered, aggrieved. "Before *me*?"

"Jamal is a very smooth talker," Bradley pointed out.

"But he knows *nothing* about the budget," I spat.

"My point exactly," Bradley said as he shoved me out to the squad room. "Be there at seven."

I fumed as I stalked to the coffeepot. I'd rather chew *glass* than let Jamal fumble in council with my carefully crafted budget. And Bradley knew that very well. I had been hoodwinked.

Herchek was behind the public service counter, waving a pink message slip at me.

"Oh, *what*?" I snarled.

"Just a message, Jo," Herchek said placidly. "You can pitch it for all I care."

"Right," I said as I snatched the slip from his hand.

He played hurt and turned his back to me.

I felt like an ass, just as he'd intended, and stomped to my desk in embarrassment with the message slip clutched around my coffee mug.

The call had come from Sandra Porter. There was no indication on the slip what she wanted, other than a request that I call her back as soon as possible. She left both a home and a work phone number.

I cradled my lukewarm coffee to my chest and exhaled so hard, my bangs fluttered on my forehead. I had been so busy with Louie Brandon that I had forgotten about Sandra. It was decidedly creepy that suddenly, *she* was calling *me*.

I plopped my mug onto my desk and dialed her work number. I got that newfangled curse on mankind called phone mail. So then I tried her home number and got nothing but ten unanswered rings for my trouble.

"Well, hell," I muttered, and thought fleetingly of tracking Sandra down in person at work.

But then Herchek was waving at me again. "Bank robbery downtown," he said.

"That's fed territory," I said automatically.

"The feds are an hour away and you're the detective on duty," Herchek intoned.

"So's Henry," I groused.

"If you hurry," Herchek said, "you'll get there first."

That would undoubtedly piss Henry off.

So I grabbed my purse and sprinted to the parking lot.

* * *

I was tied up the rest of the shift at the bank. No one had been hurt, but the robber had run off with nearly five thousand dollars. The feds eventually showed up and I dutifully tried to hand off to them, but since the perp was still at large, my presence was required just so the feds would have someone local to blame in case the robber wasn't apprehended. Fortunately, about 7 p.m., two sheriff's deputies stopped a guy for driving with stolen plates and, oh, yeah, he just happened to have a duffel bag stuffed with small bills in his back seat.

I was home by 7:30, once again snarfing up leftovers. I totally forgot Sandra Porter.

An hour later, she stumbled into the road in front of her house and was hammered by a passing pickup truck.

She was D.O.A.

CHAPTER TWENTY-ONE

I don't usually get called out for traffic fatals. Unless there's evidence of criminal intent, good uniforms are perfectly capable of interviewing witnesses, measuring skid marks and scraping the deceased off the pavement. But Adam was working an overtime shift that night and was sent to the scene for traffic control. The name of the victim sounded familiar to him, so before he started bossing around the gawkers, he called me. I nearly beat the ambulance to the hospital.

Sandra Porter was parked in an examination room, still zipped up in a body bag. There was no one attending to her because the short-staffed emergency room crew had better things to do with the living, including the driver of the pickup that had hit Sandra. So no one stopped me when I stole into the examination room and quickly unzipped the bag to shoulder level.

It wasn't one of my wiser moves. I had just wanted to assure myself that the victim was *my* Sandra Porter. The damage to the right side of her head was extensive, and my stomach heaved noisily at the sight of her. I shakily rezipped the bag, but not before I was reasonably certain that the salt and pepper hair and the one undamaged eye belonged to Sandra.

I scurried from the room before anyone could accuse me of abusing a corpse and went in search of the driver. He was moaning in a room down the hall because he didn't believe in seat belts and had smashed his forehead on the steering wheel after he had slammed into Sandra. Several people in scrubs were jabbing him with needles and asking him what day it was, so I didn't get anywhere with him. But one of our patrolmen was observing from a corner where he wouldn't get in the way if the patient went into cardiac arrest, and he slipped out to the hall to brief me.

I didn't know him well. His name was Schafer, and he'd been a highway patrolman for ten years before switching to us a year before. I'd heard he'd grown bored in his old job because he was handling mostly traffic cases, but I for one was happy he'd caught this traffic call. At least I knew someone with experience had examined the scene.

So we meandered down the hall to a coffee pot reserved for staff and he filled me in.

"The driver is Ed Harper, twenty-five, a mechanic specializing in tractor repair," Schafer said, so confident that he never once referred to his notes. "His story is he was driving home after a late job at a farm five miles out of town, and he never saw the victim. He felt a thump, hit the brakes and skidded into a tree, which is when he walloped his head on the steering wheel."

"Drunk?" I asked as I stirred white crystals that passed as cream into a plastic coffee cup.

"The emergency room docs are running a blood test, but I didn't smell alcohol on him," Schafer said as he wisely declined the "creamer."

"Speeding?"

Schafer shook his head. "The skid marks don't look like he was going that fast, and neither does the damage to the truck. He'd have probably walked away if he'd been wearing his seat belt."

"The guy doesn't look too coherent to me," I observed. "When did you question him?"

"While we were waiting for the fire department to arrive and pry him out of his truck," Schafer admitted. "So he might have been distracted by thoughts of escaping the wreckage when he talked to me."

I smiled into my coffee cup. I liked the way this guy thought. “Does he know the victim is dead?”

“Given his injuries, I didn't think it was the appropriate time to apprise him of that fact,” Schafer said gravely. “Besides, no one had declared her dead yet.”

I thought of Sandra's crushed head and grimaced. “Bottom line,” I said, shaking the image out of my head, “what do you think happened?”

Schafer contemplated his coffee. It was really wretched, but I didn't think that was the cause of the sour look on his face. “I think,” he said after a slow swallow, “Mr. Harper was driving sober, but maybe five miles above the speed limit. I think that for reasons unknown, the victim stumbled out into the street at precisely the moment Mr. Harper was tooling by, and I think his right bumper crushed her skull. I think the coroner ought to do a tox screen on the deceased, because a rational woman would know better than to dash out into the middle of traffic.”

“What if there was something on the other side of the road she was frantic to reach?” I asked, toying with possibilities.

Schafer cocked his head as he considered. “There is no indication of any such thing.”

“What if she stumbled on the curb in the dark?”

He nodded slowly. “Older woman. It's possible.”

Schafer dropped a few notches in my estimation. *Older* woman?

“What if she was pushed?” I asked, just to be ornery.

Schafer shook his head emphatically. “No way. *No* one saw anyone else on the scene. There's no indication of a struggle. The victim fell into traffic all on her own.”

“You're sure of that?” I pressed.

Schafer hesitated as he weighed the possibilities. “Ninety percent,” he finally said.

I liked the way he was covering his butt. Even an experienced traffic cop can make a mistake.

But I also respected his training.

"A sad accident," I concluded as I dumped my undrinkable coffee down the sink.

Schafer emptied his coffee on top of mine. He didn't presume to disagree with me.

My life would have been so much simpler if he had.

*   *   *

I drove to Sandra's house. The fire trucks and the gawkers and most of the squad cars were gone by then. Only Adam was left, sitting alone in his cruiser as his lights flashed lonesomely on the surrounding houses.

I leaned into his window. "Why are you here alone? Rookies are supposed to have *partners*."

Adam's eyes were weary. It had been seventeen hours since he'd come on duty. "I'm on overtime, Jo. There's no one left to baby-sit me."

"Well, maybe you could find the energy to baby-sit *me*," I said crisply and nodded at Sandra's house. "I'm going inside. I'd like to have backup."

Adam's spirits perked up immediately. Not because either of us expected to surprise an intruder. Adam was just tired of guarding a deserted accident scene all by himself. Poking around a dead woman's house was much more interesting.

We locked our cars, but Sandra hadn't been nearly as conscientious with her house. It was wide open and just begging strangers to trespass.

The house was a Cape Cod with an addition on the back that housed a sun room and greenhouse. Sandra, I remembered, had been a botany instructor at the university, so the greenhouse made professional sense. If I also remembered correctly, she had never married and never produced children.

The house had the feel of a single woman. There was one recliner in the living room, with newspapers and books stacked haphazardly on both sides. One breakfast bowl and one coffee mug sat in the dish rack. Single servings of macaroni and cheese and beef lasagne were stuffed in the freezer. The one bathroom held only feminine toiletries. And, although the master bedroom had a queen-size mattress, there was only one night stand. Sandra definitely lived alone.

There was an empty wine bottle on the kitchen counter, and a nearly empty wine glass sat on the coffee table in the living room.

"That's a lot of wine," Adam said, nodding at the bottle.

"*If* she drank it all this evening," I cautioned.

"If she was drunk, it makes the accident more feasible," Adam persevered. "She wasn't thinking clearly. Her reflexes were off. She steps into the street, but her reactions are slow and the truck hits her before she can scramble back to the curb."

"I can buy that, but why did she go into the street in the first place?"

Adam shrugged helplessly. "Who knows why a drunk does anything?"

"That's what we're here to find out," I said, and grimly turned into the spare bedroom Sandra used as an office.

There was a basic desktop computer, but I didn't even try to mess with it. I know my limits. Adam has no such self-doubts. He immediately sat at the desk and began pounding the keys.

I preferred to work around him, poking in the desk drawers. They held little to arouse my curiosity – bills neatly filed in folders in one drawer; computer paraphernalia in another; standard stationery and envelopes in a third; grade books and lesson plans in a fourth.

That was disappointing. But there was a manila folder on the window sill. I grabbed it and nestled into a cozy upholstered armchair beside a pole lamp to leaf through its contents.

The folder was filled with things I didn't particularly want to remember.

The first item was a clipping of the local newspaper article and photo from our Girl Scout reunion. Underneath was a group photo of our troop, taken the day we had planted the trees up on the hill. Even though I was already sensitized to the discrepancy by Sandra's mournful observations at the reunion, it was still shocking to see how many of us had been involved in planting the trees and how few of us had showed up for the reunion. Obviously, some of the girls had simply chosen not to attend. But the number who were missing because they were dead was unsettling.

The photos were followed by newspaper clippings of obituaries: Nikki Hocevar, killed in a traffic accident; Debbie Gauer, dead of a drug overdose; Becky Freeman, lost to breast cancer; Carol Jennings, who committed suicide after her divorce; Linda Thornberry, who died in her thirties while skiing with her husband in Colorado; Angela Marino, who picked up a raging infection at the hospital after minor back surgery; Sharon McCarthy, who was killed just the year before when a wildfire descended on her California home.

I shivered. So many dead from such a small group. And now Sandra was among them.

I thumbed again through the obituaries. There were handwritten notes on the articles about Nikki and Debbie, information that probably had been cribbed from their death certificates. A telephone number was scribbled on Carol Jennings' obituary but nothing to explain it. The other obituaries were note-free.

Another piece of paper plotted the deaths chronologically, from Nikki's in 1967 to Sharon's in 1993. Stapled to it was a map of the Midwest, with arrows pinpointing the location of many of the deaths. Most were within miles of our town.

I idly scratched an itch beneath my glasses. What in *hell* had Sandra been trying to prove?

Adam shoved himself back from Sandra's computer. "I can't get past her password. Maybe we should hand it over to Berger."

"Why?" I asked, irritated that he had hauled me back to the present. "Sandra was hit by a truck. Her computer didn't kill her."

"Maybe her emails will tell us why she was disturbed enough to jump out in front of a truck," Adam said reasonably.

"Who says she was disturbed?" I countered.

"Well, she was trying to get in touch with you, wasn't she?"

My eyes narrowed. "How do you know *that*?"

Adam had the good grace to blush.

"I'm waiting for an explanation," I said evenly, the folder temporarily forgotten.

Adam squirmed.

I slapped the folder onto the desk. "Spit it out, rookie."

"Okay, okay," he said, raising his hands in defeat. "I sat at your desk on my dinner break."

"And?" I asked icily.

"I didn't touch your drawers," he assured me.

"You damned well better *not*," I said. Adam pawing through my drawers had *way* too many kinky connotations.

"It was lying right on top of your desk," he said hastily. "A message to call Sandra Porter. That's why I called you when Herchek sent me out here. I recognized the name and thought you ought to know."

"That was the right move. You *always* call me first," I said automatically. "But why were you reading my messages?"

"Jesus, Jo," Adam protested, "it was right there beside your coffee mug. What else was I supposed to read?"

"Maybe your police manual," I said pointedly, "while eating at someone else's desk."

Adam grunted and went back to the computer, punching impossible passwords at random. I leaned back in the armchair and tried to picture what had prompted Sandra to run out into traffic.

Even if she had drunk a snoot full of wine, she shouldn't have been so delirious that she ignored oncoming traffic.

The wine bottle bothered me. It was a work night. A glass of wine or two with dinner wasn't out of line, but an entire bottle seemed excessive for someone who had to work in the morning.

Unless she hadn't been drinking alone.

I was toying with that tantalizing thought when Adam, still playing with the computer, asked, almost offhand, what Sandra had wanted from me.

"I have no idea," I admitted distractedly. Half of my mind was downstairs, trying to remember whether there was a second wine glass in the house.

"You didn't return her call?" Adam asked.

"I did, but I never reached her. I left messages but never heard back."

"When did you last see her?" he asked. He was still focused on the computer screen, but I could hear the gears grinding in his head. Like a good detective, he was trying to nail down the victim's recent contacts.

"Until the reunion, I hadn't seen her since high school graduation – twenty-five years ago."

Adam turned from the computer to me. "So why in hell was she looking for you now?"

I shrugged, tired of his questions. "I don't know. Maybe she was feeling nostalgic." I glanced at my watch. It was closing in on eleven o'clock and Sandra's house was stubbornly revealing no secrets. "Let's clock out, Adam."

His face brightened as his stomach growled, detecting conveniently forgotten. "You think Ma saved any leftovers?"

I patted his shoulder. "Mother *always* has leftovers."

"All right," Adam said, and he shut down the computer with all the flourish of a concert pianist.

I stood in the doorway, hand on the light switch as my eyes swept the room for anything we might have left out of place. Adam rose from his chair to follow me. "You forgot – " he started, then froze.

"Adam?" I prodded. "It's time to go home."

"Aw, shit, Jo," he said, and his voice was oddly mournful.

I followed his gaze to the desk, where I had slapped Sandra's folder of newspaper clippings while sparring with Adam over his impertinent habit of reading my message slips. Some of the clippings had slipped out of the folder so they fanned a bit over the desk. Debbie Gauer's obituary photo stared out at us, as did Nikki Hocevar's.

And so did my daughter's.

I sucked in my breath. This was very, very wrong. *No* one had the right to harbor a photo of my dead daughter.

I shakily reopened the folder. A clipping of the newspaper story about the fire that had killed my husband and daughter was lying beneath the obituaries of my dead classmates. The article included a photo of Steve, my husband, and if that part of the story had poked out of the folder, Adam would have never noticed. There are no pictures of Steve in our house.

But Elizabeth's portrait was sitting on our mantel, and Adam saw it every day. It had been shot a month before she died. There was a bright red ribbon in her curly black hair, and she smiled into the camera with all the impish glee of a four-year-old. In the old days, before I met Dave, just glimpsing that photo could break my heart.

"Jesus, Jo," Adam managed, "what the hell is going on?"

I carefully slipped the clippings back into the folder and slid it under my arm. "I don't know," I said as I shepherded him out of the office, "but I think we'll take this folder home and keep it in the family."

Adam's eyes were troubled. "Is that smart? You aren't – you know – *objective* about Elizabeth."

"No, I'm not," I agreed. "But your dad is. We'll let him sort it out."

Adam reluctantly acquiesced. His stomach really was grumbling. So he let me walk off with evidence from a possible crime scene.

On the way out, I detoured to the kitchen, located Sandra's stemware in one of the cabinets and hastily ran a finger around the rims of the three wine glasses stored there.

It was probably my imagination, but I could have sworn a tiny drop of water clung to the edge of one of the glasses.

I said nothing to Adam.

The night was getting curiouser and curiouser.

CHAPTER TWENTY-TWO

Dave and Mother thoughtfully pored through Sandra's folder, wordlessly swapping pages as they read through the clippings. I paced around them, guzzling beer, while Adam hunched over the kitchen counter, distractedly shoveling cold pasta into his mouth. Emily slept blissfully unaware upstairs. No one had thought it necessary to awaken her.

Both Dave and Mother had been asleep when Adam and I had stormed into the house, but they had cleared their heads quickly when we'd rousted them out of bed. They're morning people, so they wake up fast. And even though Adam and I were rambling a bit, they had gotten the gist of our problem and settled themselves at the kitchen table to sort through Sandra's notes.

Mother flinched at the photo of Elizabeth but said nothing as she passed the clipping to Dave. His mouth tightened as he recognized the photo, but neither spoke as they resolutely plowed through the folder.

Adam got seconds on the beer. I didn't dissuade him.

Mother and Dave simultaneously pushed themselves back from the table. Mother pinched the bridge of her nose. Dave rubbed his hairy jaw.

"Well?" I demanded. Now that I was home and didn't have to act like the cool-headed, unflappable detective for Adam's benefit, I was getting peevish.

"It's a peculiar collection of newspaper clippings," Dave said.

"On the morbid side," Mother added.

"And obviously disturbing to you," Dave said.

"You *think*?" I shot back. "That photo is my *daughter*!" And I gripped my beer bottle till my knuckles turned white.

"Which isn't necessarily sinister," Dave said calmly. "The folder is full of stories about dead people. Your daughter is sadly dead."

"Thank you for reminding me," I snarled. "Obviously, I'd forgotten that fact."

Dave sighed and wordlessly went to the refrigerator to get a beer of his own. I stepped away from him so he couldn't touch me.

"Of course, it's shocking to find Elizabeth's obituary while investigating the death of a woman who certainly never knew her," Mother said. "But is it really significant?"

"Are you *serious*?" I asked, appalled.

"Deadly," Mother replied.

I gulped some beer to steady myself. Mother was supposed to be on *my* side. "Sandra Porter was snooping around dead Girl Scouts," I insisted. "She was obsessed with members of our *troop* who died. Elizabeth has no business in her folder. She wasn't a *Scout*."

"Then you didn't study the folder very thoroughly," Mother said.

I narrowed my eyes suspiciously. The second fast beer made it easy to squint. "What do you mean?"

"There are several obituaries of people – not just Elizabeth – who weren't Scouts," Mother said as she shuffled through the clippings again.

"Like who?"

"Whom," Dave muttered.

I growled.

"Like Ginny Edgerton's grandson," Mother said, producing the appropriate clipping. "Sudden infant death syndrome, last year."

I gingerly fingered the clipping. "I remember that," I admitted grudgingly. "I should have sent a card."

"Yes, you should have," Mother said. "And, of course, there was Marci Gibbs' second husband."

"I didn't know she had a first," I sniffed.

"Jo, you really need to keep up with people," Mother sighed as she handed over another obituary.

I passed the first to Adam and skimmed the second. Marci's husband had died three years before while awaiting a liver transplant. He had been – oh, *shit* – only forty-two.

I edged away from my beer bottle. Perhaps I'd guzzled enough for one night.

"And there's Christine Pope's father," Mother said, waving a final clipping. "Heart failure, six months ago."

"Oh, well," I said, "that doesn't count. He was *old*."

"I beg your pardon?" Mother asked frostily.

"In a male kind of way," I said hastily.

"Excuse me?" Dave asked.

Adam grinned foolishly into his beer.

"I mean," I said, bravely trying to get both feet out of my mouth, "*his* death wasn't accidental or unexpected. Older gentlemen unfortunately die of heart attacks."

Mother and Dave weren't mollified.

But Adam rallied nicely on my behalf.

"Jo has a point," he said, studying the clippings with a surprisingly sober eye. "All of those obituaries are for people who died young – relatively speaking."

"Except for the late Mr. Pope," Dave said thoughtfully.

"And he just might be a mistake," Mother agreed.

"Mistake?" For the person who presumably had a point, I was lost.

"Sandra wasn't obsessed with dead Scouts," Mother said.

"She was tallying premature deaths *connected* to Scouts," Dave clarified.

"Specifically, this troop," Mother said.

"Exactly," Dave said.

And they beamed at each other.

"Wow," Adam said, or maybe that was just the pasta burp erupting from his throat.

"No way." I shook my head. "You're not saying – you aren't even *thinking* – all these deaths are really related – are you?"

"Sandra seemed to think so," Dave pointed out.

"But for God's sake," I protested, "they're mostly natural causes. Cancer. Liver failure. SIDS."

"Drugs," Mother said sadly. "Suicide."

"Not so natural," Dave agreed.

Nobody said fire. I refused to go there.

"This is preposterous," I sputtered.

"But not entirely impossible," Mother said.

"Although highly improbable," Dave amended.

"Kinda weird, though," Adam admitted. "All those dead people."

"I came home asking for *help*," I objected. "*Rational* suggestions. I wasn't expecting lunacy."

Mother smiled wearily and patted my hand. "Then you asked the wrong people, dear."

Dave grinned and toasted Mother with his beer bottle.

The clock chimed midnight.

And their brains turned into pumpkins right before my eyes.

I got another beer.

CHAPTER TWENTY-THREE

The blonde ground her teeth as she waited for the nurse/receptionist to slither back into the cubicle with her discharge instructions. There was a mild ache in her gut, but it was no worse than a monthly bout with cramps. And the pad shoved up between her legs was taking care of the blood. The blonde was not in distress. She simply needed to get home before her husband.

She had parked her son with his grandparents for the day. The boy – nearly two years old – was damned near perfect. He was beautiful, with golden curls and an unbelievably sweet disposition. Other mothers bemoaned the terrible twos. The blonde was not so lucky. *Her* boy was not only intelligent but also obedient. He was precious. He was endearing. Strangers stopped her on the street to fawn over him in his stroller. Both sets of grandparents battled for the privilege of sitting with him. He slept soundly through the night and was always bubbling and charming when awakened. He was already toilet trained and had an extensive, polite vocabulary.

The blonde loathed him.

It hadn't always been that way. When he was born and the nurse placed his slimy, wet body in her arms, she had been enthralled. *She* had produced this life, and he was beautiful. The blue eyes staring at her vacantly in those first few minutes mesmerized her. He was apart from her, yet they were one. She loved him madly then.

But everything changed when they went home. In the hospital, she was pampered as much as he was. Visitors asked solicitously after her well-being as often as they asked about him. *She* had mattered.

But once they were home, once her role of *incubating* had ended, all the attention switched to him. The grandparents no longer waited on *her*; they were all attuned to *him* and *his* mewlings. Visitors were effusive in their reactions to *him*. They never asked about *her* – the sleepless nights, the demands of caring for a helpless little monster, the stress of keeping him healthy and safe. *She* was relegated to the background as everyone else fussed over his colic, his teething and his first precious attempts to crawl.

Her husband was no better than the others. He doted on the baby (although he couldn't deal with diapers that leaked or feedings that turned into milky globs of spit on his shirt). He came home every day and asked how the boy was doing. He never asked about the dark circles under her eyes or the exhaustion that tinged her voice. He wanted sex before her stitches dissolved. He didn't have the slightest *idea* what she was feeling.

The new mothers in her circle were no help. They were so absorbed in the progress of their own perfect offspring that they couldn't comprehend her frustration. They were *happy* to sublimate their own desires for the needs of their babies. They couldn't imagine doing anything more constructive each day than catering to a helpless animal. They were nauseatingly content to let their ignorant children steal everyone's attention. They basked in their neglect.

The blonde couldn't stand it.

So when she accidentally allowed her husband to impregnate her again, she knew what she had to do.

It wasn't an easy decision. After all, if she let her family and friends know that she was pregnant, she could benefit from a surge of solicitous attention. They would again be focused on *her*. Perhaps they would be distracted somewhat by her precocious son, but overall, they would be thinking of *her* again, and the blonde liked that idea.

But she also knew what would happen as soon as she popped the second baby out. She would again be overshadowed by a stupid baby. And she just didn't think she could tolerate that.

Of course, if she happened to miscarry, there would be family and friends flocking to her side to offer sympathy and encouragement. She could earn high marks for her courage and perseverance in the face of tragedy. People would be inspired by her strength and resolve.

She would matter again.

But she couldn't count on a miscarriage, no matter how many times she punched herself in the gut.

So at roughly eight weeks, she sneaked into an out-of-town clinic and aborted her second child.

She had no qualms about her own safety. After all, she had talked Sandra into the same procedure just a few years before, and *she* had come out of it swimmingly. Okay, there had been the infection that had pretty much killed any chance of Sandra ever becoming pregnant again, but the abortion had taken care of all the unmarried woman's immediate problems. And if there had been no public glory for the blonde for being by Sandra's side through the entire tawdry procedure, there had been a private reward. Sandra had become her slave for life for standing by her in her hour of need. And antibiotics had eventually cured her of the unfortunate post-procedure complications.

The blonde felt no regret as the nurse/receptionist prepped her for departure. She barely listened to the woman's warnings of dire consequences if she didn't follow the clinic's instructions. She knew all about consequences from Sandra, and if perhaps a few complications did come her way, they might even prove advantageous.

Because the blonde's plan was to go home, stagger into the house in case any neighbors were watching, and tearfully call her husband to come home *now*. By the time he arrived, she would be artfully displayed on the bathroom floor, the pad removed so she would be bleeding through her panties. And when her husband fearfully gathered her in his arms, she would gasp the awful word: "Miscarriage."

She would be pampered for months.

CHAPTER TWENTY-FOUR

The coroner's report on Sandra Porter set off no alarms. The pathologist who conducted the autopsy concluded that she died when the pickup truck crushed her skull. The paramedics called to the scene didn't have a chance of saving her.

Her blood alcohol level was high enough that she could have been cited had she been driving, but she wasn't roaring drunk. She was just fuzzy and probably a little off balance. It appeared to be just her bad luck that she happened to stumble into the street at precisely the moment the pickup was driving by.

The coroner's office issued a preliminary ruling of accidental death, pending toxicology reports. I called the pathologist to clarify.

"Just checking whether drugs could have been combined with the alcohol," the pathologist assured me. He was under contract to the coroner and I was usually relieved when he was called in to conduct an autopsy. An old politico named Doc Sweitzer was the official coroner, courtesy of a blithely ignorant electorate, but it had been years since he'd handled an autopsy that could have criminal consequences. He wisely delegated the heavy lifting to forensic pathologists, and the one who had been assigned to Sandra Porter was a guy I had learned to trust. So when he seemed to shrug off the toxicology tests as routine, I was inclined to believe him.

"Did you find *anything* unusual?" I asked.

He hemmed and hawed, reluctant to feed my inherent need to be suspicious, then admitted that Sandra had the liver of someone twice her age.

"Meaning?" I prodded.

"Her alcohol intake the night she died probably wasn't an aberration," he said delicately.

"She was a drunk?"

"Certainly on that road."

I pondered that for a moment. If Sandra liked to hit the bottle, then her collection of obituaries could be merely the result of a morbid fascination fueled by alcohol. *Facts* could have had nothing to do with it.

Or alcohol could have enhanced her perceptions.

"Anything else?" I asked testily.

The pathologist cleared his throat. "She had only twenty teeth – which could simply be the result of a radical approach to orthodontia."

I winced at the memory of my own travails with braces.

"And there was a good bit of scar tissue in her uterus."

I instantly forgot about teeth. "Recent?"

I could almost hear the pathologist shaking his head. "Definitely old scar tissue, and substantial."

"How substantial?"

"Enough that I doubt she could have ever become pregnant."

I chewed on my lip. This information had absolutely nothing to do with a truck crushing Sandra's head. But it was *so* intriguing.

"What could cause such scarring?" I asked.

"You're asking me to speculate," the pathologist scolded.

"Humor me," I begged.

He sighed. "I'll never say as much in a report," he warned.

"But?" I pressed.

"Given the victim's age and the legal restrictions before *Roe vs. Wade,* I wouldn't be surprised if she had a back-street abortion that caused permanent injuries."

"Naw," I said, "not Sandra."

"I know nothing about the living Sandra," the pathologist said. "I just know what the autopsy tells me."

I thanked him for sharing.

And stared vacantly at the squad room walls as I imagined Sandra Porter, knocked up and alone as a teenager.

* * *

I was debating ducking out early – with Bradley on vacation, it seemed only fair to give myself a little treat – when for no logical reason, I remembered the unexplained telephone number Sandra Porter had scribbled on the obituary for Carol Jennings. I sincerely doubted it would shed light on Sandra's sudden dive into traffic, but it was a loose end, and the more I thought about cutting my shift short, the more it nagged at my conscience. I *owed* my fellow Scout a thorough investigation.

So I dug the number out of Sandra's file folder and checked it against the city directory. It matched up with a Dorothy Jennings on a modest street on the opposite edge of town as the university. I assumed Dorothy would be a relative of Carol.

She turned out to be Carol's mother.

And she was not inclined to talk to me.

"You had no use for my Carol," she rasped in the gravel voice of a lifetime smoker. "I remember you."

"And I'm sorry for the bad feelings," I said hastily. "But this isn't a personal call. I'm a police detective now, and I'm calling in relation to the death of Sandra Porter."

"I know what you are," she huffed, and I could picture her reaching for her pack of cigarettes. "I don't recall you bothering to investigate my *Carol's* death."

"With all due respect, Mrs. Jennings," I said patiently, "I wasn't a police officer back when your daughter died."

"No," she agreed, "you were just a drunk."

I sucked in my breath. Carol had hanged herself shortly before the fire that had killed Elizabeth. Obviously, my method of coping with tragedy hadn't been the secret I had thought.

"I understand your bitterness," I said haltingly as my mind flailed away at a barrage of memories best left buried, "but I'm looking for information about another senseless death – Sandra's."

"Carol's death *was* senseless," her mother said, "but you Scouts couldn't have cared less."

"I beg your pardon?" I said, startled by her reference to the Scout troop.

"I remember all of you," Mrs. Jennings assured me. "You all called my little girl names, you made her cry because she wasn't as smart or as pretty as you. You were mean and nasty kids."

I bit back the urge to defend myself – and not just because everything Mrs. Jennings said was true; we *had* picked on Carol because it had been so easy. But if I launched into a debate with Mrs. Jennings over the purity of my intentions as a snotty teenager, the conversation would become all about me and Carol and not about Sandra.

So I let Carol's mother vent some more, and when she finally stopped to inhale, I said, "You're right. We were nitwits. I apologize."

Mrs. Jennings coughed in surprise, but was not immediately taken in by my charms.

"You girls *hurt* her," she insisted. "Even when you were all grown up, you couldn't stop."

It was my turn to sputter in surprise. "What do you mean?" I asked. It was hard to imagine the spiteful teasing of kids surviving into adulthood.

But apparently it had – at least in Mrs. Jennings' mind. "You don't have a clue why my daughter killed herself, do you?"

“I heard she had difficulties adjusting to her divorce,” I said diplomatically.

Mrs. Jennings snorted. “Try *adjusting* to the destruction of your entire life. Her husband left her, her boy had problems – they call it autism now, but back then they just said he was retarded – and then those blond bitches made sure he got thrown out of the only school that seemed to help him.”

I didn't have to ask her to name names. If she was talking Scouts, she could only mean Marilyn and Patty. “What happened?” I asked.

“It was a private school – all the rich kids went there so they wouldn't have to be around the migrant kids in the public schools.”

I vaguely remembered a short-lived experimental school that had been wildly popular in the days when I had been a young parent, but it had also been wildly expensive. I was impressed that Carol could afford it.

“She couldn't,” Mrs. Jennings snapped. “Her husband could. But when he left, he took the money. Carol tried to keep the boy in school because the teachers there were actually reaching the kid, but she just couldn't handle the cost. She was pleading with the school to let her skate a little on the bills, and maybe they would've, but then your Scout friends made sure he got thrown out.”

Mrs. Jennings was leading me far astray from the death of Sandra Porter, but her story intrigued me. Despite the wisdom of forty-plus years, I wasn't above dishing dirt about my old rivals. “How did they manage that?” I asked.

“Money,” Mrs. Jennings snarled. “It's always about money. They threatened to pull their kids out – and tell their friends to pull *their* kids out, too – just because Carol's boy was acting out, and sometimes he picked on their kids. He wasn't a *bully*. He just didn't know how to behave around other kids, and sometimes, he pushed them around. But instead of letting the kids work it out themselves, the mothers stepped in."

"And got your grandson expelled," I said. I could just imagine the demands Marilyn and Patty would have put on the school. They would have never allowed Carol Jennings to get preferential treatment over them. They would have never allowed Carol's son to get preferential treatment over their kids. They would have insisted that Carol's son go.

And a private school on shaky financial ground would have quickly caved to parents who religiously paid their bills.

"They *said* it was because of how much Carol owed," Mrs. Jennings said, "but it was really the pressure of the other parents. My grandson got the boot, and then his dad got custody because Carol couldn't provide for him. She lost *everything* when her boy was expelled. She couldn't support herself, she didn't have a husband, she didn't have her son, she didn't have her *dignity*. So she hung herself."

I closed my eyes and shuddered. I had come very close to drinking myself to death after the fire. Who could blame Carol for choosing a rope over life without her son?

"Where is the boy now?" I asked, my voice noticeably ragged.

Mrs. Jennings' voice was flat. "Dead."

"I'm sorry," I said automatically.

"Don't bother," Mrs. Jennings said over the scrape of another match. "Carol's ex couldn't control the boy any more than Carol could. He jumped from the roof of his dad's apartment house. It might have been his medication."

We both sighed and pondered old hurts. Our heads were filled with dead children.

But eventually I remembered the purpose of my call. "And you told all this to Sandra?" I asked.

"You mean the Porter girl who just died?" Mrs. Jennings shot back.

"Yes, Sandra Porter."

"Never talked to her in my life," Mrs. Jennings said blandly.

I was shocked for half a beat – why in hell had Mrs. Jennings prolonged the conversation if she'd had no contact with Sandra? – but years of obstreperous witnesses had taught me to mask my dismay in polite doubts. "Are you sure? She had your phone number in her personal files."

"I can't imagine why," Mrs. Jennings said firmly. "I never once heard from her – not when she and Carol were in Scouts, not when they were in school together, not even when Carol died."

There was a sharp exhale over the phone line, so distinct, I could nearly smell the smoke puffing from the receiver.

" 'Course," Mrs. Jennings said, "I never heard from you, neither."

And the line went dead.

CHAPTER TWENTY-FIVE

Henry caught me in the parking lot as I was going out and he was coming in.

"You still got something going with Louie Brandon?" He lit up his last cigarette before clocking in and squinted at me through the flame of his lighter.

"Louie?" I repeated, surprised. "No longer my best friend."

"Yeah?" Henry said and politely exhaled above my head. "He thinks otherwise."

I winced at the thought and leaned against my back bumper. "Spill it," I said in resignation.

Henry was happy to oblige. It gave him more time to savor his nicotine fix. "I stopped at the Arc last night before heading home." The Arc was a student bar, but it welcomed cops in hopes of keeping its young clientele under control without paying for bouncers.

"And?" I prodded dutifully.

"Mr. Brandon was making a scene in the back room." Henry sucked hard on his cigarette, then shot out a plume of gray smoke. "The staff asked me to have a word with him."

"Unofficially?"

Henry spread his hands. "I was off duty, Jo. Didn't even flash my badge."

That was quite a concession from Henry. He *loved* to flash his badge.

"And?" I wearily repeated. An ache was suddenly pulsing behind my eyes and I pinched the bridge of my nose behind my glasses.

"Mr. Brandon was soused," Henry said. "His lady friend –"

"Jenny," I interrupted.

"Yeah, Jenny," Henry said. "She was trying to get him to go home, but Mr. Brandon wasn't inclined to leave. Said he needed to drink while he still had a job to pay for it. You know what that might be about?" And he gave me the kind of look he usually reserved for uncooperative witnesses.

"He's a video store clerk," I said quickly. "He could lose his job when Blockbuster moves in."

Henry grunted. "Blockbuster has good prices."

"Thus Mr. Brandon's dilemma."

"Whatever," Henry said and sucked on his cigarette some more. "Bottom line is, I told Mr. Brandon it was time to go home. He responded that I couldn't lean on him 'cuz he had a friend in the police department."

I groaned.

"You still his *friend*?" Henry asked, and his voice was tinged with disappointment.

"Only in Adam's nightmares," I assured him.

"Well," Henry said as he stomped out his cigarette, "Mr. Brandon's still using your name."

"I shall abuse him of that notion at the first opportunity," I stoutly promised.

That should have been enough to send Henry on his way – he had delivered a disagreeable message and I had responded without biting off his head – but he hung back. "There's something else," he admitted.

I warily raised an eyebrow.

"The girl – Jenny? She had a split lip."

"And you did *nothing*?" I asked, instantly appalled.

"Back off, Jo. I didn't *see* him punch her out, and the injury wasn't fresh. For all I know, one of her kids slugged her."

"Fat chance," I growled.

"Hey," Henry protested, "it happened to my wife with our middle boy. Nearly knocked out one of her teeth. Kids are *wicked*."

I shook my head. "Not as wicked as Louie Brandon."

"If I coulda hauled him in for it, I woulda," Henry said. "But I had no proof."

"So why are you telling me this?" I countered.

" 'Cuz maybe you might want to talk to this Jenny – seeing as how you've got a relationship with her and I don't." And the look he gave me was the poster child for sound reasoning.

I snorted. "So instead of following up yourself, you're easing your conscience by dumping what could be a dicey situation into *my* lap. Is that about right?"

Henry slapped my shoulder as he slid into the station. "I *knew* you'd understand."

And I could see him clocking in with a perfectly clear conscience.

Mine, on the other hand, was suddenly wracked with doubts.

* * *

Jenny was downright sullen as she opened her front door. She was dressed in a worn navy blue cashier's smock with her name stitched in red across the pocket. It nicely matched the scab on her lower lip.

"I gotta get to work. I don't have time to talk to *you*." And she shoved Jason away from the door with her hip as she leaned into the knob.

"And how are you *getting* to work?" I countered and wedged myself into the six-inch gap between door and jamb.

"I gotta walk – like you don't know. You took back your car."

"Louie returned it," I corrected.

"Same difference. I still gotta walk." And she tried to squeeze me out onto the porch.

"What if I drive you?" I offered. "Fair trade-off for losing the car?"

"Not hardly," she sniffed. But the pressure of the door against my shoulder eased a little.

"It's raining." I pointed to the drops spattering the driveway. "Wouldn't a ride be nice?"

Jenny wanted to tell me to go fuck myself, but the gray clouds hovering beyond the porch were threatening to burst. A dry ride quickly won out over injured pride. "Give me two minutes. I gotta tell the sitter I'm leaving." She shut the door in my face.

I paced the porch as the drizzle segued into a spring shower. I could hear the baby howling inside – or maybe it was just the television. The breeze ricocheting off the front of the duplex was chilly and I shivered in my denim jacket. If I hadn't run into Henry, I could have been home by now, cuddling with a warm dog with bad breath.

Instead, I was waiting in the damp to give a ride to a woman who clearly did not want to speak to me. It isn't always easy to be a generous cop.

Jenny popped out of the door and skittered down the porch steps, holding a jacket over her head to keep her hair dry. She was wearing jeans with her smock, so I couldn't see whether her legs were checkered with bruises.

She hopped into the car with the enviable agility of a female in her twenties. I hopscotched to the driver's side like a 43-year-old worried about spraining an ankle. It gave Jenny the upper hand as we started our drive.

"I'm not saying a single word about Louie," she informed me as I backed into the street. "I don't care how nice you're being to me."

I kept my focus on the street instead of her lip. "And why would I ask you about Louie?"

"Oh, puh-leeze," she said, and I could imagine her rolling her eyes. "I'm not *stupid*. I know that cop at the bar last night talked to you. Why else would you show up at my house?"

"Maybe because I'm worried." I headed the car in the right direction and allowed myself to glance at her. She was shaking raindrops out of her hair before reknotting it at the back of her head. Her ministrations revealed a fading thumb-size bruise on the side of her neck.

I sighed and drove.

The store where she clerked was only a five-minute drive away. It didn't give me much time to wheedle my way back into her confidence. But she was a basically polite girl, and as I swung into the parking lot, she swallowed her resentment long enough to thank me for the lift. The shower had grown insistent during our short drive and was pelting the roof of the car. Jenny weighed the distance between the car and the store and came up drenched.

I reached behind my seat and yanked out the little umbrella I kept for stakeouts that go bad.

"Take it," I said. "Stay dry."

The look she gave me nearly broke my heart. Young. Vulnerable. Aching to be treated like an adult, but in no position to turn down the kindnesses of nosy cops.

She grabbed the umbrella. "Louie would *never* hurt me or the boys," she said fiercely. "He's under a lot of pressure right now, but he *loves* us. He's tryin' to take *care* of us."

"Jenny, *please*," I quietly pleaded.

Her eyes sizzled with misplaced passion as she dashed out into the rain. "Just leave us *alone*," she hissed.

But, of course, I couldn't. I called the social worker and reported Jenny's split lip.

CHAPTER TWENTY-SIX

A warm wind from the Southwest drifted in after the rain, gently fanning the town dry and nudging temperatures up to the point that it was almost uncomfortable to pull on a suit jacket for Sandra Porter's funeral. Dave whistled when I shimmied into my skirt. I rarely showed my legs in public, and I certainly didn't fancy flashing winter white calves at the cemetery, but Mother had imposed a rare dress code for the funeral: no jeans and no guns.

Well, no *visible* guns.

Mother snorted at the heft of my purse but deemed me presentable. I reciprocated by allowing her to drive us to the cemetery.

Sandra was survived by only two distant cousins, and they had no desire to diminish her meager estate with a big shindig at the funeral home. So there were no calling hours, no church service and no expensive coffin. The body had been cremated and her ashes were delivered to the cemetery in an urn as plain as Sandra. About fifty people gathered in the sun to listen to the minister, who had clearly never met Sandra, deliver a eulogy that had little to do with the girl I had known.

Mother stood to my left, speaking quietly to my old Scout leader, Mrs. DeWitt. Her daughter, Marilyn, and best friend Patty stood behind us, whispering caustic comments that they thought no one else could hear. I was still smarting from the disturbing conversation with Carol Jennings' mother and glared at them, but they didn't notice. Sandra's cousins huddled across from us, glancing at their watches and telling the minister with their body language to move things along. No one seemed particularly distraught over the deceased.

Except the pickup truck driver, whom I spotted at the edge of the crowd, where he tried to blend in with the tombstones. The hospital had kept him for two days, then had released him with a big white bandage on his head and stern admonitions to return to the emergency room if he felt dizzy or nauseous. He was leaning heavily on a woman about his own age, and the one time I caught his eye, he struck me as a man in extreme pain. I gave him points for showing up at the funeral. If Sandra had left any relatives who had cared, he could have been pummeled with abuse. Instead, he shrank ignominiously behind the bushes, but I was the only one who noticed.

The Scout troop was well-represented. In addition to the DeWitts and Patty, Ginny Edgerton was chattering in the back row with Diane Hearne and Christine Pope. Nikki Hocevar's mother stood with Debbie Gauer's family. Behind the cousins were Becky Freeman's parents. The only obvious absence was Marci Gibbs, and as Patty muttered for most of us to hear, Marci had had no use for Sandra. It might have been a subliminal gay thing.

I pondered that thought as the minister droned on and eventually decided it was inconsequential, the damp wine glass in Sandra's cupboard notwithstanding.

The minister mercifully ended the service by inviting the bereaved to a reception at the student union, where Sandra's botany department colleagues were hosting a modest potluck buffet in her memory. Ginny Edgerton and Diane Hearne perked right up, but the cousins had already turned their backs on the urn and were hoofing it toward an airport taxi. Potluck apparently wasn't on their menu.

Mother and Mrs. DeWitt were striding purposefully toward the minister to thank him for the service – well, in the absence of the cousins, *someone* had to – so I put my cop hat back on and edged around the crowd toward the pickup driver. Most of the mourners were lining up to file past the urn before it was entombed, but he and his female companion – wife? girlfriend? – were slowly moving in the other direction, toward the cars parked along the driveway. I was easily able to cut them off before they could escape in a Ford sedan that had seen better days.

"Are you serious?" the woman complained when I flashed my badge. "You're gonna harass Ed at the *cemetery*?"

The truck driver – Ed – tried to shush her, but his efforts were feeble. Most of his energy was focused on getting into the Ford before he fell over.

I smiled brightly and opened the passenger door for him. After all, my duty was to protect and *serve*.

But once he painfully settled himself in the car seat, I blocked the door so he couldn't close it without wrenching his broken ribs.

The woman, who was on the driver's side, glared at me over the roof of the car.

"Ed," I said, trying to sound sincere, even though inside I was hating myself for invading his privacy, "it was very brave of you to show up here today. Most guys wouldn't be able to do it."

"Got that right," the woman muttered.

Ed grimaced. "The counselor at the hospital said I had to face up to what I done. Even if I didn't mean to, I killed that lady." And he nodded fiercely, more for his own benefit than mine.

"It's important to remember," I agreed.

His mouth was a grim line, and he stared pointedly over my shoulder. His companion rolled her eyes at the sky.

"Look, Ed," I said before he could fold up on me, "you were kind of fuzzy when our officers first questioned you. You were in pain and in shock, and there just weren't many details in your statement. So I have to ask – is there anything else you remember?"

Ed pulled his gaze from the graveyard to my face. “You mean other than I killed someone I never even met before?”

His eyes were deep pools of pain. I tried not to gulp. “I mean, any details that can help us reconstruct the accident.”

He squeezed his eyes shut as he obediently relived the moments before his truck crushed Sandra's head. His face reddened and his breathing accelerated.

His companion swore at me.

When Ed's eyes opened, they were wet. “Ma'am, I never saw it coming. I'm driving down the road – and I swear to God, I *wasn't* speeding – and I sorta see a woman on the sidewalk up ahead, and I look away from her, and then there's a thump and my whole world turned upside down, ya know? I don't know how she got in front of my truck so fast, but she did, and there wasn't a damn thing I could do to stop it.” And tears spilled down his cheeks.

“You goddamned *bitch*,” his companion hissed. “Go *away*.”

I swallowed hard and patted Ed's shoulder. “You're right, Ed. There was absolutely *nothing* you could do.”

I stepped back and gently closed the door. Ed was crying into his shirt. His companion gave me the finger and slid into the driver's seat. She did a U-turn to flee from the cemetery and tore up a little lawn in the process.

I did not cite her.

* * *

Mother and Mrs. DeWitt were in serious conversation with the Hocevars and the Gauers, and I knew it would be awhile before I could drag her away, so I wandered north through the tombstones and finally heeded the ghost who had been tugging at me ever since we had entered the cemetery.

Elizabeth's modest tombstone sits near a grove of trees that had been only saplings the day we buried her. She was surrounded by Ferrises – mostly aunts and uncles she had never known, but my dad was beside her now, and someday, Mother would keep her company, too. In the wretched months after Elizabeth had died, I would stagger to her grave – usually drunk – every day just to be near her. After Bradley cleaned me up, the visits became less frequent, not because I loved her less but because I didn't hate myself quite so much. It had been nearly a year since I had last stopped by the grave, and although the pain was everlasting, it was no longer so crippling.

I sat on my heels in front of the tombstone and pulled a few weeds. Mother, who was responsible for tending family graves, would come out on Memorial Day and do a proper job of taming the gravesites, but I thought it looked more presentable if the grasses didn't obscure the vital statistics on Elizabeth's gravestone.

She would have been eighteen, almost nineteen, I thought as I tossed the weeds into the wind. She would have been in college. Maybe she would have had a boyfriend. Maybe they would have practiced safe sex, or maybe I would be perilously close to grandmotherhood about now. I could have lived with that, I thought as a tear spilled out of my eye and the world as I knew it blurred. I could have lived with anything my little girl would have done.

But before I could sink into an old, familiar despair, a hand clapped my shoulder.

I squinted up into the relentless sun. Two shadows hovered over me.

"We're so sorry, Jo," Marilyn said.

"Scooter shouldn't have died," Patty sniffed, and her hand tightened on my shoulder.

I forgot Carol Jennings.

And for one moment, the three of us were at peace.

CHAPTER TWENTY-SEVEN

The blonde pursed her lips as she looked down at Steve. He had passed out, sated, as soon as he had rolled off her. His mouth hung open and a foamy speck of spit dribbled from the corner as he snored. She shuddered in disgust. Whatever had possessed her to even start this affair?

Well, when he was conscious and on the prowl, he was a stud. The hair was beginning to recede from his temples, and when he was naked, he had a softer stomach than his well-cut jeans advertised. But the eyes had been ornery with promise, and the hands had caressed a beer bottle like it was a woman. He *smelled* like sex.

And the blonde had been feeling a little crazy after her "miscarriage." Friends and family had indeed doted on her, just as she'd planned. Her husband had immediately refocused on her instead of his job and the boy, presenting her with diamond earrings and a solemn promise to get her pregnant again, as soon as her "doctor" signaled his approval.

She had been so giddy with attention for a while, she had even felt some affection for her son.

But it wasn't *enough*. She was twenty-eight years old. She felt she deserved more than a three-bedroom house, a husband with rising prospects, a perfect son, a solid job of her own and the admiration of her parents and in-laws. It was all very respectable, but life wasn't nearly as glamorous or exciting as she had expected.

So she went slumming.

And one night ran into Steve.

In a nightclub in the next county.

They were both avoiding acquaintances from home. Like her, Steve was married and had a child. Unlike her, he apparently wasn't new to this sort of thing. He expertly guided her through the small talk, the first glancing touches, the heavy rounds of drinks, and then he fucked her brains out in the back seat of his car, rocking it over a dark corner of the bar parking lot.

That had been two months ago. Now he was sprawled in his own sweaty bed and the blonde was busily scanning the room to make sure she was leaving nothing of her own behind.

It wasn't the first time they'd had sex in his house, and the thought of it gave the blonde a little shiver of excitement even now. She knew Steve's wife – in fact, had grown up with her – and was immensely pleased that she had fucked the arrogant little prig's husband in their own bed.

But now it was over.

Steve had been revealing his faults the last couple of weeks. He really had no ambition and very little appreciation of her own talents outside of bed. He had also grown impatient with the constraints on her time and a bit careless with his body language when they were in public. They were going to get caught, and although he was great fun in bed, he just wasn't worth the humiliation of exposure.

So when he had phoned that night and invited her to his house – his wife had been called out on a family emergency and the child was safely in bed – she had reluctantly agreed. One final romp, she thought, then she would tell him it was over.

Only he had beaten her to the punch, announcing even as he was mounting her that sadly, this would be their last night together. His wife was getting suspicious.

She was too aroused at that particular moment to retaliate.

But now as he snored lustily, she knew she had to teach him a lesson. Because no *man* dumped *her*.

The blonde retrieved his pack of cigarettes from the nightstand and lit up. She allowed herself one greedy lungful of smoke, then coolly dropped the cigarette on the pile of socks beside the bed and marched out of the bedroom.

She slowly felt her way down the unfamiliar hall in the dark. She had no intention of *killing* him. There would be no satisfaction in *that*. What she really wanted was to have the bastard forever in her debt.

So she would walk sedately to her car, which she had parked around the corner where the neighbors wouldn't see it, then drive around the block back to the house. By then, she calculated, there would be enough smoke to capture the attention of a passerby like herself, and she would be justified in pounding frantically on the front door to rouse the occupants.

She might even be deemed a hero for saving the louse.

A floorboard in the hallway creaked loudly as she passed the child's bedroom door. Teetering on tiptoe, the blonde strained to hear whether the child had awakened. There was only silence, and the blonde relaxed. She noted before sliding down the stairs that the youngster's bedroom door was firmly shut. The child shouldn't be harmed if the smoldering socks produced more smoke than the blonde intended.

She hoisted her purse onto her shoulder and exited by way of the front door, striding confidently like a guest who had every right to be leaving the premises at such a late hour. She really had no fear of being recognized. The nearest streetlight was two houses away and Steve's porch was in deep shadow.

She maintained her unhurried pace to her car. She wanted the cigarette to have enough time to create a noticeable amount of smoke. She wanted Steve to awaken in *panic*. And she wanted *hers* to be the first face he saw when he fled the house. So she took her time unlocking the car and sliding into the driver's seat, where she carefully adjusted the rearview mirror. After all, didn't her husband *always* remonstrate with her when she neglected to check the mirror?

And for good measure, she used the mirror to touch up her lipstick. If she was about to become a hero – again – she wanted to look good for the newspaper cameras.

She was humming as she eased the car from the curb. Poor Steve had thought *he* was dictating the terms of their affair. He would be horrified when he realized that *she* was the one who was really in charge. And perhaps he'd be just a little bit frightened of her cold-hearted daring.

She eased the car down the street behind his house, wondering whether she should allow him to grovel and perhaps bed him one more time.

Or would it be better to cut him off coldly, as though he had never meant a thing to her? She couldn't decide.

She slid the car around the next corner. The street was empty, and she tensed with excitement. The stage was all hers. This was going to be *so* good.

It wasn't until she turned onto Steve's street that she got her first hint that everything was going to hell.

A blurred figure in knotted bathrobe darted across the road in front of her, running frantically toward Steve's side of the street.

Another figure erupted from the darkness and threw itself on Steve's house, pounding on the siding.

The blonde looked up at the house, and her foot slipped off the accelerator. The car slowed to a crawl as she gawked.

Clouds of black smoke rolled from the eaves and the attic. The upstairs windows glowed with a fascinating orange light, and tiny flames licked at the curtains. The blonde opened the driver's door and her nostrils were accosted with a hot, acrid smell, and her ears were pummeled with the crackle of burning wood and the gush of wind being sucked into the inferno. Bits of glowing ash swirled into the car and stung her cheek. She cried out in surprise and feverishly batted the ash from her face.

A fist pounded on the hood of her car. “Move it, lady! The fire trucks are coming!” Then the owner of the fist, a meaty man in a wife beater and sweats, charged up Steve's porch, dragging an ax behind him.

More people were staggering out of neighboring houses, some barely dressed as they swarmed toward Steve's yard.

The blonde's hopes of heroic acclaim disintegrated in the same heat that was chasing neighbors back from Steve's porch. It was too late to rescue him.

Or his little girl.

The blonde fled.

She needed a new plan.

For life.

CHAPTER TWENTY-EIGHT

The afternoon newspaper brought unsettling news.

Mother was reading it at the kitchen table as I perspired delicately over the spaghetti sauce. I had skipped the rest of my shift after the funeral, so in atonement, I had volunteered to make dinner. Mother had appreciated the offer, but hadn't felt quite comfortable leaving me alone in the kitchen with all those sharp utensils, so she had scooped the newspaper off the front porch and settled herself at the table with a nice Chianti while I waited for the sauce to cook down.

Dave and Adam weren't home yet. Emily was napping upstairs (I fervently hoped she wasn't preparing for an all-nighter). The cats were draped around Mother's feet and Barney was sitting obediently in front of the stove, his snout pointing straight at the meatballs.

I was thinking of adding a dash of oregano when Mother sighed, “Oh, my.”

“What?” I barked, afraid she was making an editorial comment about my choice of spices.

But she wasn't looking at the sauce pot. She was tapping the local business news page with her finger. “I think our Louie is in trouble.”

“He is not *our* Louie,” I said tartly. “He made that abundantly clear when he returned your car.”

Mother was temporarily sidetracked. “That *was* unfortunate,” she agreed.

“Especially to your suspension.”

“Which your father especially appreciated,” Mother said brightly.

I chose to blush.

“Not *our* Louie,” Mother acquiesced, “but *Jenny's* Louie is in trouble.”

I reconsidered the oregano and contemplated garlic powder instead. Maybe *that* would turn Adam and Emily off. “What'd Louie do now?” I asked in resignation.

“Nothing that I know of,” Mother admitted, “but his video store is closing.”

“Oh, no,” I groaned, and in my dismay, dumped onion powder instead of garlic powder into the sauce. Oh, well.

Mother pretended not to notice. “It says here the store will close in a week, giving customers time to return their videos.”

“And Louie time to apply to Blockbuster?” I asked.

“We can hope,” Mother said.

I sampled the sauce. I thought the extra onion made it robust. “This is not good news for Jenny or the kids,” I allowed.

“He won't be out of a paycheck until next week,” Mother pointed out.

“But he may already be drowning his sorrows with *this* week's check,” I countered.

“Perhaps some extra patrols in his neighborhood might be warranted,” Mother suggested.

“I was thinking the very same thing,” I said as I reached for the phone to call Herchek.

“And some garlic bread to overpower the sauce?” Mother added.

I snarled.

CHAPTER TWENTY-NINE

Louie started drinking Thursday night after work. Quinlan discreetly trailed him home after last call at a student bar, and although he didn't walk in a perfectly straight line and he may have been disrespectful to his fellow pedestrians, Quinlan didn't see enough to justify hassling him. Adam called Quinlan a wuss, but he just smiled benignly as he explained it to me the next afternoon, and I gave him points for restraint. Once upon a time, I had feared Quinlan would be a hotdog like Henry, but lately he had been displaying a shocking amount of good judgment. I hoped Adam was paying attention.

On Friday night, Louie switched bars, this time a workingman's tavern in a part of town that students rarely penetrated. Herchek concentrates weekend patrols downtown, so Louie dropped off our radar. But he apparently had the money to drink hard, and walk home pissed after the bar closed. His neighbors in the duplex finally called 911 about 3 a.m. because the pounding and the shouts next door were getting scary.

Louie had conveniently passed out by the time the uniforms responded, and Jenny assured them everything was under control. The way Jason clung to her when he should have been tucked away in bed gave them pause, but Louie was snoring on the couch, and only one foot stool had been knocked over, where it almost fit in with the mess of toys underfoot, and no one was bleeding. So the uniforms departed without bothering to rouse Louie from his stupor, although they did urge Jenny to lock Louie out the next time the bum erupted. Jenny hastily promised there wouldn't be a next time.

I gleaned all this by reading the uniforms' incident report Saturday morning. They hadn't called me during the night because, unlike Quinlan, they didn't know Louie was a special case. I would have to educate them otherwise.

Saturday was supposed to be my day off, but with Bradley due back in town Monday, I had moseyed down to the station after cleaning up the breakfast dishes to see whether there were any squad room messes that needed cleaning up, too. Fortunately, a cold front had moved in on Friday, chilling some of the usual springtime fervor downtown. So far, there were no catastrophes awaiting Bradley's return.

But Louie's misbehavior was troubling.

So instead of going straight back home, I detoured to his duplex. I wanted to see with my own eyes that Jenny and the kids were all right.

Except Jenny wasn't home.

A rancid Louie opened the front door a crack. It had been eight hours since the uniforms had responded to the neighbors' complaints, but the smell of alcohol and sweat still rolled off Louie's beer-stained clothes. His hair hung in greasy clumps and his skin had an oily sheen. Although his eyes were focused, they were as red as his nose.

“Get the fuck outta here,” he growled, and leaned into the door to close it.

But I wedged it open with my purse. (I had learned the hard way not to use my foot.) “I want to see Jenny.”

“She don't wanna see you,” he said around a drunk-dry mouth and leaned a little harder on the door.

My purse withstood the pressure nicely.

“I want to hear Jenny say she doesn't want to see me,” I insisted.

“Too bad for you,” he said. “She's at work.”

I stood on tiptoe to peer over his shoulder. “Where are the kids?”

“At the sitter's,” he said swiftly.

“You aren't watching them?”

“Lady, do I look in any condition to watch two little kids?”

I had to agree he didn't look healthy enough to watch snow melt. “But have Jenny call me when she gets home,” I instructed as I shoved my card through the crack in the door.

“The fuck I will,” Louie snarled, and he crumpled the card and flicked it over my head.

Then he slammed the door so hard, the porch rattled.

I conceded defeat. Jenny and the kids weren't home and Louie didn't want to talk to me. So I stepped down from the porch to the driveway and caught the flutter of a curtain in a second-floor window.

I shaded my eyes with my hands and stared hard at the window. It had been cracked open to catch a little spring air, and no doubt the curtain had simply floated in the breeze. Certainly nothing human was peering out of the window at me.

Now.

But I hate liars. So I drove to the store where Jenny worked and was told it was her day off.

I returned to Louie's duplex in a decidedly nasty frame of mind, but no one responded when I pounded on the door – except the neighbor, who said Louie had just taken off with some buddies. He didn't have a clue where Jenny and the kids might be.

So I went home to work off my frustrations on Dave.

It was, after all, my day off.

CHAPTER THIRTY

It was the middle of the seventh, and Dave was stretching for another beer. Normally, I would have stretched, too, but I had been voted the designated driver. We had wandered down to the Farmhouse after our own calisthenics to grab a burger and watch the ballgame because no one at home felt like cooking. Mother was too busy writing a term paper, Emily was engrossed in a project for an elementary education class that involved a lot of orange and pink construction paper, red glitter and glue, and Adam was cruising downtown with Quinlan on overtime. So Dave and I decided to eat out.

It was supposed to be a cozy supper for two, but the Farmhouse draws a lot of university faculty, and pretty soon we were shoving tables together to accommodate a crowd of professors who were shouting with distressingly poor grammar at the umpires on TV. Dave was in the mood to party, so I switched to Coke and watched contentedly as he acted like a college kid instead of an angry vet with a permanent limp. It was worth giving up the alcohol buzz.

Which meant I was stone-cold sober when my cell phone went off. I recognized Adam's voice at the other end, but Dave and Friends were in the middle of a sloppy and loud rendition of *Take Me Out to the Ballgame*, and I couldn't understand a thing Adam was saying. But his voice was definitely urgent.

So I shoved through the crowd around the Farmhouse TVs and popped out into the relative quiet of the parking lot. “Say again, Adam?”

There was some static – cell reception at the Farmhouse end of town was not good – then Adam babbled something about a Code 19.

In city parlance, that was a domestic violence call.

And that's an awful call for a cop. There's always a lot of anger roiling at the scene, and the combatants are often inclined to shift that anger onto the police. So even without knowing where Adam was heading, I felt the muscles in my stomach tighten into a knot.

“Where are you going, Adam?” I demanded, unable to keep the dismay out of my voice.

More static crackled over the phone, almost drowning Adam out.

I stuck a finger in my ear, trying to drown out ambient noise. “Repeat that, Adam.”

The phone sputtered, and I thought it was going to die. Then Adam said clearly, “We're pulling up to Louie Brandon's duplex.”

No, no, no, I thought. This just won't do.

But I couldn't get any response from Adam.

“Do not go in until I get there,” I shouted into the phone, as though loudness would overcome atmospheric interference. “Do you read me?”

The phone laughed at me with its static.

“Adam?” I pleaded.

There was still no response. I frantically felt my pockets. Had Dave given me the keys to his van, or would I have to waste valuable time squeezing back into the bar to retrieve them? And would Adam even wait for me to get to Louie's duplex before he charged in?

Louie took the debate out of my hands.

"Shots fired," Adam yelled into the phone. "We're going in."

A little part of me died.

CHAPTER THIRTY-ONE

I slammed the van to the curb behind Adam's cruiser just as the backup I had called for squealed to a halt from the opposite direction. Blue lights from Adam's cruiser and the backup ride bounced off the duplex, shimmering in the windows and catching the neighbors in a psychedelic dance as they scrambled from the relative safety of their porch steps to the street behind the cruisers. It was just dark enough to twist the house and yard into disorienting shadows. The only sound was another siren wailing blocks behind us.

Adam's cruiser was empty and neither Adam nor Quinlan was in sight. The front door to Louie's half of the duplex was ajar, but I could see no one in the shaft of light spilling from his living room. I'd left my cell phone on, but I'd heard nothing more from Adam.

I duckwalked around vehicles to the backup cruiser. Schafer, the former highway patrolman, was crouched behind the driver's door. Perry was on the passenger side.

"We have contact?" I asked quietly. My gun was in my hand. I never traveled – not even to the Farmhouse – without it.

"Their radio's been dead," Schafer said.

That was bad news, but I lectured myself not to let it rattle me. "Adam said they were going in."

Schafer nodded. "Quinlan radioed the same to dispatch."

I peered at the duplex over the driver's side of the cruiser. “So which way did they go?”

“Quinlan would have gone to the back,” Perry said. “He would've figured he'd have the better chance of taking the perp by surprise.”

Leaving the front to Adam. “That would've put Adam in a vulnerable position,” I said tersely.

Perry just shrugged. At this point, it wasn't about saving the rookie. It was about neutralizing the perp before he had a chance to cause any more harm.

“Do we know if anyone's hurt?” I asked.

“Only that the neighbors called 911 because of the noise of a fight,” Schafer said. “And then shots were fired, prompting Quinlan and Adam to move in without backup.”

“Where in hell *are* they?” I asked, more to myself than anyone else.

But Schafer felt obliged to answer. “I agree with Perry. I think Adam went in the front,” he said, nodding at the gaping door, “and Quinlan went to the back.”

“And why haven't we heard from them?” I hissed.

Schafer raised his hands to deflect my heat. We all knew the answer couldn't be good.

And then Jenny howled. “Oh, God, no, you *can't*!”

Schafer and I stared at each other.

“Louie, *no*!” Jenny screamed.

“I'll take the back,” I snapped, sliding away from the security of the cruiser.

“Maybe I should,” Schafer offered. He probably had as many years in law enforcement as I did. His scores on the shooting range were probably as good as mine, too. And he had no dog in this fight.

But I stared him down. “Give me a radio,” I said to Perry. “And call for more backup.”

And with a radio in one hand and gun in the other, I slithered around the cruiser and up the driveway to the blind side of the duplex.

I could hear Jenny sobbing and the rumble of a reasonable male voice – maybe Adam? – and the fussbudget whine of a baby as I crept past the porch toward the back of the building. All three sounds were reassuring. They meant Jenny and baby and possibly Adam were still alive and coherent. But it troubled me that I couldn't hear the boy Jason or Quinlan.

Well, I couldn't hear Quinlan because he lay crumpled on the back stoop. He'd taken a shot in the center of his chest, but it had been nicely blocked by his vest. Unfortunately, the impact had knocked him off his feet and he may have struck his head on the concrete steps as he went down. There was a modest amount of blood smeared on the back of his head, and he was most definitely unconscious.

I quietly radioed for an ambulance, then stepped over him through the back door.

The kitchen was dark, but light oozed in from the living room by way of the dining room. I could still hear Jenny crying indistinctly and the baby whimpring, but over it the male conversation – Louie and Adam – was becoming more pronounced.

" – can work this out, man" – Adam.

" – fucking had it in for me from the start" – Louie.

I shuddered. The anger dripping from Louie's voice did not inspire confidence.

I tiptoed into the dining room. I assumed Schafer was easing up onto the front porch. I hoped a career nurtured on traffic stops didn't make him averse to drawing his gun.

I was hidden by shadows in the dining room, but I could clearly see Louie in the living room. He was swaying slightly and sweating, and he clutched the boy Jason roughly to his waist. Jenny was off to his left, sobbing in time with the baby. Adam was standing to the right of the front door, his hands raised in surrender. I couldn't see his gun.

"Let the boy go," Adam said.

"Don't wanna," Louie slurred. Then he raised the gun above his head and fired into the ceiling.

Jenny screamed and sank to her knees with the baby.

Adam lurched involuntarily toward Louie.

Louie nestled the gun behind Jason's ear. "Uh-uh, Mr. Policeman. Back up."

Adam's eyes flared and his fists clenched. I could see he wanted to wring Louie's neck.

Louie saw it, too, and he laughed mercilessly.

Adam obediently backed up a step.

I stared through the gloom of the dining room, but couldn't see whether Schafer was in position.

More sirens screeched on the street as an ambulance joined the cacophony.

Louie twitched. The alcohol spewing from his pores was so strong, I could smell him from the dining room. His eyes rolled and his grip on Jason was perilous. Maybe I could pull the boy free.

Maybe I couldn't.

"Louie," I said calmly, and moved to the archway to the living room so he could see me.

He flinched, and the fist gripping the boy tightened. Jason squawked. His mother moaned.

"Louie, " I repeated, "let the boy go."

Louie's eyes danced over Jason, then flashed drunkenly to Adam. "Which boy, Detective?" he asked, almost gleefully.

Adam blanched. Jason squirmed.

Louie's gun circled Jason's head.

"Louie," I said firmly, "you fire and I'm going to shoot you."

The look he gave me was plaintively mad. “But you gave me your *car*.”

“That was a mistake,” I admitted.

“Then shoot me,” he taunted. “The boy'll be dead before you can pull the trigger.”

Jenny moaned.

No, I thought as I steadied my gun, he will *not* shoot Jenny's boy.

Adam gave me a look of angry resignation.

But he *will* shoot –

Louie grinned as the barrel of his gun swung from Jason's ear toward Adam's chest.

Not *my* boy, I thought fiercely.

And I fired.

My aim was a little low. I hit Louie in the neck instead of the head.

He died anyway.

PART TWO

CHAPTER THIRTY-TWO

The jet carefully lowered itself over the River Shannon like a mother hen, and just like that, I fell in love.

It was a brilliantly clear dawn and the fields spreading back from the coast were so intensely green, they hurt the eyes. We were so close to the ground now, we could easily distinguish the lanes and hedgerows separating each farm. Sheep dotted the pastures. Freshly scrubbed shirts flapped on clotheslines. A farm wife feeding the pigs shaded her eyes against the rising sun and waved. I idiotically waved back. It was so damned *peaceful.*

Mother, who had used the prerogatives of age to claim the window seat, smiled at me in pure delight and didn't even mind that I was nearly sitting on her lap to peer out at the emerald patchwork below. We were both enchanted.

Behind us, Marilyn DeWitt groaned. “Aren't we *ever* going to land?”

We were a strange traveling party: Mother and me, Marilyn and her mother, and Marilyn's pal Patty. If anyone had told me two months before that Mother and I would be traipsing off to Ireland with Patty and the DeWitts, I would have seriously questioned their sanity.

But two months ago, I hadn't killed Louie Brandon.

Mother had decided I needed a change of scenery.

I had to agree as I peered out the jet's window that Ireland was a stupendous change.

I just wasn't comfortable yet with Marilyn and Patty as our traveling companions.

Mother and Mrs. DeWitt had come up with the idea of an Irish holiday. They both claimed Irish ancestors, and they had told each other for years that they should go back to the Old Country to explore their roots. They would have never gone beyond the wouldn't-it-be-nice stage if I hadn't shot Louie and Marilyn's third husband-to-be hadn't taken off with a woman twenty years younger. The mothers had a hankering to see their homeland, their daughters needed a distraction and the trip was arranged before I had a decent chance to protest.

Our foursome quickly became a fivesome when Patty's long-awaited promotion fell through. The mothers solemnly agreed that a trip abroad was just what all three traumatized girls needed to get over their disappointments.

I wasn't sure I agreed with their logic. I had fired in the line of duty before and hadn't felt the need to flee the country. However, the aftermath of this shooting was admittedly wearing on my nerves. Even Emily, who held me in some awe for saving Adam's hide, told Mother (who immediately told me) that I was becoming *acerbic*. (Emily would toil forever in the A's of the dictionary world.)

Well, I had a right to be. If I had watched Louie's eyes instead of his gun, Adam's blood would have been spattered all over the living room along with Louie's.

Jenny and the kids had indeed been upstairs when I had stopped by the duplex that afternoon to check on them. Louie had insisted that they hide. He didn't want to put their newest bruises on display. And just to emphasize that Jenny shouldn't try to contact me later, he had knocked her around some more before heading downtown to drink off his hangover.

When she was interviewed after the shooting, Jenny swore that the last beating had finally convinced her that she and the kids had to get away from Louie. Losing his job had changed him from a sometimes belligerent drunk into a violent crazy man. But Jenny had few friends of her own and even fewer resources, so even though she had managed to pack one bag by the time Louie stumbled home, she had no real plan for getting out.

Louie didn't give her a chance to improvise. He saw the bag and tore into her.

And this time, he had brought home a gun so he could *really* terrify her.

The neighbors had grown so tired of his antics that they had called 911 almost as soon as Louie and Jenny raised their voices, so Quinlan and Adam were on the scene before Louie could do any real damage. But he couldn't resist showing off to Jenny by firing his gun into the ceiling, and that had drawn Quinlan and Adam into the house.

If Adam hadn't called me first, it would have been the death of both of them.

Louie had taken Quinlan by surprise on the back porch. As Quinlan told us later at the hospital, Louie hadn't hesitated. He'd seen Quinlan on the stoop and had fired. Then he had slithered back into the house to confront Adam before he could spirit Jenny and the kids out the front door.

Louie was drunk and a grandstander. He should have dispatched Adam immediately. But he had to taunt the boy instead, and Adam had learned enough on the job to keep Louie preoccupied with talk of his misunderstood greatness. Ten minutes must have passed from the time Quinlan was shot and I showed up in the dining room, but Adam held everything loosely together, playing Louie and trying to get Jenny and the kids safely out the door. He did nothing *wrong*. Louie was just determined to kill him.

So I felt no guilt over shooting Louie first.

I did feel a little irritated with Quinlan. He should have known better than to charge the house without backup, even after a shot was fired. But he paid for his rashness with excruciating bruises on his chest where the bullets hit his vest and a nasty concussion suffered when he fell and smacked his head on the back steps. He was off work for three weeks, and when he came back, he still looked a little green. Herchek handed him over to Henry for some reindoctrination.

I wisely handed Adam over to Herchek for the same. I was much too close to the cause to make sure Adam's head was screwed on straight. I needed too much counseling myself, and since Dave and Mother were initially torn between Adam's needs and mine, I looked to Bradley.

Once upon a time, that would have been a prescription for disaster. But Bradley had come back from vacation itching to take charge, and if that meant cleaning up the political fallout from a domestic gone bad, he was psyched for it. He whisked Jenny and the kids into a secret safe house for victims of domestic abuse; he whipped the prosecutor's office into a speedy ruling of justifiable homicide; he bullied the mayor and the vultures on council back into line before they could use the shooting and its resulting publicity as an excuse to decimate the police budget; and he kept the media off me. We spent many long evenings in his office, hitting the Jameson he kept in his bottom file drawer and speaking obliquely of the occasionally violent consequences of protecting the innocent. Bradley had been there several times himself. He knew how to talk the talk.

Dave knew our history and wasn't crazy about our private debriefings, but he's also a war vet and knew I needed to talk it out with someone who understood. So he never grilled me when I came home late reeking of whiskey. But Mother knew my addictions, and before Dave's patience snapped and Bradley and I could wander across the line, she had us booked on the flight to Shannon.

I initially objected. It was deep summer by then and the department was seriously suffering from vacations. I argued that I couldn't leave my colleagues so short-staffed. And I pointed to my backlog of cases and insisted that I couldn't possibly take off for a two-week excursion overseas. I had *way* too many obligations.

But the truth was, left to myself, I wasn't making any headway on the backlog. Administrative procedure required that I be placed on paid leave until there was a ruling on Louie's death, and even after the prosecutor declared the shooting justified, protocol called for Bradley to place me on desk duty until the department doctor declared me fit for action. That didn't happen for a month. In the meantime, I studied old case files and occasionally helped Herchek direct the dance of the patrols downtown. It gave me a lot of opportunities to fret that perhaps I had fired at Louie prematurely.

I could have squelched the Ireland trip if it had been only Mother pushing it, but everybody ganged up on me – Bradley, who couldn't afford a damaged cop; Dave, who was reluctant to leave my mental health entirely in Bradley's hands; Adam, who was sincerely grateful that I hadn't hesitated to shoot Louie but was somewhat conflicted that his quasi-mother had to save his ass; even Herchek, who was sick of dealing with my sour mood in the squad room. *Everyone* wanted me out of the country.

So there I was on a bright Sunday morning in July, sinking inevitably into Shannon, and the weight of two months of brooding was rising off my shoulders. I watched a small flock of sheep meander across a lane, so close to me I could almost bury my fingers in their wool.

Mother beamed at me. "It's magical, isn't it?"

Behind us, Marilyn snorted from sleep deprivation.

I grinned and squeezed Mother's hand. "This was your best idea *ever*."

And we both gawked out the window as Ireland rushed up to greet us.

CHAPTER THIRTY-THREE

"Why is it so *cold*?" Patty groused as we waited for the lad from the car rental agency to retrieve our vehicles from the back lot.

We were all quietly shivering in our Midwest summer clothes. It had been baking in the 90s when we had taken off on the first leg of our journey. No one had warned us that it would be 30 degrees cooler when we landed at Shannon. We really should have done more research, because there were more tank tops in our luggage than sweaters. But we smiled through chattering teeth – well, *some* of us smiled – and pleaded with the rental agency gods to produce our cars *soon*.

Five women on vacation in a foreign country have five very different ideas of how to spend their time, so we had agreed early on to rent two cars. It wasn't until the cars were finally brought to us that we realized how smart a move that had been. European rental agencies operate with small, fuel-efficient cars. Even with two vehicles, it was tough to squeeze in all of our luggage and still leave room for five grown-ups.

"You could have done with fewer shoes," Marilyn scolded Patty as they wedged suitcases into the boot of their car.

Patty planted her hands on her hips. "And what about your hair dryer? I *told* you it wasn't compatible with the electrical outlets here."

"I'll get an adaptor," Marilyn muttered.

"And when will you do *that*?" Patty demanded. "It's Sunday. Everything's *closed* on Sunday in Ireland. They're *religious*."

Mrs. DeWitt intervened with words of conciliation, but I shook my head as I stowed Mother's suitcases and my own in the second car. I was afraid the quarreling between Marilyn and Patty would be the hallmark of our vacation.

But Mother was determined to keep everyone jolly.

"Ladies," she said, "it's eight o'clock in the morning. We can't check in to our bed and breakfast until noon. I propose we drive the short distance to Limerick and do a little sightseeing before we head to our lodgings."

"Here, here," Mrs. DeWitt agreed. "Let's see a castle!"

"Let's see a *bed*," Patty muttered.

Marilyn glanced at her friend and wrapped a protective arm around her mother.

Patty rolled her eyes.

Mother and I stayed out of it. It was a strategy that would prove useful as we wandered deeper into Ireland.

Marilyn took the wheel of the first car. I climbed into the driver's seat of the second.

"Marilyn *does* know they drive on the wrong side of the road here, doesn't she?" I asked Mother.

Mother grunted as she stared at the map. "I'm just trying to get us to Limerick," she said. "I can't be bothered with Marilyn."

I sighed and fired up the ignition. Jet lag was creeping into my brain. We had flown all night with very little sleep. Now we had four hours to kill before we could crash at our B&B. Despite the enchantment of our aerial approach to Shannon, I wasn't sure I could handle Ireland on the ground without a nap.

Marilyn certainly couldn't. She zipped out of the car rental lot onto the right side of the highway – which was the wrong side in Ireland. Brakes squealed and horns honked.

Mother smiled weakly at me. “Perhaps you, at least, can avoid an international incident?” she suggested, nodding at the driver raising his fist at Marilyn.

“Perhaps we should have signed up for a tour bus,” I grumped.

But I gamely nosed the car out onto the highway and diligently kept it on the wrong side of the road.

We chugged past out buildings for the airport – on the ground, it was *not* a scenic introduction to Ireland – and Mother noted wistfully that it was almost like driving through the industrial end of our own town.

But then we hit our first roundabout.

In the States, they're called traffic circles and wisely are used only in extreme circumstances. In Ireland, they pop up at nearly every intersection. But we didn't know that as we puttered out of the Shannon airport. We naively thought this roundabout was a once-in-a-lifetime challenge.

Ha.

Marilyn tooled confidently ahead and briskly drove past the turnoff to Limerick. I glanced at Mother. She just shrugged. So we obediently followed Marilyn, who, without any better direction, continued around the circle. When she missed the exit the second time, I muttered, “Screw this,” and turned toward Limerick on my own.

Marilyn eventually fell in behind us and I tremulously took the lead to Limerick.

In the airplane, I'd had a nonstop opportunity to breathlessly view the landscape below. On the ground, behind the wheel, I felt the loss of that luxury sharply. I was a stranger in a stranger land, trying to negotiate the highways to an unfamiliar destination. I didn't have time to absorb even a smidgen of the passing scenery.

Mother did, and as she traced our route on the map, she had only one observation: “It looks like home.”

Which was very disappointing. Why travel thousands of miles for countryside that's reminiscent of your own back yard?

Ah, we hadn't seen the soul of Ireland.

Yet.

* * *

Limerick should have been a 30-minute drive from Shannon. It took us 60. Along the way, we passed a festive little castle called Bunratty with colorful pennants fluttering from its turrets that tempted us to stop and indulge our tourist urges. And we probably would have if we hadn't sailed past the exit before anyone had time to change our itinerary. But the deeper we got into the dark town of Limerick, the more we regretted giving up Bunratty's blatant grab for tourist dollars.

Limerick sounds like a jolly place. After all, what drunken college party revs up on *sad* limericks? But Limerick the city is depressed, and its streets on Sunday morning were dreary and empty. The green of the Irish countryside faded to gray at the city limits, and the bright blue sky was suddenly pocked with gritty rain clouds. We couldn't find any of the gay cafes that our guidebook promised, or the quaint shops, or the gracious Georgian terraces. The only attraction we could spot was the hulking King John's castle, which fortunately did offer tours on Sunday.

"All I want is a hot cup of coffee," Patty whined as we locked our cars in a nearly empty parking lot at the castle. "Is that too much to ask?"

"Don't act like a crabby tourist," Marilyn carped.

I surreptitiously made a face at Mother.

She slapped my hip to put me in my place, then took Mrs. DeWitt's arm and led her up the path to the entrance of the castle. I quickly followed. I had no desire to be caught in a cat fight between Marilyn and Patty.

Besides, the wind whipping off the river was definitely chilly. It would be warmer and drier indoors.

Well, only marginally. King John's, after all, *was* a castle, and castles aren't known for being cozy. We had missed the only guided tour of the morning, but the little lady at the ticket window assured us we could guide ourselves through the castle using its nifty brochure. At least I *thought* that was what she said. We were quickly discovering that the Irish don't speak American. The only thing we really understood was the price of admission, which we would have balked at if we hadn't had so much free time on our hands. Besides, it was our first castle. How could we let a little thing like money keep us out of our first castle?

King John's castle (that's King John of England, not Ireland) dates from about 1200 A.D. It's a dark, imposing structure with all the towers and narrow passageways you'd expect in a castle. Despite the rather tacky dioramas constructed at regular intervals to illustrate castle life, we were all suitably impressed by the thick stone walls and the narrow slits that passed as windows, barely wide enough to admit an arrow. The castle was large but felt claustrophobic. It was a relief to climb up to the parapets and stride along the top of the walls.

It was about 10 o'clock by then and traffic on the roads below had picked up somewhat. Church bells pealed across the way at St. Mary's Cathedral, the oldest building in the city. But the clouds had darkened and we could smell rain approaching from the coast. Still, after the dark hours on the plane and the cramped car ride from Shannon, it felt good to lean against the battlements and feel an alien wind in our faces.

Patty huddled in a corner of wall near me and furiously flicked her Bic until her cigarette ignited.

"I don't think smoking is allowed on the grounds," I said to the breeze, declining to face her.

"If they don't like it," Patty said around her cigarette, "they can throw me out."

“They might deport you,” I said hopefully.

Patty snorted. “They want my dollars too much.”

Which was probably true. An older gentleman in the vest of a castle volunteer squeezed past us and didn't even raise an eyebrow at Patty's cigarette. In fact, he might have hesitated a moment to inhale before marching to the next tower.

“See,” Patty said, flicking her ash over the side, “we're nothing but cash to them.”

“We could be cousins!” I said in exasperation, waving at his receding back.

“Oh, my Lord, I hope not,” Patty groaned. “The thought of being Irish makes my skin crawl.”

“Then why in hell are you even here?” I demanded. “You've done nothing but piss and moan since we left the States. Why make the trip?”

Patty stared out over the Shannon as she sucked her cigarette down to the filter, and her expression softened with the nicotine. “I'm here to take care of my best friend.”

“You?” I hooted. “You've been quarreling with Marilyn all morning.”

“And she hasn't thought once of that prick who walked out on her, has she?” Patty shot back.

“You're not serious,” I objected. “You're picking fights with her to make her feel *better*?” And disbelief dripped from my voice.

Patty smiled as she dropped her cigarette and ground it out with her shoe. “Trust me, Jo, I know how to handle my girl.”

And she swaggered along the wall to join Marilyn.

Leaving her smoldering butt behind.

CHAPTER THIRTY-FOUR

The morning turned into a full Irish drizzle as we left Limerick and headed north to Ennis, our home for the night. It was an hour's drive, and the route took us back past the gay flags of Bunratty and the exit for Shannon airport. By then, the countryside was wet and gloomy under gray skies. As I drove, my mind kept flashing to the blinding green landscape that had stretched out below us as we approached the airport. Where had it gone? Everything around us now was bleak and dismal, and despite myself, I began wondering, just like Patty, what we were doing here.

But at least I didn't have to worry about where we were going. Marilyn was so jetlagged, she unwittingly allowed me to lead, and Mother was just super reading a map. She even figured out how to direct me around those damned roundabouts by reading them like the face of a clock. She'd tell me to exit at nine o'clock and I knew exactly where to go.

So the church towers were just striking noon when I pulled into the front car park at a stone-faced bed and breakfast in suburban Ennis. It looked more modern than quaint, but by then we were craving convenience more than authenticity. The innkeeper, a fading redhead with a nicotine halo, cheerfully assigned us to three rooms that would become a standard division of lodging during our trip: Mother and I in one room, Marilyn and

Mrs. DeWitt in a second and Patty in a third. In this particular B&B, that meant we had the run of the second floor.

But we weren't doing any running. As soon as the landlady handed us our keys, we locked ourselves into our rooms and collapsed. Jet lag slammed us into our beds.

It was late afternoon before we resurfaced.

* * *

Ennis is a market town, which means it is packed on Saturdays with shoppers and sellers. But on Sunday evenings, its cobbled streets and squares are nearly empty. However, we managed to find a pub that hadn't yet closed its kitchen – "We've nothing left but stew," the barmaid warned us – and we whetted our appetites with our first taste of Guinness.

Marilyn officiously ordered a round as we appropriated a table near a fireplace that was smoky with peat.

"I'm not a beer drinker," Mrs. DeWitt protested mildly.

"It's not beer," Marilyn said authoritatively. "It's stout."

"Is there a difference?" Mrs. DeWitt asked Mother.

Mother just shrugged. "You'd have to ask Dave," she admitted.

"Don't worry, Mrs. DeWitt," Patty said, patting her hand, "it goes down smooth and easy. You'll hardly know you're drinking."

Mrs. DeWitt ceased her fussing. "Oh, well, if it isn't strong...."

Marilyn glared at her friend for getting between her and her mother; Patty simply smiled beatifically. Despite Patty's declaration at the castle that she had made the trip to Ireland solely to watch Marilyn's back, there were discomfiting undercurrents swirling around their end of the table. I was happy I wasn't rooming with either one of them.

The Guinness turned out to be creamy and shockingly warm, but it soothed the harried souls of five ladies who just twenty-four hours before had been comfortably ensconced in their Midwest America homes. We even loosened up enough to giggle at the foamy mustaches the Guinness left on a bunch of inexperienced drinkers. The sight prompted Mother to recall the first time she surreptitiously sipped hard liquor at a USO dance, which reminded Mrs. DeWitt of teenage raids on the jugs of homemade wine stashed in her neighbor's backyard shed. Patty confessed to sneaking a nip or two from the bottle her mother kept – "for medicinal purposes" – on the top shelf of her closet. I admitted to sneaking out of high school sock hops to guzzle warm cans of beer in the parking lot with other unruly kids.

The stew arrived before Marilyn could give up her own story.

We'd gone twenty-four hours with nothing but freeze-dried airline food, so even though the stew was from the bottom of the pot and the hunks of brown bread were getting stale, we tore into the meal. The barmaid had called it mutton stew, and the taste was a little musty to our American tongues, but we lapped it up like the Last Supper. The barmaid added a platter of what we called french fries but she called chips to the center of the table, and somewhere along the way, a second round of Guinness arrived. We did not go hungry.

We had landed in Ennis at the height of summer, so even though we took our time with dinner, the sun was still slanting through the pub door as we polished off the second round of drinks. Well, some of us did. Mrs. DeWitt and Mother didn't touch their fresh mugs. They hadn't acquired the taste.

"There's a friary down the road," Mother said, reminding us that as tourists, we had an obligation to *tour*.

"It's very famous," Mrs. DeWitt said, nodding vigorously. "It was built by the Franciscans in 1240."

"So it will still be around tomorrow," I said. The thought of leaving the cozy pub to traipse around ruins wasn't at all appealing. Guinness has that effect.

"Tomorrow," Mother reminded me, "we are going to the Cliffs of Moher and up the coast to Galway."

"I really don't want to see a friary," I said stubbornly.

"Me neither," Marilyn agreed.

I was not pleased to have her as my ally.

"Well, I want to go," Mrs. DeWitt insisted.

"And you shall," Patty hopped in. "The moms and I will go sightseeing and you party poopers can stay behind."

I eyed the untouched drinks in front of Mother and Mrs. DeWitt. "I can live with that," I decided.

Marilyn was loath to let anyone else lead her mother on an adventure, but she had slipped into the wrong shoes for bopping around a friary. They were tight and narrow and perched on impractical heels. "If you want to keep the moms out of trouble – "

"The *moms* don't need chaperones," Mother said tartly. Then her voice lightened as she turned to Patty. "But if you'd like to accompany us while these sluggards guzzle stout...."

"Why else are we here if not to see ruins?" Patty gushed. "To the friary!" And she clapped her hands noisily.

Mother and Mrs. DeWitt disengaged fussily from the table, trying to retrieve sweaters and handbags without dipping them into the dregs of their stew. Patty chatted gaily about a lifelong desire to climb among the ruins of medieval monasteries (a desire she had successfully hidden from Marilyn and me) and asked solicitously whether Mother and Mrs. DeWitt had remembered their cameras as she shepherded them out to the street.

Marilyn and I quickly slid the unappreciated Guinnesses to our end of the table.

The bar and a couple more tables had filled up by then, mostly with locals, although a middle-aged couple at the table next to us definitely spoke German. There was a small area on the other side of the fireplace reserved as a makeshift stage, and fliers fluttered on the walls advertising upcoming acts, but none was scheduled for that night.

"It's Sunday," the barmaid said when I asked why.

"Ah," I said wisely, "you observe the Sabbath."

"No," the barmaid said wearily as she cleared our dishes, "our ears need a night off."

Well, I *think* that's what she said. Who could tell?

"I really wanted to hear Irish music," Marilyn pouted.

"You can't escape it," the barmaid assured her. "Except tonight." And secure in her logic, she swept the empties from our table.

Marilyn and I slouched in our chairs, giving in a little to the exhaustion of traveling, and nursed our mugs. I felt a wee bit guilty for sending Mother out to explore strange streets without me, but each sip of Guinness helped ease my conscience. Marilyn seemed to be relaxing as well. The pinched lines around her nose were fading (or perhaps the fluttering light from the fireplace simply masked them) and the harsh shape of her mouth softened (or perhaps it just seemed that way because she wasn't uttering any venomous thoughts). We weren't friendly enough for conversation to be automatic, so we sipped in silence and watched a couple of older gents throw darts.

Until Marilyn asked with no warning, "What's it like to kill a man?"

I choked on an otherwise fine mouthful of Guinness.

Marilyn was still watching the dart match and didn't see my eyes water as stout dribbled onto my chin.

"I mean," Marilyn said, oblivious to my shock, "I lost patients when I was a nurse. I've *watched* people die, but I've never actually caused their deaths. Well – " she chuckled as she darted a glance at me – "least not that anyone can *prove*." And she drained the last of her mother's Guinness.

I stared at the fire and said nothing. It had been twelve hours since we had landed in Ireland and I hadn't thought once of Louie Brandon. That was some kind of record.

"Oh, come on," Marilyn prodded after some moments had passed in silence, "you aren't going all sensitive on me, are you?"

"It's really not something I care to discuss," I said, but just to demonstrate that I hadn't allowed her to upset me on our first night of vacation, I grabbed our empty mugs and bellied up to the bar to order two more. I figured that by the time the fresh Guinness had built a proper head, Marilyn's brain would have moved on to other obsessions.

No such luck.

She lustily slurped at the foam on the fresh mug, but her eyes were maliciously probing. "I'm serious, Jo. How does it feel to snuff out another life simply by pulling a trigger?"

I stared at her coldly over my own mug. "Is there a *reason* for dredging this up?"

"Professional interest?" she countered.

"I doubt it," I snapped. Marilyn was strictly an administrator these days. She had no contact whatever with patients.

"Morbid curiosity, then," she acknowledged with a smile.

"More believable," I agreed, "but still *way* out of line."

"Why?" Marilyn demanded. "Are you ashamed of what you did?"

I thought of Louie's gun swinging toward Adam and vigorously shook my head. "Not in the least."

"Then why not tell me?" Marilyn asked as she distractedly ripped open a bag that was labeled "crisps" but looked like potato chips to me.

"Because you're a civilian," I said without thinking it through.

"Whoa!" Marilyn protested. "I'm not a member of the police fraternity, so I don't have a right to know?"

I carefully swallowed some Guinness to blot out the image of blood spurting from Louie's neck. “My job is to protect the public,” I said. “Exposing you to the information you request would be a disservice.”

“To whom?” Marilyn challenged. “Me or you?”

“Both,” I admitted.

Marilyn munched thoughtfully on a crisp. “All right,” she finally acknowledged, “that's a fair trade-off – in *your* mind. But I'm an adult, and I think I'm stable enough to handle the truth. So what's it like to be the one who decides it's okay to end a life?”

“I did *not* decide it was okay to *end* a life,” I said tersely. “I decided it was *necessary* to *save* one.”

“Your stepson,” Marilyn said, nodding.

“Dave's son,” I corrected.

“Same difference,” Marilyn said dismissively.

And who was I to argue?

“So you decided it was all right to kill one man to save another man.” Marilyn was speaking more to the peat fire than to me as she pondered the decision I had made in a split second. “It could have easily gone the other way. You could have sacrificed your stepson to save his assailant. *You* could have gone either way. I suppose your personal attachment to your stepson decided things in his favor?”

“That and the fact that Louie Brandon was lethally deranged and had to be stopped,” I said hotly.

“Now, now,” Marilyn said, wagging a finger at me, “let's not take this personally.”

“How else *should* I take it?” I demanded. “You imply that I killed a man for selfish reasons – that perhaps he wouldn't be dead if I didn't have a personal connection to Adam – but you weren't there, Marilyn. The man had already shot one officer and he was holding a gun to a child's head. What would *you* have done?”

Marilyn had eased out of her left shoe and was methodically kneading her bruised toes. “Honey,” she said without bothering to look at me, "I wouldn't have been there in the first place. I don't like drama, and I don't like blood. Why do you think I'm in administration?"

"Because it pays more," I said automatically.

She chuckled. "Yes, it does. But it's also a bureaucracy, and the blood shed in *my* office is all theoretical."

"So you're getting your kicks through me?"

She paused ever so slightly, then resumed massaging her foot. "That's part of it," she admitted.

"What else is there? You certainly aren't qualified to critique my professional performance."

"No," she agreed, and she slowly raised her eyes to mine, "but I *am* qualified to judge whether you are a danger to the other people on this trip."

She was deadly serious, and I was so shocked by the notion that I was speechless. Why would *anyone* feel the need to protect people from *me*?

"As soon as I heard you were part of this trip, I tried to talk Mother out of going. When that didn't work, I invited myself along."

"But your fiance left you," I protested feebly. "You were devastated. *That's* why you're here."

Marilyn dismissed the gentleman with a flick of her wrist. "He was already a bore. I was happy to see him go. Especially when it gave me an excuse to join the tour."

"But *why*?"

"Don't take this the wrong way, Jo," Marilyn said in a tone that meant that was exactly how I should take it, "but you *kill* people. I know you have a badge that allows you to shoot a gun, but I don't think you're very stable. And I couldn't leave you alone with my mother."

I gaped.

And felt rather icky. As though I'd just been caught torturing a fluffy litter of kittens.

Marilyn slipped her foot back into her shoe and stood. The breeze wafting through the pub door had turned frosty, and so did her smile. “I just wanted you to know. I'm watching you.” And she strode from the pub as haughtily as any woman can with sore feet.

Leaving me with the tab.

* * *

I caught up with Mother on a bridge across from the friary, peering into the reedy River Fergus.

“Are you planning to jump?” I asked.

“Looks like I'd simply land waist-deep in muck,” Mother said.

“This is Ireland,” I reminded her.

“Poetic muck,” she amended.

I leaned on the stone balustrade beside her. “And how was the friary?”

“In ruins,” Mother confided. “But picturesque nonetheless – especially the finely carved alabaster panels of the 15th-century MacMahon tomb.”

“You are quoting from the guidebook,” I said wisely.

“I am,” Mother agreed. “It's Sunday evening and the gates were locked. We could see nothing but fallen stone beyond the wrought iron fence.”

I patted her hand. “It's only the first night. We'll see proper antiquities tomorrow.”

Mother allowed herself a look around the neighborhood. “This entire *town* is an antiquity. It was founded in the 13th century.”

“Makes us brash youngsters,” I said as I steered her off the bridge and back in the direction of our B&B.

“Oh, I'm feeling quite spry,” she assured me.

“Good, because I hear the Cliffs of Moher are challenging.”

Mother squared her shoulders. “Bring them on!”

I laughed and squeezed her arm. It was good to be in a foreign land with a feisty old broad like Mother.

The streets of Ennis were narrow, and in the fading light, its gay pastel shops were becoming muted and less inviting. On the way to dinner, we had stopped at every other shop window to gawk at the merchandise and guess what the prices translated to in American dollars. We had lingered on the squares and speculated on the history behind every statue. But now in the growing dark, we hustled, anxious to reach our B&B and the little bit of Ennis that was our own territory.

As we turned onto the final block, we could see Marilyn and Patty ushering Mrs. DeWitt through the door of the B&B. The sight of Marilyn so solicitous toward her mother made me sigh.

Mother's radar pinged. "Are you all right? And don't tell me it's jet lag."

I watched as Patty pulled the door shut behind the three of them, putting them safely out of my reach. I turned in despair to Mother. "Do you think I'm dangerous?"

Mother's smile was tinged with sadness as she gently patted my cheek. "Only when you have to be, dear."

The ghost of Louie Brandon howled.

CHAPTER THIRTY-FIVE

The next morning, we stumbled into the maelstrom.

A dismal rain was pattering against the windows as we sleepily filed into the dining room of the B&B. We were the only guests, so we claimed the big center table, which was dressed in crisp white linens and delicate china. You get your money's worth in Irish B&Bs.

Especially for breakfast.

The landlady, who was in a nicotine fog even at eight in the morning, asked whether we'd like a full Irish breakfast.

Lacking real coffee to clear our minds, we foolishly agreed.

Ten minutes later, the landlady delivered platters overflowing with fried eggs, ham that the Irish stubbornly called bacon, two kinds of sausage (including something with the unappetizing adjective of "blood"), broiled tomatoes, baked beans (sadly straight out of a can) and sauteed mushrooms. These were accompanied by a plate of warm bread euphemistically billed as toast and mugs of Nescafe. If we wanted a dash of healthy, we were welcome to help ourselves to a pitcher of orange juice and a bowl of apples and bananas on the sideboard.

"I can't eat all this!" Patty objected. "I'll burst out of my jeans!"

"Is that your excuse?" Marilyn inquired.

Patty glared, but it didn't stop her from defiantly spearing a sausage link.

Mother and I hunkered behind the coffee mugs and greedily attacked our eggs. We felt the need to fortify ourselves against our traveling companions.

The landlady sent us off with many Irish blessings. The weather suggested we would need them. The temperature barely reached fifty and the rain was relentless. But we were determined to see the storied cliffs.

And as often happens in Ireland, the weather changed dramatically in the course of a few miles. The cliffs were only an hour away from Ennis, but by the time Marilyn led us into a gravel parking lot for visitors, the sun had pushed brazenly through the clouds, the rain had evaporated and a rainbow was shimmering over the pastures leading to the cliffs.

"Oh, my," Mrs. DeWitt breathed, "that is astonishing!"

Even the girls and I had to admit it was impressive. Ireland hammers your heart with miserable weather, then tears it open with scenes of exquisite enchantment.

Quickly followed by mortal danger.

Although historic town squares are free, majestic vistas often are not, and we had to line up at a turnstile to shell out a pound apiece for admission. At that point, we were still downhill from the cliff tops and the breeze was pleasant, if brisk. But as the path approached a fork, leading right to a Victorian tower that looked out over the Atlantic and left to a rugged track along the top of the cliffs, the wind suddenly packed a punch, and we staggered in indecision.

"I want to see the ocean!" Mrs. DeWitt gasped, clinging to Marilyn.

"This is dangerous," Patty said, very calmly despite the wild look in her eyes.

Mother's eyes were determined. “I didn't come all this way to let a little wind stop me,” she declared, and she veered to the left to the more exposed path.

“I'm going to the tower,” Mrs. DeWitt decided, and she was blown to the right. Marilyn was dragged along like the hapless tail of a kite.

Patty shook her head. “I am not dying here,” she announced, and turned downhill toward the souvenir shop.

And even though that was the indisputably practical choice, I lowered my head into the wind and followed Mother.

It was like slamming – repeatedly – into a wall. The wind shot off the ocean, somersaulted up the cliffs and exploded in our faces. With one hand, I clutched my jacket to my throat so it wouldn't be ripped over my head, and with the other, I gripped the wooden rails that had been installed along the path to keep the unwary from tumbling into the sea. They offered only the illusion of safety. One serious misstep and even a husky adult could be hurled into the rocks below.

Mother plodded up the cliff path, fighting the voracious pull of the wind, and I breathlessly followed. As we climbed, the ocean and the cliffs opened up below us. It was a spectacular view in black and white – gray sky over white waves crashing on black rocks – and I risked all the children I would never have to balance on a slippery rock and take one photo of Mother staring out at the primeval madness swirling around the cliffs. But then I stopped playing tourist and fought my way through gusts that stung my cheeks with salt until I could grab her shoulder and shout in her ear, “We have to go back!”

Mother's wig was damp with sea spray and her skin was pummeled red. It was the height of summer, but she was shivering inside her jacket. Still, she wanted to climb higher.

“The next cliff,” she hollered back at me, and she slipped from my grasp.

I had no choice but to follow.

We had advanced no more than ten yards – the wind still battered us and the waves roared below – when Mother stumbled. It was just a little slip on damp rock, and she quickly recovered. She is remarkably agile for a woman with an artificial hip.

But in that instant as she tottered toward a fatal fall, I flashed on Sandra Porter, wobbling on the edge of the curb, flailing to catch her balance in the dark as a pickup truck bore down on her, and I screamed in warning.

The sound was lost in the cacophony of Moher. None of the other climbers even looked in my direction. But Mother glanced at me and the horror on my face must have registered with her, because she wordlessly turned back from the cliffs and we carefully descended to civilization.

The cliffs grumbled at their loss.

*   *   *

We stopped for lunch at a pub in a one-road village called Doolin. Our guidebook said it was a mecca for traditional Irish bands, but, of course, none of them was even awake at noon. We were the only customers at the pub, but the innkeeper still served up a smashing sausage and potato pie. And when he heard us bemoaning the lack of musical accompaniment for our lunch, he assured us that Galway, our final destination for the night, would be crawling with musicians and wannabes.

Mother eyed him sternly. “You aren't misrepresenting your country's musical aptitude, are you, young man?”

The “young man” was at least my age, but he blushed under Mother's scrutiny. She would have made a great nun.

“On my sainted mother's grave,” he assured her, “the pubs in Salthill are the best. Go to O'Conner's. You won't be disappointed.”

“We're coming back this way in a week,” Mother warned him. “We won't be happy if you've misled us.”

He blanched. And I think he might have given us a break on the bill.

* * *

Marilyn wanted to hit the highway straight to Galway. She was tired of the scenic route. But her mother was a more romantic soul and wanted to see more of the Irish countryside. So before leaving Doolin, Mrs. DeWitt transferred to our car, and Marilyn and Patty shot off for Galway with promises to take care of checking us in at our next B&B. I was frankly happy to be rid of them, although allowing them to divvy up our rooms in Galway was probably not wise.

While they sped along on a main highway, Mother, Mrs. DeWitt and I cautiously followed a narrow coastal road that barely had a foothold above the smashing surf. We were so close to the ocean that the spray from the waves dotted our windshield. Clouds roiled above us, frequently so low we were nearly in fog. But then we'd break free to clear skies and the dazzling waves would nearly blind us. Ireland is a land of many moods, and all of them are gorgeous.

As we headed north, the road veered inland. We could still see the ocean to our left, but it was no longer in our faces. And the landscape changed abruptly. Instead of rough green fields, we were suddenly surrounded by bare rock, from the flat beaches to our left straight up the hills to our right. There were no trees, there were no bushes, and there were certainly no homes. Within a matter of miles, we had passed from rural Ireland into the beautiful desolation of the Burren.

“It's a moonscape,” Mrs. DeWitt said in awe.

“It's certainly unlivable,” Mother agreed.

“I want to stop,” Mrs. DeWitt said. She was in the back seat and tapped forcefully on my shoulder. “I want to explore this bleak landscape.”

"I hear you, Mrs. DeWitt," I said. But it was miles, with the land growing more and more desolate, before we found a good spot to pull off. The road along the coast is so narrow that it's difficult, even in tourist areas like the Burren, to safely park beside the pavement. All it would take was one big tour bus to knock us into eternity.

But I tucked our rental car into a corner of a fairly substantial overlook and we spilled out onto the limestone. Three other cars were parked there, and we could see human dots hopping over the rocks below us. Beyond them were bigger brown dots galloping through the surf.

"Are those *horses*?" Mrs. DeWitt asked, incredulous.

Mother was furiously thumbing through her guidebook. "I believe they are," she said.

"Oh, I must go see," Mrs. DeWitt declared, and she dashed off to the many rocks between us and the sea.

"Jo?" Mother asked, looking at me.

I shrugged. "She's on vacation. Let her go."

Mother sniffed in disapproval, but eventually tottered after Mrs. DeWitt.

I thrust my hands into my jeans pockets and concentrated on advancing from rock to rock without twisting an ankle.

The Burren derives from the Gaelic word "boireann," which means "rocky land." The blocks of limestone, called plints, cover sixty-two miles of coast and hills. In between the rocks are crevices that nurture some of the most exquisite wildflowers in Ireland. There are parts of the Burren where travelers are asked to stay in their cars, so as not to damage the delicate ecosystem. But we had apparently pulled off in an area that was not so endangered. Thus the horses galloping on the beach.

I kept an eye on Mother and Mrs. DeWitt descending toward the horses, but I wasn't inclined to join them. Marilyn and Patty were out of my hair, speeding toward Galway, and Mother and Mrs. DeWitt were engrossed by four-legged denizens of the

Burren. It was a rare opportunity for me to be alone, and my first chance since the Cliffs of Moher to allow my mind to dance around Sandra Porter.

She had fallen into traffic and died, so it really wasn't so preposterous to see Mother falling into the wind at Moher and immediately think of Sandra. Both situations involved a deadly lack of balance. Mother *could* have tumbled onto the black cliffs below the path, just as Sandra had indisputably tumbled into the traffic in front of her house. Mother *could* have died, just as Sandra most assuredly had met her demise. Only luck had separated them.

And yet, as I watched Mother tiptoe across the rocks, I couldn't help but wonder *why*? Why could a woman well into her 70s keep her balance on the blustery cliffs of Moher while a woman in her 40s couldn't keep her head on her own front walk? Why could Mother, even with a Guinness under her belt, stay on her feet on the streets of Ennis, while Sandra, with only a glass of wine or two, couldn't stop herself from falling into the traffic passing her house? Mother had undoubtedly aged, but she was still agile enough to hop across the rocks of the Burren. Why couldn't Sandra deal with the traffic on a quiet residential street?

I vigorously shook my head. I was on *vacation*. These were not the kind of thoughts I should be entertaining, especially since Sandra's case was closed and I no longer had any standing to pry it open. Bradley's efforts notwithstanding, I *was* damaged. I *needed* this time away to make myself whole and legitimate again.

Mrs. DeWitt got close enough to a horse for it to snort belligerently at her outstretched hand. Then it galloped off along the shore, leading the other horses with it. Mrs. DeWitt watched in dismay as Mother caught up with her and patted her shoulder.

I looked down at a small lavender flower poking out of a crevice at my feet. In the vast expanse of limestone stretching out in all directions, today was its only shot at sunshine, its only shot at life. Part of me wanted to pluck the flower and stick it in my headband. Part of me wanted to shield it from the marauding hordes programmed to stampede it to pieces.

I caressed it with my fingertip.

Then inadvertently sideswiped it with my hiking boots as I turned back to the car.

* * *

Even in the empty expanses of the Burren, one must shop, so we detoured to the Burren Perfumery, a family-run business that was savvy enough to use the mystique of its unique location to sell its soaps and fragrances. We walked in searching for a restroom, were seduced by the tea room and departed with bags of aromatic lotions and oils that would require precious space in our luggage.

Then being tourists, we had to backtrack to the Poulnabrone Domen, an austere but striking stone portal to a tomb dating to 2500 to 2000 B.C. And then we had to stop at Ailwee Cave, where we caught the last tour of the afternoon. I worried about the older ladies losing their footing in wet underground passages, but Mother and Mrs. DeWitt were charged up. They had flown thousands of miles to the Old Country and, by golly, they were going to tour everything that made it old.

I vetoed Leemanagh Castle. It would have meant backtracking yet again, and the afternoon was disappearing. I could picture Marilyn and Patty lounging at our B&B in Galway, sipping adult beverages. We, on the other hand, still had to find the main highway that would shoot us around the bay to Galway.

The drizzle descended as we passed from the Burren to greener countryside, and gray sky seemed to press down on us, blocking out the afternoon light. Mother and Mrs. DeWitt slumped in their seats and drifted off. I was left to navigate on my own, fighting foreign traffic on the wrong side of the road, with visibility roughly equivalent to pea soup. But the alternative was negotiating the highway with two old ladies stridently instructing me to drive in two different directions, so I let them doze, even when Mrs. DeWitt began to snore. Despite the navigational challenge, it was a relief to be dealing with a problem that didn't involve good guys and bad guys with guns. There were only drivers who knew what they were doing and those who didn't, and I was squarely among the latter.

We had just safely entered the Galway city limits, probably an hour behind what an Irish driver would have managed from the Burren, when Mother roused herself, frowned at the rain and took over the directions to our B&B. We were at the height of Galway's rush hour (which I'm told isn't nearly as bad off season), but Mother efficiently guided me through town and west toward the Salthill neighborhood. Our B&B was several blocks off the Promenade, making it a long walk from downtown but a short hop to some of the more popular pubs.

The B&B turned out to be a modern-looking one-story house with brick facing, sitting on a street with many similar houses, all fronted by fussily tended gardens that bloomed brilliantly in the chilly sea air. Many Irish houses are just one floor – no basement and no bedrooms tucked up under the eaves. Our B&B had two generous guest rooms in front, a dining room and kitchen in the middle, and private living quarters squeezed in the back. I tried not to think of our ample landlady and her husband existing in just a third of the house.

Marilyn and Patty had indeed divided the two guest rooms to their liking. They took the larger one and consigned Mother, Mrs. DeWitt and me to the other – meaning Mother and Mrs. DeWitt got the twin beds and I got the rollaway cot. We were staying in this B&B for two nights. I eyed the cot and resigned myself to an aching back.

The afternoon drizzle amped itself up to a downpour as I was hauling our luggage out of the car. I was drenched by the time I staggered indoors.

Galway was not stirring my heart.

CHAPTER THIRTY-SIX

We not only hadn't packed for cool weather, but we also hadn't come dressed for rain, but our landlady was awash in umbrellas and convinced us to take a "wee walk up the road" to a seafood restaurant for dinner. We were discovering that "wee" can cover a multitude of sizes and we were squishing in our shoes by the time we found the restaurant, but it smelled so mouthwatering as we shook off our umbrellas and stepped inside that even Marilyn and Patty dialed down their complaints to one wrinkled nose at the portly customer smoking a pipe in the corner and one raised eyebrow at the coffee that turned out to be instant. I wasn't affected by that particular outrage because I was drinking Guinness.

Dinner was exquisite. After all, it had been swimming in the ocean just that morning. But then we felt the need to walk off our excesses and we headed to the Promenade, a two-and-a-half-mile walkway along the coast. It was rumored that swans sometimes hung out there.

Not on our shift. We staggered half a mile up the coast and witnessed a brilliant sunset thanks to the clouds that intermittently blessed us with cold sprinkles, but we didn't spot a single swan. Boats occasionally honked on the bay, but even ignorant foreigners couldn't mistake them for birds. So we retraced our steps to our starting point, where Mother and Mrs. DeWitt called it a day.

The younger generation went pub hopping.

After much bickering, we finally wandered into O'Connor's, the pub that the innkeeper in Doolin had recommended. I was immediately intrigued because it was packed with old stuff. Marilyn and Patty were enthralled because it was filled with old men who would be particularly defenseless against them. We decided to stay.

I grabbed my Guinness as soon as it had built a proper head and roamed around the rooms, gawking at the owner's amazing collection of outdated things. There were mundane displays of old shot glasses and coasters and there was a lot of shell-studded fishnet hanging from the rafters, illuminated by strings of Christmas lights. But there were also more unusual decorations for a pub, like the rusted implements used to tend peat fires and the board games that had amused children generations back and religious icons that actually meant something to the practicing Catholics cozying up to the bar. I poked through the dim lighting, hoping for a flash of the red glass that I scarfed up at auctions back home, but nothing sang out to me among the displays of glassware tucked into corners here and there. Ireland is renowned for its crystal, particularly on the southern coast, but its talents don't extend to my favorite Ruby Red.

I downed the first Guinness just being nosy (a button collection mesmerized me as the pub filled up for the night's entertainment), so my mug was sadly dry when the lights suddenly dimmed and three shadows moved to the corner reserved for the band. I groped through the gloom to the table (actually, an old treadle sewing machine) Marilyn and Patty had confiscated just to the right of the band, and as the Celtic whistle soared into the dreadfully tragic territory of Irish music, I slipped onto a stool beside the girls and focused – minus Guinness – on the musicians.

It was our first opportunity to hear a traditional band, and I was intrigued. Left to my own devices, my musical talents wouldn't have evolved past the British Invasion. But Dave is much more adventuresome, and he has exposed me to more ethnic sounds, including Celtic, so I blotted out the chatter between Marilyn and Patty and sank into the music.

The whistle player was a stout graybeard probably ten years my senior, but he still had a good pair of lungs. He was accompanied by a youngster who was so energetic on the fiddle that he made my heart race. And pulling it together was the salt-and-pepper tenor on guitar. They played nothing I knew, but it didn't matter. The slow tunes were universally mournful, the fast ones were raucously gay, and both wormed their way into my brain. By the end of the set, I was pounding the table and stomping my feet in time, just like a Galwegian.

But I really needed another Guinness.

Marilyn and Patty were totally focused by then on the table of Canadian tourists next to us – so much so that they ignored my offer to buy a round. They could afford to ignore me. Their mugs were full, suggesting to my suspicious mind that they had loaded up on refills without counting me in.

Well, it was my own fault for getting lost in the music.

So I pushed my way to the bar to get a Guinness of my own. I found the Irish custom of placing your order at the bar instead of waiting for a server to come round to your table a little disconcerting. It meant jostling for the bartender's attention with patrons who were just as thirsty as you were. Like the evening's guitarist.

We locked eyes for a second, and he *almost* gallantly stepped aside to let me order first, but then a tipsy couple stumbled between us, pushing me even farther from the bar, and he just shrugged and placed his order.

Oh, well, I thought, he had *tried* to be a gentleman.

And I meekly waited my turn.

The second set was as energetic as the first, and since the Guinness had had more time to ferment the crowd, the response from the audience was much more raucous. I still didn't know the lyrics, but by the end of the set, I was again rocking and swaying to the tunes right along with the locals. The musicians had struck a chord with their listeners, and everyone was crying and shouting and spitting in their beer. I was used to the Farmhouse at home, where patrons might dance euphorically to the music, but they never crossed the psychological line between them and the band. Here, it was all one big bleeding of the soul, and when the band stopped, we were all exhausted.

"Well," Marilyn said primly as most people surged to the bar to get in their last call, "that was primitive."

Patty snorted and nodded at the next table, which had emptied quickly. "You're just pissed that the Canadian gentlemen didn't invite you along."

"Like you wouldn't have gone if they'd asked?" Marilyn countered.

"The only place I'm going is to *bed*," Patty said.

"Alone again," Marilyn taunted.

Patty's eyes flashed. "You forget, I'm *married*."

"For now," Marilyn chided.

"Ladies," I sighed.

"Oh, Miss Holier Than Thou," Marilyn sniped, "shacking up with the guy who can't be bothered to marry you."

Patty tut-tutted.

But I just stared curiously at Marilyn through the fumes of Guinness. Whoever said it was *Dave* who wouldn't tie the matrimonial knot?

We were forced to take our disagreements outside. Irish pubs close earlier than American bars, and the staff was cheerfully but efficiently moving the clientele out to the street. I found myself squeezing through the door at the same time as the salt-and-pepper guitarist.

"We play again tomorrow," he said with no introduction.

"I'm married," I babbled.

His eyes twinkled. "Of course you are, lass."

The crowd carried him off to the Promenade. Marilyn and Patty steered me toward our B&B.

I mentally rolled my eyes for Dave's benefit. It's hard to be a good girl when you're so damned alluring.

CHAPTER THIRTY-SEVEN

We woke to hangovers and a pounding Irish rain. But the landlady assured us the sun would come out because this was Ireland and the weather changed by the hour. And by the time we were tucking into our eggs and bacon, a rainbow was indeed dancing over the bay.

Which led to a dispute over the day's tourist traps. There was a cruise up the River Corrib that appealed to ladies of a certain age with aching knees. But there were also many shops downtown that called out to women with credit cards who were woefully underdressed for Ireland's capricious climate. So after much dithering, Mother and Mrs. DeWitt launched themselves toward the Quay, where they hoped to catch a boat, and Marilyn and Patty girded themselves for some serious shoe shopping. I smiled broadly and waved both groups off on their adventures, hoping to take my throbbing head back to bed.

The landlady had other ideas. It was cleaning time at the B&B, and guests weren't particularly welcome. But since I *was* paying for another night's lodgings, she reluctantly allowed me to take over her private patio behind the house. The chaise longue wasn't nearly as comfy as a bed, but it promised the opportunity to doze.

Except my brain was tired of doing nothing. It was our third day of travel, and though it was nice to see new places and cope with new customs, they weren't enough to keep me from thinking about the problems I had left at home. There was no mystery about Louis Brandon – I knew *exactly* why he was dead – but Sandra Porter's accident still gnawed at my peace of mind.

Which was why I had reserved a precious corner of luggage space for her case file.

If Bradley ever learned I'd taken it out of the country, he might not let me back in. But I was fairly confident the file wouldn't be missed. The case was officially closed. Based on my own department's investigation and the coroner's report, the prosecutor had decided not to take Sandra's death to the grand jury. Ed Harper didn't get so much as a ticket.

And I had no problem with that. Schafer had checked out the accident scene with a skilled eye. His final report had held Harper blameless. His speed had been perfectly legal. The roadway had been dry and in good repair. Although the accident had occurred past sundown, the streetlights outside Sandra's house had been working. Visibility had been as good as it was going to get that night, and if Harper had been a truck length back of the spot where Sandra had stumbled into the road, he probably would have been able to swerve enough to avoid hitting her, or at least avoid killing her. Harper couldn't have done anything to stop the accident.

But could Sandra? Even drunk, could she have jumped back to the curb? Could she have seen Harper's truck in time and twisted out of the way?

Or did she choose to fall into its path?

I wearily rubbed the bridge of my nose and the pleasant Irish garden where I was lounging receded. Instead of a riot of roses growing incongruously next to a palm tree, I saw Sandra, flushed from the wine, darting out between two parked cars directly into the path of the truck, and I tried to picture her eyes. Were they wide with surprise and – belatedly – terror? Or were they determined to stare into Harper's headlights until the impact killed her? Could the accident have been a suicide?

Sandra *had* displayed some bizarre behavior in the days before her death, especially at the recorder's office, where I had run into her, and at the drugstore, where she had confronted Patty. Her recounting of the dead at the Girl Scout reunion had certainly been morose. But I hadn't seen or heard anything about her that indicated she was dangerously depressed. Schafer had interviewed neighbors and co-workers in the course of his investigation and hadn't picked up any hint that Sandra was unstable, either – perhaps a bit odd, maybe even obsessive, but not on the brink of doing herself harm.

Yet what if she had fooled us?

I hadn't given the idea much serious thought until the night before Mother and I left town. I was working late at the station, organizing my files so others could cover for me. As I worked through the stack of folders, I came across Sandra's file and put it to the side. There was no need to pass her case along to anyone. It was dead.

Ellen Graham clocked in as I worked. She was on nights that month and normally wouldn't be due to start her shift for a couple of hours yet. However, Berger was winding up his vacation just as I was starting mine and the squad was short, so Ellen was picking up some overtime. Laboring under the cost of babysitters and pediatricians, she was in a constant battle with Henry for overtime hours.

She frowned at the empty coffee pot. I smiled apologetically but didn't offer to start a pot. I'd hit my caffeine ceiling two mugs ago.

Normally, she would have needled me for letting the pot run dry, but she cut me some slack instead. Most people had been cutting me slack since I'd killed Louie Brandon. But it was a good thing I was leaving the country. I could tell by the way Ellen sighed as she filled the coffee pot that her patience, like everyone else's, was wearing thin.

I was stacking files according to who was best suited to handle them in my absence. Berger was a no-brainer for the check-kiting scheme, and I figured I could count on Henry to lean on the deadbeat dads I had accumulated. I assumed that when Ellen gravitated to my desk while waiting for the coffee maker to do its magic, she would thumb through the cases I was leaving for her. There was a dandy sexual assault with a victim who wouldn't ID her assailant, and I knew that was just the kind of thing that would trip Ellen's trigger, but when I looked up from my work to gauge her outrage level, I found her staring instead at Sandra Porter's file.

Specifically, at the local newspaper photo from the Girl Scout reunion.

I was unaccountably defensive. “Is there a problem?” I demanded, barely on the proper side of polite.

Ellen had been tracing her finger across the faces in the photo, but froze at the sound of my voice, her finger coincidentally on Sandra's face. “Well, yes,” she said. “Isn't this group of Scouts awfully small?”

“It's a small town,” I countered idiotically.

Ellen thoughtfully considered that, then dared to disagree. “There are – what? Eight former Scouts in this photo? I was a Girl Scout. We had nearly twenty-five girls in our troop.”

“We had twenty-three,” I said swiftly, eager to defend my troop's honor.

“So only eight out of twenty-three showed up for your reunion?” Ellen shook her head as she sidled back to the coffee pot, which was hissing at the end of its drip cycle. “You must not have liked each other much.”

“That's ridiculous,” I said. “Some of the girls have moved out of state, some had other commitments that day.”

“Fifteen of them were too busy to attend?” Ellen asked. She was always quick at math.

"Well," I admitted, "Sandra Porter isn't the only one who's died."

Ellen's look as she poured coffee was skeptical, so I hastily listed the other dead, from Nikki Hocevar's car accident at sixteen to Sharon McCarthy's death in a California wildfire just the year before. I thought I made my point quite nicely.

Ellen was stunned. "How old are you, Jo? Forty-five?"

"Forty-three," I stiffly corrected.

"And out of 23 women roughly 43 years old, eight are dead? Don't you think that's a little *high*?"

I shrugged irritably. "People die." Just ask Louie Brandon.

"But in these numbers?" Ellen persisted. "I think that's statistically unlikely."

"Maybe unlikely," I conceded, "but certainly not *criminal*."

Ellen leveled her mathematically curious gaze on me. "Are you sure?"

"Be serious, Ellen," I protested. "Cancer is a killer, but it isn't a crime. Wildfires don't kill with criminal intent. They were all deaths by natural causes or *accidental*."

"It does look that way," Ellen agreed.

"But?" I prodded.

Ellen hedged. "Really, I don't mean to stir up painful memories, but your Girl Scout troop has been extremely unlucky. Don't you find it *odd*?"

"Not in the least," I said stoutly.

"Of course not," Ellen sighed, and she wandered back to her desk.

End of conversation.

I pursed my lips, wishing I had paid more attention to statistics and probabilities in college.

And ultimately smuggled Sandra's file out of the station for the long flight to Ireland.

* * *

Marilyn and Patty found a friendly group of Australian tourists downtown and wandered off with them for the rest of the night. Mother and Mrs. DeWitt were so worn out by their river tour that it was all I could do to keep them awake long enough for some takeout fish and chips. Which left me wide awake and alone in a strange city at eight o'clock. So I clutched at the familiar and wound up nursing a Guinness at a treadle sewing machine at O'Connor's.

I've been alone in American bars and felt extremely out of place. Either the guys think it's a clear invitation to hit on you or the women think you're pitiful and need their makeover advice. But it's different in an Irish pub. Perhaps it was because I was a foreigner, but no one seemed to think it particularly odd that a woman of my age was occupying a (small) table by herself. I slouched comfortably in the chair, nibbled on crisps, sipped my Guinness and watched the crowd. It kept my mind off dead Girl Scouts and the occasional flash of blood bursting from Louie Brandon's neck.

And eventually the band mates from the night before turned up and set their instruments on fire.

The set was alternately lively and morose. The musicians may have been playing exactly the same songs as the previous night, but the patrons didn't care. They clapped and hooted and stomped their feet, and I jumped in with them because I was on vacation and I wanted to have some fun. The band certainly was enjoying itself. By the time the set ended, the musicians were glistening with sweat and their mugs were dry.

I fought the crowd to the bar for a fresh Guinness. When I finally made my way back to my treadle sewing machine, Sean, the guitarist, was sitting in the chair opposite mine and chatting happily with tourists.

“Did you bring any more crisps?” he asked between questions from his admirers.

"I ate them all myself," I said gravely.

"You'll get uncommonly fat, lass," he warned, and turned his warm smile on an American couple begging him to autograph their map of Ireland.

I leaned back in my chair and sipped my Guinness. It was my table, but since he was the invader, it was his play. So I watched him with some caution as he chatted up the tourists and eventually accepted their pen so he could sign the map.

He grinned sheepishly as they happily exited with their trophy. "It's grand being famous," he said, and greedily slurped some Guinness.

"Are you a star in Ireland?" I asked.

He held his thumb and forefinger about an inch apart. "Maybe a wee bit in Galway."

"But in County Donegal?" I asked, pulling a name out of the air.

He shrugged. "Maybe not as much."

And if I hadn't had Dave in my life, his twinkling eyes would have torn into my soul.

"Are you staying with us for long?" he asked.

It was such an obvious play, I nearly laughed. The man was working me like the rest of his audience. I couldn't begrudge him the pound or two he was making off the house by sweet talking the ladies in the crowd.

"We're leaving tomorrow," I said. "Heading up the coast to Clifden."

In a flash, he dropped all pretense of playing with the patrons. "Stop in Cleggan," he advised, quite seriously.

"We want to hike in the Connemara," I countered. "We may not have time."

"Make time. Go to Oliver's in Cleggan and order the fish chowder. It is orgasmic."

I raised an eyebrow. A total stranger was telling me to buy something *orgasmic*?

“Seriously,” he said, tapping his finger on the table as the lights flickered to signal the next set, “it's *absolutely* the best chowder you'll ever eat.”

“And you know this because?” I challenged him.

His eyes flashed as he rose to go back to the makeshift stage. “I'm Irish, lass. Don't doubt me in my own land.”

And I pondered his advice and his motives as he tuned up for the next set.

I had already downed much Guinness and I had a long day of driving ahead of me, but the first song of the set crept under my skin, and even though I knew sleep rather than another Guinness was the better way to go when driving left-handed in a foreign land, I ordered another pint and allowed myself to float on the music. As a guitarist, Sean was overwhelmed by the fiddle and the whistle, but his voice was the strongest of the three, so he dominated the vocals. I was so stirred by the passion of his delivery that I forced myself to think hard instead of Dave. Naked.

Which was why I was already a little hot and bothered by the end of the set, when Sean strode to my table and cupped my face in his hands.

“I have business to tend to. Go to Cleggan.” And he leaned in and kissed me fiercely.

Then he was gone.

Just like a leprechaun.

CHAPTER THIRTY-EIGHT

Mother strongly suggested the next morning that she take the wheel. I wouldn't hear of it, but I got her message. Guinness is best savored in moderation.

It was a brilliantly clear morning as we left Galway. The bay sparkled on our left. The hills rising to our right were bright with yellow gorse. The sky was so blue, it hurt the eyes.

But this was Ireland, and as we drove inland from the bay, clouds moved in, hinting of stormy nights and smoky peat.

Mother amused me by recounting her trip up the River Corrib with the very earth-centric Mrs. DeWitt. Suffice it to say, one should never take an ocean cruise with Mrs. DeWitt. Even within touching distance of the river banks, she was in mortal fear of sinking. So it hadn't been a relaxing outing for either Mother or Mrs. DeWitt.

But even as Mother gently took jabs at Mrs. DeWitt's fears, she was watching me rather than the scenery unfolding around us.

"What?" I asked, as moody as the hills.

"Are you obsessing over Sandra Porter?" she asked.

"Why would I do that?" I scoffed, keeping my eyes on the road as it twisted with the landscape.

"Why would you bring her file on vacation?" Mother countered.

I risked a sharp glance in her direction. "Are you snooping through my luggage?"

"Of course," she said unapologetically. "I *am* your mother."

"Christ," I muttered, and it had nothing to do with the oncoming tour bus that was forcing us to the side of the road.

"There is no need to be profane," Mother remonstrated.

"There is if that bus squishes us into the gorse."

"Marilyn doesn't seem to be having a problem," Mother said, nodding to the car ahead of us. Marilyn had squirted through the pass to a slightly broader stretch of road before the bus could bear down on *her*.

"You're quite free to ride with Marilyn if you like," I snarled.

"And miss the opportunity to hear *why* you're working on your vacation?" Mother sniffed. "I think not."

I refrained from retorting as I concentrated on slithering past the bus without losing a mirror. Mother was an excellent navigator, but she had no idea how difficult it was to drive around the maniacs who had been issued licenses in Ireland.

The road was somewhat curvy and the bus wasn't the only large vehicle traveling toward us. So it was a while before we hit a section of roadway where it was safe to ask Mother why she was monitoring the contents of my luggage.

"Because," she said, uncharacteristically miffed, "you are supposed to be *healing* on this trip, not wallowing in more crime."

"Sandra's death wasn't a crime," I said automatically.

"My point exactly!" Mother crowed. "She died in a traffic accident. Why are you obsessing on it?"

"Because she *called* me," I said without thinking, "and she died before I could get back to her."

"Ah," Mother said, and she visibly relaxed. "I *see*."

My eyes narrowed at the temporarily benign traffic. "You see *what*?"

"It isn't just that Elizabeth's picture was in Sandra's folder," she said, nodding placidly. "It's the fact that *you don't know what Sandra wanted*, and since she's dead, you'll *never* know."

I chewed on my lip. It was so like Mother to home in on my less honorable motivations. Of *course*, it was killing me that Sandra had died without telling me her secrets. I was a *cop*. What cop *wouldn't* suspect criminal misbehavior on *someone's* part?

"Nine o'clock," Mother said blandly as we approached a roundabout in mid-debate.

I just as blandly negotiated the exit. Marilyn, of course, had missed the turn and was zipping around the roundabout again to catch up.

"If I had gotten back to Sandra sooner, she could have told me what was on her mind before she died," I admitted.

Mother nodded. "She might not have died if she'd been on the phone to you."

I flinched.

Mother shrugged. "Who knows what else she could have been doing at the moment Mr. Harper's truck drove by if she had talked to you first?"

"So it *is* my fault she died," I said glumly.

"Don't be an ass, Jo," Mother sighed. "You failed to return a phone call but you didn't get her drunk that night and you didn't push her into the road."

I sucked in my breath, but it wasn't entirely because of the tank truck barreling at us from the opposite direction. I had flashed back on the damp glass in Sandra's kitchen cupboard, the one that matched the wine-stained glass we had found in her living room.

"*I* didn't get her drunk," I said as I swerved to the side of the road rather than challenge the tanker, "but what if someone else did?"

"Why would you think that?" Mother asked, bravely focusing on me rather than the truck.

I gripped the wheel and squeezed my eyes shut as the tanker scraped past us with barely inches to spare. Giddy at escaping a fatal encounter with the truck, I babbled to Mother about the wine glass.

Mother was thoughtful as I pulled back onto the road to Roundstone, where we planned to stop for lunch. Eventually, the highway crested a hill and suddenly we were back in sight of the ocean. Ahead of us was a small harbor, hugged by a string of pastel houses. Our stomachs growled for a pit stop.

I parked along the harbor. As Marilyn slid into the space beside us, Mother leaned over conspiratorially. "You believe someone got poor Sandra drunk?"

I stared at the waves gently slapping the stone pier at the center of Roundstone. I was thousands of miles away from home, thousands of miles away from the road where Sandra died, thousands of miles away from anyone who could help me with an investigation. Yet I surprised myself by saying to Mother, "I do."

She patted my hand with confidence. "Then you'll find out who, dear. It's what you do."

And she climbed out of the car in search of boiled cabbage.

* * *

We settled for lunch in a hotel overlooking the harbor because it was the only place in town that offered food. Calling it a hotel might have been an exaggeration. The first floor was taken up by a lobby with a pub to the left and a dining room to the right. Guest rooms occupied the two floors above. The building *was* larger than our first B&B in Ennis, but not by much.

The innkeeper offered Guinness, but it was barely past noon and we all ordered coffee or tea. We thought we'd go light with soup and sandwiches, but the innkeeper threw in a bowl of mashed potatoes and a platter of chips to bulk us up for the drive north. There was a basket of fresh brown bread as well, flanked by loaves of soda bread studded with raisins. The amount of food that came out of his kitchen threatened to topple the table.

We weren't inclined to rush the meal. A storm swooped into the harbor and lashed the hotel with gray sheets of rain, and the wind turned cold enough to prompt the hotelier to dash around closing windows and doors. So we lingered over coffee and pudding and waited for rainbows to brighten the bay.

"I wish," Mrs. DeWitt sighed over her delicate china coffee cup, "that we had booked a tour bus instead of renting cars."

Marilyn bristled. "Do you have a problem with my driving?"

Patty snorted. "Doesn't everyone?"

Marilyn glared.

Mrs. DeWitt smiled indulgently at her daughter. "It has nothing to do with *you*, dear. It's this *place*." And her sweeping arm took in the entire northwestern coast of Ireland.

Patty snorted again. I wondered uncharitably whether the house was spiking her tea.

"I don't understand at *all*," Marilyn protested. "We've had some *lovely* drives."

"When we weren't staring death in the eye," Patty muttered to me. I just happened to be sitting next to her.

Marilyn hissed.

"Really," Mrs. DeWitt insisted, "wouldn't it have been so much simpler if we had let a tour guide handle all of our arrangements? No arguments over getting lost. No debates about where to go." She turned beseechingly to Mother. "Don't you agree, Ruth? It would have been *so* much easier."

Mother hated to be put on the spot, but she rallied nicely. "We are a bit disorganized," she agreed, "but I think it's exciting never knowing from one day to the next *exactly* what we're going to do."

"But if we were on a bus," Mrs. DeWitt said, just a shade peevishly, "we wouldn't get lost."

"That's Patty's fault," Marilyn interjected. "*She's* supposed to be the navigator."

"You try doing any better," Patty shot back. "The road signs aren't even in *English*."

"Which is why the navigator is supposed to be paying attention," Marilyn said tersely. "The driver doesn't have *time* to translate road signs."

I unwittingly nodded in sympathy with Marilyn. Just keeping the car on the wrong side of the road took all of my concentration. I didn't have a brain cell to spare for signage in any language.

Patty's eyes narrowed at me. "You think you could do better?"

"Wha – ?" I sputtered eloquently.

"Of course she could," Marilyn snapped – arguably the first time she had ever come to my defense. "Jo's a *detective*."

I failed to see her logic.

So did Patty.

Marilyn threw up her hands. "She follows *trails*. Get it?"

No, but Patty didn't care. It gave her the opening she wanted. "Then we'll just test that theory. We'll switch roles."

"Oh?" Marilyn asked. Her voice did not drip disapproval, but I could tell by the way she dropped her napkin onto the table that she was not overjoyed at the prospect.

"I will drive and Jo will navigate," Patty decided.

"Aren't you having this argument with *Marilyn*?" I objected.

"And isn't her argument that you're a better navigator because you're a great detective?" Patty countered.

"Absolutely," Marilyn said firmly.

I looked at Mother. "This is all wrong."

Mother turned to Mrs. DeWitt. "I think I'll ride with you."

And when the rain disappeared inland, Mother squeezed into the back seat of the DeWitt car and we left Roundstone for Clifden with Patty in the lead and me riding shotgun.

CHAPTER THIRTY-NINE

Clifden, our home for the next few nights, should have been a leisurely drive up the coast. But the road was slick and curvy, and Patty was getting her first taste of left-hand driving. It didn't help that her navigator was grossly unfamiliar with the map. So there was a lot of sniping as we tried to follow a road that twisted around coves that existed only in folklore. The scenery was spectacular, but we didn't have time to pay it any mind.

Patty lasted until Ballyconneely Bay, where we headed inland to cut across a small peninsula. Just as we rounded a bend (perhaps too fast), we met our first Irish sheep. It was standing in the middle of the road, apparently weighing the nutritional value of the vegetation on the west side of the road with that on the east. It must have been a serious matter, requiring all of its concentration, because the sheep showed no inclination to move despite tons of metal bearing down on it.

Patty leaned on the horn and the brakes.

The sheep twitched its tail but refused to acknowledge our existence.

The brakes locked and the car slid toward quick-fried mutton chops.

Fortunately for the sheep, our forward thrust petered out about a foot from its hooves. We stopped grill to nose.

The sheep didn't even blink.

"Jesus *Christ*," Patty hissed.

Marilyn pulled up sedately behind us and honked her horn. The sheep paid no more attention to her than it had to us. In fact, two more critters wandered into the road to join the first, and all three stared placidly at us.

"I hate this country," Patty groaned, and she pressed her forehead onto the steering wheel.

Marilyn continued to blare her horn. It did nothing to motivate the sheep, but it apparently alerted a higher authority. Suddenly, a blur of black and white border collie landed on the roadway and began barking and nipping at sheep legs. The sheep immediately scattered to the eastern side of the road.

"*Go*!" I urged Patty.

She raised her head, saw her chance and pushed forward. We weren't exactly free of sheep – there were dozens of them hugging the hillside right down to the pavement – but no others were actually in the road. Patty carefully drove past them and gingerly picked up speed as we left the herd behind.

But a hundred yards down the road, she whipped into a scenic turnoff.

Marilyn dutifully followed us off the road, and wound down her window as she pulled abreast of us.

"Photo op?" she asked, waving at a landscape that was pleasant but not nearly as striking as other spots we had passed up.

Patty raised a cigarette and wriggled it at her.

Marilyn wrinkled her nose. "We'll keep going," she said, and unceremoniously pulled back onto the roadway.

Patty snorted. "There's nothing more sanctimonious than an ex-smoker." But in deference to me, she climbed out of the car to calm her nerves with a nicotine fix.

I climbed out after her. The encounter with the sheep – with another driver in control of my life – had been surprisingly rattling. I needed to escape the confines of the car.

So I joined Patty on a rock overlooking a steep hillside dotted with even more sheep.

Patty exhaled rapturously.

I felt pitifully excluded.

“Oh, for God's sake,” she said, and tossed me the pack.

“I haven't smoked in years,” I protested.

“When was the last time you stared death in the face of a sheep?” she countered.

I couldn't begin to argue that point, so before my conscience could take over, I plucked a cigarette out of the pack and lit up.

And tried not to cough.

“There now,” Patty said, slapping me on the back, “don't you feel better?”

My throat was burning, but it didn't stop me from taking a second hit. Because I could already feel the jangly edges of my nerves quieting.

Or maybe I was just hallucinating.

Patty chuckled. “Marilyn says you're a hopeless prig. I told her you weren't nearly as bad as some of the other girls we used to know.”

“Me? A prig?” I sputtered. “I live in sin, for God's sake.”

“With your mother,” Patty pointed out.

“And *Dave*,” I reminded her, “and his *son*.”

“Which somehow makes it all seem legitimate,” Patty said with the logic of a sleep-deprived tourist.

“And what was wrong with all the other girls?” I demanded.

Patty snorted smoke – *most* unattractive. “We're talking about the Scouts, right?”

I nodded as I hungrily inhaled again.

“Was there ever a more compliant, pedestrian group of girls?” Patty asked. “Come on, Jo. War protests, civil rights demonstrations, battles for women's rights were erupting all round us, and all our fellow Scouts could think of was accumulating badges. Sarah even mounted her badges on her sash and hung it on her living room wall!" And Patty rolled her eyes.

I felt a mild discomfort – no doubt a nicotine overdose. "Be fair," I admonished. "All those protests came along when we were in college. When we were in Scouts, the world was still benign."

"But you know what I mean," Patty countered as she raised her cigarette for a final hit. "Our troop was full of Pollyannas."

"And you prefer Cassandras?"

Patty sighed. "You know that's why the girls never liked you, don't you? You were always bringing up something from our classes – like Cassandra – to prove *you* were studying, even if the rest of us weren't. You really *were* a prig." And she sucked her cigarette down to the filter, then crushed the butt out on the pavement.

I was rather stunned. *None* of the other girls liked me? I thought Patty was overstating the case.

But she was done discussing.

And driving as well. She tossed the car keys at me. "I've proved my point. Now I intend to nap."

And she circled around to the passenger side of the car.

I happily jiggled the keys as I took my own final hit. I did not trust other people to drive me around foreign lands. If I was destined to be flattened by a tour bus, I wanted it to be my fault, not because someone else was distracted at the wheel. So despite the many oversized vehicles on the road, I was quite relieved to be back in the driver's seat.

I just wasn't as giddy as I should have been. Something Patty had said was nagging the back of my brain. Something significant. I just couldn't identify it.

So I drove distracted to Clifden and, while Patty dozed, I missed a storyland of Irish scenery.

*   *   *

"You've been smoking," Mother sniffed with disapproval as we unpacked at out Clifden B&B.

"Patty was smoking in the car," I hedged.

"Don't prevaricate like a teenager," Mother scolded, and disappeared into the bathroom with an armful of pharmaceuticals.

We were staying in a downtown B&B that looked cramped and small from the street but twisted and climbed around courtyards to offer ten rooms, all but three on the top floor ensuite. It was especially nice that Patty and the DeWitts were at the other end of the house and a labyrinth of corridors and stairs separated us.

While Mother scoped out the bathroom, I bounced on the two beds to see which mattress might be more suitable for a tired driver. The bed next to the window would catch the night breeze, but it would also be subjected to the noise of deliverymen using the back alley. Did I want to sleep cool or undisturbed?

Mother wasn't thinking about sleep. She bustled out of the bathroom and nailed me. "I may be ancient, Josephine, but I still know tobacco when I smell it, and I recognize discord when I hear it."

I had been staring out at the alley, quiet now in the absence of deliveries, but turned away sharply to look at Mother. "What discord?"

Mother looked mildly pensive. "I hate to gossip."

I hooted.

Mother blushed. "I hate to gossip without *reason*," she amended.

I rolled onto my side and propped my head on my hand. "Oh, spill it," I begged. "I *love* to talk trash." Especially if it would take Mother's mind off cigarettes.

"It isn't *trash*," Mother said as she lowered herself onto the bed opposite me. "It's just – an odd disagreement."

"About what?"

"That's what is so odd," Mother said. "It was Nikki Hocevar."

I stared at Mother blankly. We were gossiping in a B&B in northwest Ireland. The name of a girl dead since I was a teenager did not compute.

Mother nodded. "Nikki Hocevar," she repeated. "Why in the world would Marilyn and Mrs. DeWitt argue over *her*?"

"Perhaps if you started at the beginning?" I prodded.

"Oh, right," Mother said. "You weren't there. You don't know what I'm talking about."

Mother scanned the room as though searching the rafters for her thoughts. I snuggled into a more comfortable position on the bed to hear her out. The fact that we were supposed to meet the others for dinner in just a few minutes was temporarily forgotten.

"We were talking about the Scout troop," Mother said. "And all the deaths came up. Well, they do when you discuss *this* troop anymore, don't they?"

"Absolutely," I agreed.

"Someone mentioned Nikki – I think it was Mrs. DeWitt – and that led to the accident, naturally. You remember, Marilyn and Patty were in the car?"

"Patty reminded me," I said, remembering our conversation outside the emergency room months ago, back when Sandra and Louie Brandon were still alive.

"Did she mention who was in the front seat?" Mother asked.

"We didn't get into specifics," I admitted.

"Too bad, because Marilyn and Mrs. DeWitt don't agree on the specifics."

I raised an eyebrow.

"They were arguing because Marilyn said she was in the back seat and Mrs. DeWitt insisted she was in the front with Nikki. I don't see how it matters either way, but the difference seemed to be very important to them."

I frowned. “Who cares? Everyone but the driver survived. Why should it matter where the others were sitting?”

“My thoughts exactly,” Mother said.

“But Marilyn is arguing with her mother over it?”

“More stridently than seems necessary,” Mother assured me.

I chewed on my lip. I couldn't imagine why anyone would care where Marilyn was sitting as long as she survived the crash. So why was Marilyn battling her mother over the point?

“I'll have to think about this,” I decided.

“Yes, do that,” Mother said. “And stop smoking.”

I couldn't put a thing past that woman.

CHAPTER FORTY

We ventured out of Clifden early the next morning and discovered the Ireland of fable.

The sky was a brilliant blue, the temperature was uncommonly warm and, for the first time since landing at Shannon, we were comfortably wearing shorts as our two-car caravan headed into the Connemara. It is billed as one of the wildest areas of Ireland, punctuated by the Twelve Pins (or Bens), windswept mountains that separate the coast from Ireland's largest inland lake, Lough Corrib. Our plan was to succumb to the tourist trap known as Kylemore Abbey, vindicate ourselves by hiking around Connemara National Park, then circle back to Clifden for dinner. Along the way, we'd stop at any ruins that beckoned to us.

Unlike most plans, everything went just as expected. We paid the outrageous admission to Kylemore and were captivated by the abbey. At the park, we climbed higher than anyone under 30 had a right to expect and were bowled over by the views of the Connemara spread out below us. And then famished by our exertions, we veered off at the road sign for Cleggan for a late lunch.

The first indication that Cleggan wasn't a tourist trap was the cow.

It was dead.

It lay in a pasture next to the road and its feet were sticking straight up in the air and its belly was bloated, advertising that it had been a while since the poor animal had passed on. Several men stood around the corpse, rubbing their chins and perhaps contemplating how to remove the beast from the main entrance to the village.

"Oh, my," Mother said, "I hope that isn't an omen for lunch."

I gave her a smile of false cheer. "It's life in the country, Ma," I said. But I resolved not to order beef for lunch.

We puttered into Cleggan, which was a one-road village nestled at the head of Cleggan Bay. There were two pubs, a general store and a pretty little monument to 25 local fishermen who drowned in a disaster at sea in 1927. We parked by the memorial and tottered up the road to Oliver's, the restaurant that the guitarist from Galway had recommended. It was inconsequential, I told myself, that we were stopping there. Of the two pubs in town, it was the only one serving lunch.

We settled at a large table overlooking the wharf. Then taking a cue from our nightly pub crawling, I went up to the bar to order coffee and tea (it was too early for Guinness, even for me) and reassure the bartender that eventually we'd ask for real food. We just needed time to decipher the menu.

"I told you, lass," a familiar voice said from a bar stool, "you'll be wanting the fish chowder."

I slowly turned toward him. He was wearing a fisherman's jersey and ratty dungarees and looked like he'd just arrived with the morning's catch – well, what did I know? Maybe he had. But the smile was just as rakish as what he'd worn at O'Connor's in Galway.

"What are you doing here?" I groaned.

He raised his hands in self-defense. "A man has to live somewhere."

"In Cleggan?" I countered. "There can't be a hundred souls in this village."

"Two hundred sixty-three," Sean corrected, "and I am one of them."

"You could have warned me," I pouted.

"How was I to know you'd actually come?" And the smile he flashed at me rated as beatific in Ireland.

"I told you," I said strongly, "I'm *married*."

"Your ring finger says otherwise," he pointed out. But he politely held his tongue as the beleaguered proprietor/cook/waitress appeared.

I ordered fish chowder all around, menu be damned.

Sean beamed.

I glared and stomped back to our table.

"Isn't that one of the musicians from Galway?" Marilyn asked. She had obviously been paying more attention at O'Connor's than I had suspected.

"It's the guitarist," I admitted.

"He must have liked something he saw," Marilyn purred.

Patty bristled. "Meaning you?"

"I don't recall *you* paying attention to the music."

I squeezed in next to Mother and serenely allowed Marilyn and Patty to bicker. I could afford to be serene. After all, *I* had been the one he had kissed good night.

Dave watched sourly in my thoughts.

I was seriously hoping Sean would leave for a fishing boat or something equally smelly when he sauntered up to the table with a loaded bread basket in each hand. "Ah, ladies," he crooned as he placed the baskets on the table, "you can't fully appreciate the chowder without brown bread."

"What chowder?" Patty asked. "Did I order chowder?"

"How could you pass it up?" Sean asked as he insinuated himself at the table between Marilyn and Patty.

If I had been at home and wearing my gun, I would have shot him.

"I was hoping for fish and chips," Patty pouted.

Sean shoved a basket of bread under her nose. "It's hot from the oven, lass. A smear of butter and you'll be thinking of leprechauns."

I rolled my eyes. Sean caught it, and his grin was ornery.

But Patty missed it entirely and dipped her hand into the basket. "Well, I don't mind if I do," she simpered, pleased that at least the natives appreciated her worth.

Mother aimed a disapproving look at me. I excused myself for the restroom.

Mother followed.

"Is there something you wish to share with me?" she demanded from her stall.

"Toilet paper?" I asked, offering a roll beneath the divider.

Mother unceremoniously kicked it back at me. "You know what I mean," she said in accusation. "That *musician*!"

"He's very good on guitar," I pointed out.

"And why has he followed you here?" she demanded.

"Technically, I believe *we* followed *him.* It's *his* village."

"And he just happened to be haunting *this* restaurant?" Mother's voice was highly suspicious.

"Oh, really, Ma," I said, while half of my brain tried to figure how to flush the confounded toilet, "how many restaurants in Cleggan can he haunt? There's only one."

"Dave wouldn't like it," Mother declared.

"Dave has nothing to fear," I assured her.

But it would have been helpful if Dave had been along to keep my mind off Sean's energetic mouth.

*   *   *

Sean was still at the table when Mother and I returned, and he was charming the pants off Marilyn and Patty. They were giggling like teenagers as he regaled the table with stories about life on the northwestern coast of Ireland. Mother and I barely rated a glance from him as we slipped back into our seats. But I was pretty sure that the hand squeezing my knee under the table didn't belong to Mrs. DeWitt.

The man hadn't lied. The fish chowder was sinfully good – he smiled modestly, as though personally responsible for the freshness of the fish – so we all had seconds, which meant our waistbands were digging ruthlessly into our guts as we pushed back from the table to leave.

Sean may have lived in a small village, but he had an unsettling sense of what ladies of a similar age were feeling, so he offered to lead us on a walking tour of Cleggan to ease the weight in our bellies.

Marilyn and Patty fell over each other to accept.

And they each latched onto one of his arms to be squired about town.

Not that I cared.

Sean led us to the wharf and a brief tour of a fishing boat (an excursion granted to us free because the captain was Sean's cousin – or perhaps nephew – or former in-law; it wasn't entirely clear). He guided us to stone cottages older than our hometown and, through another vague relationship with one of the elderly residents, fast-talked us inside her home for a quick look around. (Money may have changed hands for that indulgence.) Then he marched us up the road to a pebbled beach where patrons of the local riding school galloped their horses. And when Mrs. DeWitt quietly expressed her weariness, he shepherded us back to the drowned fishermen's monument.

He gave a dramatic account of their demise as Mrs. DeWitt sat on a rock and fanned her face. Marilyn and Patty listened rapturously while Mother compared the data on the monument to

Sean's emotional re-enactment of death at sea. I could tell as she crossed her arms in disapproval that there were many discrepancies.

I nudged the ladies in the direction of our cars before Mother could challenge him.

"Are you heading back to Clifden?" Sean asked. I was pretty sure he was asking me, but Marilyn butted right in.

"We're staying another night. Will we find you playing at a pub?" And there was promise in the way her eyes roamed south of his chin.

Sean sadly admitted that he had no gigs in Clifden that night. "I'm a working man," he said, waving vaguely at the bay. It implied that he would be leaving too early with the fishing boats tomorrow to go pub hopping with us tonight. Or it could simply have meant that since he didn't have a gig that night, he wouldn't be going to town. Who could tell with an Irishman?

Marilyn and Patty were crestfallen.

Mother and I were relieved – for totally different reasons, of course.

"Will you be playing anywhere near us before we leave?" Marilyn asked.

"How could I say, lass?" Sean replied. "I don't know where you're going."

"Neither do we," I said as I abruptly pushed the girls to our cars.

"Adare!" Patty tossed over my shoulder.

"Dingle!" Marilyn shot around my ribs.

"If we don't get lost," I said, trying to muddy the waters.

"Oh, my, we never get lost," Mrs. DeWitt protested. "We're *Scouts*!"

Patty snorted.

Marilyn glared at her for taking a shot at her mother.

Sean raised his eyebrows at me.

"Seriously," I said, sweeping the horizon with my arm, "we're going north, we're going south."

"And then we're going home," Mother said sternly as she shouldered past Sean to our car. "I seriously doubt we'll ever see you again."

"Whoa!" Patty hooted. "That's *rude*, Mrs. F."

Mother ignored her.

I blushed furiously.

The girls piled into their assigned cars. Marilyn belched fish chowder as she yanked open the door and tried to pin it on her bemused mother. Patty slapped Marilyn's shoulder for her errant behavior and climbed into the back seat. Marilyn snarled.

Sean followed me to the driver's side of my car. I tried to twist away from him as he leaned in because Mother was shrewishly watching. But instead of the kiss I feared, he just whispered, "You're travelin' with banshees, love. Take care."

And he was watching us pensively as our little cars climbed out of Cleggan.

CHAPTER FORTY-ONE

We roamed around Ireland for the next three days under a shaky truce brought on by guilt for allowing a foreigner to glimpse our lesser instincts. Marilyn and Patty were suddenly best of friends again. Mother dropped her strident vigilance on Dave's behalf. And I ordered my disagreeable nature back into hibernation so I could enjoy the strange country where we had landed.

We followed the coast farther north, investigating sea ports and castles and islands along the way. We bought sweaters that had been on the backs of sheep just the week before and ate fish so fresh, it nearly swam to our plates. We got into territory where the pubs were more political than collegial and the songs were bloody and frightening. Although the Troubles were ebbing that year, there were still signs, especially along deserted stretches of shore, of the subterfuge and violence that marked relations between the bulk of Ireland and the eight counties of the North. Although we never ventured across the border, we could feel the tension, even as shopkeepers and publicans and hoteliers assured us that everything was fine. There were rumors of a Celtic tiger poised to pounce on the Irish economy, but as we traveled north, we felt, if not despair, then extreme caution, and we were relieved when our itinerary turned us south.

We left the bleak, harsh country along the coast and drove down the middle of Ireland through fields that were so green, they were blinding. Mother said it reminded her sharply of Amish country near our home. Mrs. DeWitt compared it to rolling Pennsylvania farmland. Marilyn and Patty agreed it was beautiful, but we felt isolated from the real world.

At Adare, we pooled our resources to bunk in a lavish room in a restored Irish manor house. In Cork, we escaped the rain by touring the Jameson distillery. And then we drove west for our final stop before heading back to Shannon. Our destination was a bed and breakfast in Dingle, where I finally figured out the tragedy of Sandra Porter's life.

*   *   *

We arrived in Dingle early on Tuesday afternoon. We had been in Ireland just over a week and would stay in Dingle until Saturday afternoon, when we would take a leisurely drive up to Shannon for a night at the airport inn and an early Sunday flight home. We were open to adventures in Dingle, but we had been on the road long enough that a few quiet days on the peninsula would be okay, too. I was missing Dave, Sean's attentions notwithstanding, and the other members of the party were beginning to tire of the nuisances of life abroad as well.

So it was reassuring to discover that our Dingle B&B was a white stucco home with green shutters that could have been planted on any Midwestern plot if it hadn't been for the two palm trees framing its back door. Palm trees pop up all over Ireland because of the Gulf Stream. Unfortunately, they aren't accompanied by a sunny tropical climate.

Since we had missed the weekend traffic, the B&B was empty except for us, so we again had the run of the house. Patty scored a single room on the first floor, but the rest of us had to drag our luggage upstairs. Marilyn and Mrs. DeWitt won the coin toss and got the bigger room, but they had to use the bathroom that opened off the main hall. Mother and I got a much smaller room, but a cramped bathroom was part of the suite. I gloated over our good fortune. Marilyn curled her lip.

The house had a spectacular garden, and rather than waste sunshine unpacking, I scurried to a bench under trees that smelled obscenely sweet and broke into the complimentary wine from our bedroom. It wouldn't go well with the Guinness planned for dinner, but I couldn't turn down a free drink.

I was shocked to be joined by Mrs. DeWitt, who demanded wine as well.

I scrambled for another glass and eventually we were both sipping from fine examples of the house crystal.

We had taken a leisurely drive that day from Cork to Dingle, stopping frequently to view local sights and shop for souvenirs, so the sunlight was already dying. Mrs. DeWitt and I were marking time until the others were ready to walk into town for dinner. I expected nothing significant in small talk with Mrs. DeWitt.

But she shattered my illusions by asking whether I thought anyone was trying to kill us off.

I spit out a mouthful of perfectly fine wine. "I beg your pardon?" I sputtered.

Mrs. DeWitt looked at me with guileless eyes. "The Scouts," she said. "You're a police detective. Do you think someone is trying to kill us?"

"Why in the world would you think that?" I asked. Mrs. DeWitt was the last person in our troop I expected to have a suspicious mind.

But she calmly took a sip of wine and smacked her lips. The vintage met with her approval. "So many dead girls," she said, looking at me over her glass. "Is it normal?"

"We're getting older," I said ineffectually. "People die."

Mrs. DeWitt nodded in happy agreement. "That's what I told Marilyn. *Statistically*, I don't think our numbers are an aberration."

Part of me was stunned by Mrs. DeWitt's grasp of numbers. Part of me was appalled by my shallow estimation of her understanding of statistical probabilities. And part of me was ashamed that I, despite discussing the possibilities with Ellen Graham weeks ago, had dismissed our death toll as the unfortunate low end of a logical spread of numbers.

"Marilyn disagrees?" I prodded.

Mrs. DeWitt snorted. "Marilyn doesn't think I should talk about it. She says everyone died naturally. Even your poor daughter."

Her words, so unexpected from a normally kind soul, kicked me in the chest. "My daughter?" I gasped.

"Oh, my, yes," Mrs. DeWitt said without looking at me. "She's part of the pall hanging over our troop, don't you think? She died with her father, who, of course, was running around."

"He was *what*?" I shrilled.

Mrs. DeWitt was astonished. "Oh, goodness, you *must* have known, dear."

"I did *not*!" I said fiercely, even though my gut said otherwise.

"Everyone saw what he was up to," Mrs. DeWitt insisted, leaning over to pat my hand. "You *must* have seen it, too."

"You are *wrong*," I hissed, and snatched my hand away.

Mrs. DeWitt sighed and hugged her wine glass. "So many tragedies in our troop," she muttered. "It's no wonder Sandra died. It drove her to distraction."

"Sandra had *nothing* to do with my husband," I said, so stridently that the birds in the garden were suddenly silent.

Mrs. DeWitt looked at me over her glass. "They are both dead, dear, aren't they?"

I stared at her in consternation. Of course, the fire had nothing to do with Sandra's death in traffic. But all deaths apparently were linked to the troop in Mrs. DeWitt's mind. She was old and addled by the exhaustions of travel. There was no point in discussing her musings further.

So I topped off her glass and went in search of Mother.

* * *

Mother was still in our room, arranging clothes in the bureau. At each B&B, she had felt the need to make our room a small version of home, and that meant unpacking as much as she could. She even put a souvenir cup from Galway on the window sill.

I accosted her with a half-full wine glass sloshing in my hand. It didn't bode well for the conversation. “Was Steve cheating on me?” I demanded.

Mother looked a lot like a deer caught in headlights as she raised her head from the bureau. “Was he what?” she asked, but without the proper amount of outrage.

“Mrs. DeWitt says he was running around. She says everyone knew. Is that *true*?” And I pinned her to the wall with my glare.

Mother dropped her eyes and slowly closed the drawer she had been filling with underwear. “We're on vacation, Jo,” she reminded me.

“Yes,” I chattered, “to get away from the nastiness of killing Louie Brandon. I *get* that. But am I running away from something else?” And I shivered in the Atlantic breeze slicing through the window.

Mother sighed. “It's been fourteen years, Jo. We're thousands of miles from home. Do you really want to have this conversation now?”

“Can we just *ignore* it?”

“You have for years,” Mother said gently.

“No,” I protested, “I have *not*.” And my knees gave out and I plopped gracelessly onto one of the twin beds.

Mother dutifully sat beside me and took my hand. “That fire was everything. It burned so much out of your memory.” And her thumb skillfully kneaded my palm.

“What are you saying?” I asked, my voice raw.

Mother chose her words carefully. “You were angry long before the fire. You were *suspicious* before the fire. Don't you remember?”

I stared at her in disbelief.

“Jo,” Mother said, “you cried in my arms a week before the fire because you thought Steve was betraying you.”

I shook my head numbly.

“Ah, my poor little girl,” Mother said as she cradled me in her arms again. “You knew. You knew long before anyone else. But the horror of Elizabeth's death drove it out of your memory.”

“No,” I objected feebly.

“Yes, child,” she said softly, and she held me as an old pain slammed through my body.

My dead husband was a cheat.

And my only child had died.

Just like Louie Brandon had died.

Did I mention I kill people?

And without Dave to hold me together, I melted down in a badly furnished room on the fickle coast of Ireland.

CHAPTER FORTY-TWO

We dined that night at a pub by the sea. It started as a subdued dinner – not only was the pub half empty because it was a weeknight, but also our troop was tense, and for once, we dealt with it with silence rather than caustic remarks. The only time we engaged in semi-lively conversation was when the waitress approached our table. Otherwise, we stared blankly at the peat fire, or the corner where the band would have been playing if there had been a band on a Tuesday night.

Mother attributed it simply to the fact that we had been on the road for ten days and we were tired of each other. I thought it might have a little more to do with picking scabs off each other – I was pretty sure that was why Mrs. DeWitt and I sat as far apart as possible. There seemed to be something more than travel fatigue at work, but rather than probe the possibilities, I buried my nose in Guinness.

My traveling companions joined me.

It did nothing to lift the mood at our table, but eventually it did loosen tongues a little. By the time we were sopping up the dregs of our shepherd's pie with hunks of brown bread, we were grunting at each other in half sentences, but it was a stretch to call it conversation. It was mostly reactions.

Like the television report of another pop star found dead of a drug overdose.

"Debbie Gauer," I muttered, forgetting that officially, no one knew she had overdosed.

But we were into our third round of Guinness by then, and Marilyn and Patty solemnly joined me in raising our glasses to the TV screen.

Or when our waitress swooped down on our table with two freshly uncorked bottles of wine.

"There's been a mistake," I said diplomatically, and nodded to our glasses of Guinness. "We aren't drinking wine."

"Well, some of us used to," Marilyn corrected.

Then she and Patty looked at each other and said simultaneously, "Sannnnnnn-dra."

I looked at them in surprise – or as much surprise as I could muster while drunk.

The waitress scurried away. We were starting to resemble disagreeable Americans.

Or when we finally dislodged ourselves and, while the grownups (Mother and Mrs. DeWitt) settled the tab at the bar, Marilyn, Patty and I clumsily shrugged ourselves into sweaters and sweatshirts and nearly jumped out of our skins when a lorry backing away from the wharf blasted its horn.

"Oh, my God!" Marilyn babbled at Patty as they clung to each other. I was the odd man out and had to cling to myself.

"Just like on our bikes!" Patty chattered.

"He could've *killed* us," Marilyn said, eyes wide and solemn.

"But he *didn't*," Patty said.

And they tapped forearms like a secret sorority ritual.

Mother and Mrs. DeWitt saved us from the one-truck traffic and a slide off the wharf and shepherded us the two blocks back to our B&B. I don't know who put Patty to bed, but I clearly remember Mrs. DeWitt leading Marilyn up to their room and Mother was tending to me with much disapproval. The last thing I remember was swearing to Mother that I'd never drink another

Guinness, even though we had days left on our trip, and Mother's look of resignation as she wrestled me out of my sweater and jeans.

It was not my finest hour.

CHAPTER FORTY-THREE

Not surprisingly, only Mother and Mrs. DeWitt showed up for breakfast. In my defense, they ate at a morally reprehensible hour so they could catch an 8 a.m. tour bus for the Ring of Kerry. The other girls and I had made noises the night before about taking the tour, too, but the mothers knew very well we wouldn't be in any shape for it, and in a rare show of defiance, they refused to waste time hanging around the B&B while we nursed our hangovers. They were long gone by the time Marilyn and I, and then Patty, ventured to the garden to sit in the sun. It was much too late by then for breakfast, but the landlady obliged us with a pot of real coffee, and we slouched in lounge chairs behind dark glasses as we shakily lifted hot mugs to our mouths.

I hadn't had so much to drink in such a concentrated stretch of time since Elizabeth had died. Ireland was supposed to heal my soul, but I wasn't sure my liver could stand it.

Marilyn and Patty looked no better than I felt. Both were pale, even by Irish standards, and we had been on the road so long, Patty's gray roots were beginning to show. We looked every one of our forty-three years that morning.

But when I groaned at my reflection in the quaint little bird bath, Marilyn was the one who brought up the Scouts. “We're still the best-looking girls in the troop,” she said stoutly.

Patty eyed me critically from the fog of her first cigarette of the day. “I don't know about Jo.”

Her hair was sticking out in uncombed spikes and last night's mascara was blurred under her eyelids. "I don't know about *you,*" I countered.

Patty curled her lip, but Marilyn was thinking as positively as one could on a queasy stomach. "That leaves me, and I could pass for thirty."

"In the dark," Patty muttered.

"Oh, really?" Marilyn challenged.

"With a blind drunk," Patty said, and took a solid slug of her coffee.

Marilyn pursed her lips in anger, but surprisingly said nothing. I mentally noted that as significant, but wasn't sure why.

"Marilyn is obsessed with appearance," Patty said as she lit another cigarette. "It is *very* important for her to look young."

Marilyn blanched.

I could think of nothing to cool their hangovers, so I helped myself to Patty's cigarettes instead. It was becoming a habit.

But, oh my, it felt so *good.*

Marilyn waited until I exhaled before firing back at Patty. "*You're* obsessed with status. You have to be smarter than everyone else."

"Well, I *am,*" Patty said serenely, and blew smoke in Marilyn's face.

Marilyn glared back at her without blinking.

I began to wonder whether more than hangovers were at work here, but I was suffering such a headache myself, I couldn't really pursue that thought.

"You are a cold bitch," Marilyn said.

"I learned from an expert," Patty replied acidly.

I sucked hard on my cigarette, giving in to the nicotine fix.

Marilyn turned quizzical eyes on me. "Did you know Patty fucked the loan officer so she could get her five-bedroom Tudor next to the golf course?"

“Don't you wish it were so easy?” Patty snarled. She turned to me. “Marilyn has always envied my house. I have one more bedroom and one more bath.”

“And *I* have a three-car garage,” Marilyn said in triumph.

“And only two cars,” Patty said blandly.

I puffed, puffed, puffed madly.

“Did you know Marilyn fucked two professors so she could graduate magna cum laude?” Patty asked me. Her eyes were riveted on Marilyn, not me. “And did I mention she was a newlywed at the time?”

“I don't think I care,” I said as I stood and stabbed out the suddenly foul cigarette.

Marilyn leaned in to Patty. The look on her face was borderline insane. “Ask her about Becky Freeman, Jo.”

Patty squared off with her eye to eye. “You mean the poor girl you used while she was dying?”

“No,” Marilyn said, “the girl *you* used.”

Patty laughed.

Marilyn laughed just as evilly.

“Ladies,” I said, “this has been enlightening, but I think I'm going to barf.”

But I did manage to get back to my room before I did.

CHAPTER FORTY-FOUR

Dingle is a pleasant village and the surrounding hills are picturesque, so after a nap that settled my abused digestive system, I spent the afternoon roaming the shops downtown and the paths hugging the shore. I had no idea what Marilyn and Patty did.

The sky was cloudless and the breeze was warm, giving me the perfect opportunity to wander (and regret missing the bus to the Ring of Kerry). As I clambered around the bay, I kept one eye peeled for Fungie, the dolphin who has been a resident since 1983 and is the lure for many boat excursions aimed at tourists. I saw no sign of him as I climbed away from the wharf, but Fungie watching was a good excuse for me to plop my butt down on the hillside overlooking the bay and stare at the sea as I munched an apple.

Meanwhile, my mind tumbled over images of Marilyn and Patty and other Scouts.

Becky Freeman was a hard one to re-create. We hadn't been close in school, and when she had fallen ill, I had been engrossed in new motherhood, too obsessed with Elizabeth and me for any humanitarian gestures outside the immediate family. But I did seem to recall talk of friends keeping vigil with Becky at the hospital once her condition became hopeless. I just couldn't see why it was a source of contention between Marilyn and Patty.

Of course, contentious competition was part of what kept them so entwined. I never really thought of one without the other, and I imagined other people thought the same way. They had grown up together like sisters, and like sisters, they knew exactly how to cause each other excruciating pain.

I frowned at a blip in the bay that turned out not to be Fungie – but disappointment wasn't why I was frowning. I had grown up with a sister, and though we were no longer in-your-face close, we still knew many secrets about each other. Sometimes we even used them to our advantage – like Maureen's confident insistence that I send Mother to Boston to spend each Thanksgiving with her family, or my insistence that whenever Maureen came to town with her husband and four kids, they sleep at a motel because there was no way I could survive with six more people in my house. But we had never bludgeoned each other with secrets as Marilyn and Patty had the night before while drinking or this morning while crawling up out of their hangovers, and I found their behavior disturbing. Both had taken pains to warn me that they were watching out for each other on this trip, but their actions toward each other were neither protective nor appreciated.

Half of me was intrigued by their mutual animosity, but the other half was irritated. I was on this trip to heal myself. Conflicts between other members of the touring party were detracting from that effort.

And that was exactly where my mind was trapped when Sean plopped down on the coastal path beside me.

"What in hell are you doing here?" I yelped.

"That's hardly a polite tone for a foreigner to take," Sean admonished, but his grin was impish.

"I'm in Dingle, for God's sake," I protested. "You live in Cleggan. Why are you here?"

"I've got a gig in town tonight," he said equably. "What's your excuse?"

"Dingle was highly recommended by our Triple-A agent," I informed him.

He looked at me in bemused ignorance. "Triple-A?"

“Never mind,” I sighed.

A gull squawked overhead, and our eyes were drawn temporarily to the bay. Still no Fungie.

I knew I had to stop this *thing* with Sean *now*. It was bad enough that the man was following me around Ireland. Mother would never understand if I tried to stuff him into my suitcase to take him home.

“Sean,” I said with resolution, “I am committed to a wonderful man at home. There's no future for you and me.”

He took it very well. “My wife would quite agree,” he said, and warmly patted my hand.

I snatched my fingers away. “You're *married*?”

“Oh, aye, lass,” he said, nodding serenely at the bay, “these twenty-one years now.”

“And you never told me?” I demanded.

“Should I have?” he countered.

My God, he was so *calm*.

“Children?” I croaked without looking at him.

“Two handsome lads. Smart catches for any man's daughters.”

“Oh, my God,” I muttered, and shielded my eyes from the glare of the bay with a decidedly shaky hand.

“Perhaps an explanation is in order,” Sean ventured after some time had passed and the planets hadn't quite realigned themselves.

“Oh, please,” I begged, “explain away.”

“Shall we facilitate the explanation with a little something to relax us?” he suggested, feigning a mellow puff on a joint.

“For God's sake, Sean,” I snapped, “I'm a *cop*!”

“But not here,” he reminded me.

“You do what you like. Just leave me out of it.” And I turned to the bay and hugged my knees.

Sean shrugged and pulled the requisite accoutrements out of his backpack. We were sitting just off the path, and visibility in both directions was unencumbered. Sean could toke up without fear of being taken by surprise.

Which he did in due time, sighing happily as he exhaled.

"You see, lass, I'm an entertainer," he said when he was significantly more relaxed. "And it pays to chat up the ladies in the audience."

"Of course," I said, trying to ignore the joint. "I *know* that. But Cleggan – wasn't showing up in Cleggan pushing things over the line?"

"It *is* where I live," he protested.

I glared.

"But perhaps I was amusing myself too much," he admitted. "My wife was off to Ballyshannon visiting her ma, and there you were in Oliver's, and I couldn't let you leave without the fish chowder." And he smiled at me with all the innocence of an Irish gentleman who has just stumbled upon a pot of pot at the end of the rainbow.

I sadly shook my head. "Your wife is a saint."

He smiled beatifically and took another hit.

"Are you really in Dingle for a gig?" I asked. "My mother will be suspicious."

He quickly crossed his heart. "My intentions are honorable," he assured me.

I looked at the joint and snorted.

Sean held it delicately between two fingers. "It's dying down, lass. There's barely a hit left."

I glanced swiftly to left and right. The path was deserted. And Sean was right. I wasn't a cop in Ireland.

So I snatched the roach out of his hand and sucked greedily. Sean chuckled as I held it in as long as my unpracticed lungs could take it, then coughed. Smoke spewed over my head in a guilty cloud.

"Now, now," Sean said, clapping my back, "isn't that better?"

And it was, in a fuzzy sort of way. Enough so that I couldn't think of a single objection as Sean rolled up another joint.

"You're a *bangharda*," he mused as he twisted the ends of the joint. "Do you kill people?"

He meant it as a joke – I know he did – but I still gasped.

Sean dropped the joint in his lap. "I am so sorry, lass." And his face was as grave as I'd ever seen it.

"Light the joint," I said shakily.

"I didn't mean – " he apologized.

"Just light it!" I ordered.

He studied me with regret. His little joke had turned into something painful, and there was scant hope now that a hit would do anything for my mood, but eventually he lifted the joint, took a token hit as he lit it, then passed it to me.

I inhaled greedily and lay back on the grass. I expected nothing and I wasn't disappointed. The here and now remained sharp and unpleasant.

Sean took a hit himself and stared at the bay. He didn't probe.

So, of course, I told him about Louie Brandon as we passed the joint back and forth. I didn't make it a long story. I had pushed myself into Louie's life, he had responded by using me for what he could get, and when he fell over the edge, I had stopped him from taking Adam with him.

Sean nodded as he ground out the roach. "Sounds like the right thing," he said.

"There were mitigating circumstances in his background," I forced myself to say – forced, because I wasn't used to toking up and it was difficult to string thoughts together in a coherent sentence.

"There are always mitigating circumstances," Sean said wisely as he stowed his paraphernalia back in his pack. "The trick is to move forward despite them."

I nodded as though he had delivered a great truth. So perhaps I *was* feeling the effects of the pot more than I had thought.

The afternoon was taking on a golden edge and Sean had musical duties to attend to, so we wordlessly turned back on the path toward town. I was fine as long as the only people we passed were hikers. Odds were they were a little high, too.

But when we descended into town and the afternoon jumble of tourists and natives hustling for home, I began to feel paranoid. I was sure our clothes, our hair, our breath reeked of grass. I was sure people were sniffing the air as we passed and turning to stare at us. I was sure Mother would have to bail us out of an Irish jail. And I mumbled as much to Sean.

He laughed uproariously.

"I don't see what's so amusing," I sputtered. We were standing at a busy intersection near the wharf, and Sean was laughing so loudly, people were, indeed, staring at us.

"Ah, Jo," he wheezed through tears, "you worry too much. No one will bother us."

"Really?" I hissed, my eyes sliding back and forth over suspicious pedestrians. Any one of them could be an undercover cop.

"Aye, really," he said, leaning in to me and dropping his voice conspiratorially. "I have a free pass."

"To break the law?" I whispered back.

He nodded happily. "My da was in the garda. They won't bother with me."

My eyes narrowed. "That's a load of bull."

"Is it now?" he countered. "Well, what about this?" And he whipped a leather case out of his pocket and flipped it open.

A shield glinted in the sun.

I bent over to inspect it. The leather was worn, the metal of the shield was hefty, the number was beginning to fade with the years. It looked and felt like the real thing.

"Your father is gone?" I asked.

"Aye," Sean said, his eyes nostalgic, "these five years."

"And you keep his badge with you?"

"It's a comfort," he said as he flipped the case shut and slid it back into his pocket.

"You are a truly surprising man," I said. "But I'm still taken." And I kissed him on the cheek and marched away to the other side of the street.

Where Marilyn and Patty were waiting, shopping bags in hand.

"Was that Sean?" Marilyn purred. Her bag screamed new shoes.

"Is he playing tonight?" Patty asked. Her bag was soft with a lamb's wool sweater.

"Back there," I said, waving at the pubs along the wharf.

"We'll have to go," Patty said.

"It's only polite," Marilyn agreed.

I groaned. "I can't take another Guinness."

Patty put her hands on her hips. "Who said you were invited?"

I opened my mouth to protest, then snapped it shut. Sean was a big boy. Surely he could handle two Girl Scouts.

So I staggered back to the B&B and crashed.

CHAPTER FORTY-FIVE

"You're drinking too much," Dave said.

"Why do you say that?" I demanded.

"Because you're calling me from Ireland. Do you have any idea how much that costs?"

"No," I giggled. "I reversed the charges."

"And thank God the phone bill is in *your* name," he reminded me.

And suddenly we laughed at each other like we were in the same room.

I was nestled in a corner of the B&B's kitchen, where the landlady kept her phone. I had initiated the call and had caught Dave at his office on campus, eating lunch. I could almost smell his tuna sandwich over the phone.

"The Guinness is good," I conceded, leaning into the nook that housed the phone and playing with the cord.

"Nothing wrong with a drink or two," Dave agreed. "How many are you having?"

"Five or six?" I ventured.

There was silence, then Dave rallied. "Maybe it's time to reel it in."

"My head's fuzzy," I admitted.

"Thus the phone call," Dave said wisely. "What's up?"

Ah, Dave, I thought. Never one to waste a penny on small talk at trans-Atlantic rates.

But I forced myself to focus, because, after all, I was the one who had reached out to him. "Something's not right in this group. I mean, I'm a killer, that's a fact, but something else is going on."

Dave swallowed uncomfortably. "*Killer* might be an overly harsh characterization."

"But true. And since killing Louie Brandon saved Adam, I'm okay with that. But I'm getting other strange vibes."

"Is Ruth all right?" Dave asked immediately.

I smiled indulgently at the phone. Some guys have big problems with the mothers of their lady friends. Dave and Mother had reached an understanding early on. Frankly, they adored each other, and the concern crackling over the telephone wire was genuine.

"She's fine," I assured him. "A little pissed off at me for drinking, but I think she's having a great time."

"Okay," Dave said, clearly relieved, "if Ruth is in good spirits, what's the problem?"

"Marilyn and Patty," I said, snuggling deeper into the nook so no one could overhear. "The way they get along is – unnatural."

"Sexual?" Dave's astonishment beamed across the ocean.

"No, no, no," I said hastily. "It's more like family – bad family."

"Love/hate?" he asked.

"Yes!" I said in relief that he understood. "But really, really intense."

"Most unpleasant for you and Ruth." It was clearly a statement, not a question.

"It's made for some awkward moments."

There was another silence, and I imagined Dave doing the math in his head. "You'll be home in what – five days? You and your mother can hang on for five more days, right?"

"Absolutely," I said firmly, despite being the one who had cracked and made the phone call. "We have our own car. Until we're home, we'll just steer clear of their unpleasantness."

"And when you get home, there will be flowers," Dave said.

That would have been a non-sequitur to most people, but one of the things that had initially prompted me to fight the trip was the timing. I would be out of the country on the anniversary of the fire. I had never – ever – missed a trip to Elizabeth's grave on the anniversary.

But Dave had prevailed by promising to take care of her grave for me.

And I had been so unhinged by killing Louie that I had given in to the pressure from all sides to leave the country.

"I will take care of Scooter," Dave promised.

"I know you will," I said in a small, grateful voice.

And since he knew I was getting weepy, Dave responded with a mildly amusing story about Adam and Emily and their adventures in the kitchen. By the time we hung up – very deeply in debt – I was laughing again, in the way only Dave could make me laugh.

But as I climbed the stairs, something he had told me about the fresh flowers for Elizabeth's grave was nagging my brain.

I just couldn't pinpoint what.

CHAPTER FORTY-SIX

We went to a pub on the wharf for a late dinner, and I shocked the hell out of Mother by ordering a Coke instead of a Guinness. Marilyn and Patty also restrained themselves. In fact, the entire table got by on tea and soft drinks.

Even when it turned out we were dining at the same pub where Sean was playing.

Mother shot me an accusing look when she saw Sean shuffling to the makeshift stage, but I was fresh from a conversation with Dave and felt self-righteously innocent as I waved to Sean. He smiled back like he might have smoked a little more before tuning up.

We'd heard enough of his performances that I feared the evening would be redundant, but he was playing with three new musicians and the sound was magically different. I clutched my Coke glass to my chest and sat mesmerized as his tenor blended with the alto on bodhran, and it was perhaps the very best Celtic performance I'd heard in our entire haphazard trip through Ireland. Even Mother stood and clapped when the set ended.

I dashed to the bar – hey, I'd lasted the entire first set dry and this *was* Ireland. Mother frowned, but not enough to deter me. Besides, she wanted a pint of her own.

So I stood three rows back from the bartender and peered over heads, looking for Sean. I knew he'd be thirsty from the set, and I thought it would be a polite gesture to buy him a Guinness, especially after he'd shared his stash with me. But his salt-and-pepper head was nowhere among the clamoring tourists pressing up against the bar.

I eventually claimed two creamy pints from the bar and tiptoed through the crowd back to our table. It would have been a crime to spill any of that Guinness.

"What are you doing?" Mother asked suspiciously as I deposited both pints in front of her. She was sitting alone with Mrs. DeWitt. Marilyn and Patty had both slinked away during the set, presumably to accost other tourists who looked like they might be someone.

"Little girls' room," I said, waggling my fingers at Mother. "Guard the Guinness."

She grunted. Sean hadn't returned to the stage; therefore, she assumed I was on his trail.

The restrooms opened off either side of a dark little hallway at the back of the pub, and the ladies' loo was packed, with a line snaking out into the hall. A couple of ladies were desperate enough to pop into the men's facilities, but I didn't have that kind of chutzpah in a foreign land. So I wandered to the end of the line.

The hall backed up against a door that opened onto an alley behind the pub. Since I was at the back of a rather long line, I had time to stare out the window in the door. The view was the dismal sort you see out the back of any bar in Ireland or the States: damp concrete littered with detritus from the pub, a single weak bulb illuminating the greasy expanses of the alley, and a man's foot in a worn Reebok.

I blinked rapidly and reminded myself I was not drunk.

And still I saw a man's foot.

I shouldered my way out the door into the alley. A cold wind, smelling of the sea, whipped between the buildings and made me shiver. I tugged my shirt around me and looked tremulously for the foot. It was attached to a leg that curled around a dumpster into the dark.

If I were back home, I would have pulled out my radio then and called for backup. Henry and a squad of paramedics would have been dashing to my location in seconds.

But I wasn't home. I was in a cold, dark alley thousands of miles away, and when I crept around the leg, deeper into the dark, I found Sean, his head puddled in blood.

And for one moment, I forgot my training and wailed.

CHAPTER FORTY-SEVEN

Sean was whisked to the local hospital and, after making a perfunctory statement to the local garda, I was told to wait in the pub for further instructions. That chafed. I was used to *leading* investigations. Sitting around until some other investigator got around to interviewing me gave me a brand-new view of the world. I didn't like it.

The officers dealt methodically with the patrons of the pub, and Mother and Mrs. DeWitt and Marilyn and Patty were eventually sent on their way while I sat at a table and fretted. I had no idea what condition Sean was in, although the wound I had seen on the back of his head was frightening, and I had no idea how competent the local police were at evaluating crime scenes. If it had been my case, I could think of a dozen things I would be doing now to advance the investigation.

But I was a foreigner, and no one asked my opinion.

Two hours passed. The pub keeper offered Guinness, but even though most of the detained took him up on his offer, I declined. I was alone in a land where my badge meant nothing. It seemed important to keep a clear head.

And eventually, an inspector who looked barely older than Adam sat down at my table and offered an Irish smile.

“Ms. Ferris?” he asked. “I'm Detective Inspector Donovan. May we talk?”

I irritably waved his pleasantries away. “How is Sean? Is he alive?”

“You know Mr. O'Riley well?” Donovan countered.

“Barely at all,” I snapped. “But I found him bleeding in the alley. How is he?”

Donovan pondered, then admitted, “Not well. He has a serious head wound.”

“*Shit*!” I hissed, and fell back against my chair.

Donovan raised an eyebrow. “That's a pretty emotional reaction for someone you barely know.”

“Barely knowing doesn't mean I don't *like* him. Have you checked my papers? Do you know who I *am*?”

Donovan nodded pleasantly. “You are a U.S. policewoman, just as you told our officer. Your chief thinks highly of you.”

I tried not to gape but failed.

Donovan smiled thinly, pleased in a small way that he had astonished me, but really more preoccupied with the need to proceed quickly with the attack on Sean.

“Your chief says I can trust your observations. Did you see anything in the alley that would help us?”

I closed my eyes as I re-created the scene in my head – and felt an odd pressure to come up with something definitive to please my interviewer. Was this how all witnesses felt?

“The alley was empty,” I said without opening my eyes. “It smelled of fish and grease from the kitchen and disinfectant seeping out of the restroom windows. Someone peed recently on the cobblestones.”

“What else?” Donovan prodded.

“It was very dark. The light from the back door reached only as far as Sean's shoes. I couldn't see anyone else. But – ” I frowned. “Maybe I heard something.”

“Such as?”

“Heels on cobblestones,” I said, and nodded as the memory became clearer in my mind. “Footsteps fading.”

"So perhaps you found Mr. O'Riley just as his assailant was running away?"

I opened my eyes in excitement. "Yes! That's *exactly* what I heard!"

Donovan leaned over and patted my hand. "That doesn't help me a bit."

And my excitement shriveled as I realized he was absolutely right. I hadn't seen – or heard – a thing that could help him.

But we talked for ten more minutes – five because I was the unfortunate bystander who found the victim and five more out of professional courtesy. I was aching to know what he thought of the attack, but he wasn't inclined to share – even when I offered the tidbit that Sean indulged in a little pot.

Donovan shrugged. "Mr. O'Riley is a musician," he said, as though that explained a multitude of sins.

"So you don't think the attack is connected to the drug underworld?"

Donovan smiled indulgently. "This is Dingle, Ms. Ferris. There *is* no drug underworld."

"How fortunate for you," I said stiffly.

Donovan sighed. "Ah, sarcasm. Your chief mentioned the possibility of sarcasm."

"He said no such thing!" I protested.

Donovan smiled wearily.

I blushed.

"Do you have any thoughts on why Mr. O'Riley was attacked?" Donovan asked.

"Robbery," I said immediately.

"His wallet is missing," Donovan admitted, "but he hadn't been paid yet for tonight's gig, so there probably wasn't much money."

That seemed to rule out a random assailant looking for a few extra pounds.

"He *is* part-owner of a fishing boat out of Cleggan," Donovan said.

"Smuggling?" I asked. "Could he have been attacked because of a smuggling operation gone bad?"

"You have a very active imagination," Donovan said.

"Is that a no?"

"No comment."

That could mean anything, but Donovan was obviously reluctant to go in that direction – at least with *me*. So I chewed pensively on my lip.

"You are missing the obvious, Ms. Ferris," Donovan goaded.

I screwed up my face in thought. Maybe robbery, but that could be just a ruse to misdirect the police. Maybe drugs, but no one seemed to think it noteworthy that a traveling musician might be toking up. Maybe smuggling with his fishing boat, but the local police didn't have a bad feeling about that, either.

So what was left?

My eyes flew open.

Sex???

"Oh, come on," I said, "you don't think Sean and I – ?"

Donovan pursed his lips suggestively.

"He's married!" I objected.

"And you aren't," Donovan noted.

"If you really talked to my chief," I pointed out, "you know that isn't exactly true."

"I see no ring on your finger," Donovan observed

"Like that makes a difference," I huffed, and blew the bangs off my forehead in frustration.

"You must understand my point of view, Ms. Ferris," Donovan said. "Mr. O'Riley is a married man. You are attracted to him. Is it not possible that you had an emotional, violent reaction when he refused to leave his wife for you?"

"Is it not possible you're dealing in fairy tales?" I asked acidly.

Donovan nodded. "Your chief predicted this reaction."

"You told Bradley I was screwing around with an Irish singer?" I demanded.

"I could have told your boyfriend instead," Donovan countered.

I groaned. "This is much worse," I said, and hung my head. "Dave would understand. Bradley never will."

Donovan cocked his head as he studied me. "Americans are perplexing."

"You really don't have time to analyze the American psyche," I said rudely. "While you sit here proposing ridiculous theories, someone is getting away with the attack on Sean."

Donovan's pleasant smile turned frosty. "I assure you, Ms. Ferris, *no one* is getting away with *anything*." He waved at me in a clear gesture of dismissal. "I understand from your mother that you will be in Dingle until Saturday. Do not attempt to leave before then without contacting my office."

Donovan needn't have bothered with the warning, because I had no intention of fleeing any farther than Sean's hospital room.

CHAPTER FORTY-EIGHT

The nurses at the hospital wouldn't let me in Sean's room, but they couldn't keep me out of the small waiting area at the end of the hallway. If I leaned to the left while sitting in one of the excruciatingly uncomfortable chairs, I could even see the door to his room.

I hadn't planned on sitting there all night when I defiantly took up my post. I was tired, and even though I had called the B&B to assure Mother I was fine, I knew she was worried and wanted me safely with her. Despite her best efforts, our vacation had landed us at a crime scene, and she fretted that I might lose all the emotional ground I had gained since blowing Louie Brandon away. But I insisted on ignoring her sound arguments and standing guard in the cramped waiting room. The police had been unable to locate Sean's wife, and I couldn't stand the thought of him lying alone in the hospital. So I stayed in his wife's place.

I alternately dozed in the wretched plastic chair and paced the hall outside his room. When the nurses weren't hiding him behind a curtain, I could see a turban of white gauze around his head and tubes sprouting from his arms. The monitors tracking his vital signs beeped erratically, scaring me with their refusal to be bold and steady.

I spent a lot of time castigating myself for not acting like a cop when I found him. I should have taken charge of the crime scene. Or I should have run to the street, chasing the footsteps that had not registered in my brain until Inspector Donovan had questioned me. At the very least, I should have had a good idea by now *why* Sean was attacked. The fact that I was a foreigner shouldn't even be in play. I was a cop in *any* language. I should be able to read the scene.

But I was clueless, and it gnawed at me as I shifted in the chair and wondered whether I could lift a blanket from one of the unoccupied beds.

Even though people were surely dying within its walls, the hospital was very quiet through the darkest hours of the night. But along about dawn, the activity in and out of Sean's room increased, and it had nothing to do with the arrival of breakfast.

I tried to corner one of the nurses, but she politely told me to go fuck myself. (Well, that's what it sounded like to me.) And when I tried to edge my way into Sean's room to eavesdrop on the serious-looking doctors, an aide grabbed my arm and escorted me back to the waiting room.

"What's *happening*?" I hissed.

"Mr. O'Riley's condition is unchanged," the aide recited.

"Oh, bullshit," I said, and plopped in a pout into my chair.

And I stared at the door to his room and wondered where in hell his wife was hiding.

Apparently somewhere at a crossroads called Maam Cross, up near Cleggan. At about 8 a.m., as my eyes crossed with exhaustion, I eavesdropped on the radio transmissions to one of the guards stationed at Sean's door and heard assurances that Mrs. Sean had been located and was speeding to the hospital.

A weary part of me thought that was my excuse to leave. Sean wouldn't be alone much longer. But another part of me thought of the drive from the wilds north of Galway down to Dingle and acknowledged it could be a while before Sean's wife showed up.

So I sat in the waiting room and fretted over Sean and another day of my vacation lost to the evil vicissitudes of human nature.

At some point, I decided coffee would really help me to focus, so I wandered antiseptic halls until I found a cafeteria selling Nescafe. The taste was abominable, but the liquid was hot. So I gulped it down as I retraced my steps to the waiting room and found the hallway in an uproar.

A woman with very long red hair tinged with gray was being led into Sean's room, accompanied by a phalanx of white-coated doctors. Meanwhile, a clutch of cops, with Inspector Donovan at its center, huddled outside Sean's room. Something was up. My cop's nose told me so. So I edged closer and closer to the guards, hoping to latch onto a clue.

But Donovan saw me before I could hear anything significant and ordered me back to the waiting room. And in case I was of a mind to ignore him, he delegated a guard to escort me back to the sinister plastic chairs.

I fumed. I was a decorated police detective. I could be *helping* these people find Sean's attacker. Instead, they were treating me like a nuisance *way* down their list of plausible suspects.

But just as sleep deprivation was threatening to transform me into an ugly American, Donovan swept into the waiting room.

"Mr. O'Riley is being transferred to Dublin," he announced. "There's no need for you to remain here."

I wrung my hands. "Is he worse?"

Donovan's eyes darted to the ceiling as he weighed what he could safely tell me. "Not worse, but not better. There are neurosurgeons in Dublin who are more experienced with this kind of injury."

"Surgeons?" I gulped.

Donovan was an Irishman and took pity on my sleep-deprived nerves. "It's a precaution," he said, and patted my shoulder, much as I had patted so many frightened witnesses myself. I *hated* this turnabout.

I looked past Donovan down the hall to Sean's room, where many people in uniform were busily preparing him for transport. His wife hung in the background in despair.

"Has he regained consciousness at all?" I asked Donovan. "Has he said *anything*?"

"He floats in and out. And what he says is gibberish."

"No names?" I prodded hopelessly. "No IDs?"

"Just one word, lass," Donovan said heavily. "Banshee."

I shuddered as memory stirred.

Donovan mistook my reaction. "He's delirious. It means nothing."

"Of course not," I agreed automatically, even as my brain began sorting through the memories of our stay in Ireland. *Where* had I heard that term before?

Donovan repeated his warning that I not leave Dingle, then hurried up the hall to Sean's room, to delegate the guards that would accompany Sean to Dublin. I hung out in the waiting room doorway, watching as Sean was carefully shifted from bed to gurney and noting that he never opened his eyes, even when his IVs became briefly and painfully entangled. And while I watched, the conversations I'd had since landing in Ireland flitted through a hole in my head until suddenly they deadlocked on the word "banshee."

I knew then who had attacked Sean.

I just couldn't fathom why.

CHAPTER FORTY-NINE

It was a gorgeous Irish morning, with the fruit trees in the B&B garden gently filtering the sunlight. Mrs. DeWitt sat on a bench with her tea, basking in the heady fragrance of the flowers. She was an innocently contented traveler, and I said nothing to disturb her as I slipped in the back door of the B&B and up the stairs.

Marilyn was frantically shoving clothes into a suitcase as I slid into her room and secured the door behind me. I could handle her; I could handle Patty. I wasn't sure I could handle both of them without my gun.

"Which one of you attacked Sean?" I asked as I leaned against the door, arms crossed. "Or was it both of you?"

Marilyn snorted but barely broke stride as she ripped clothes out of the closet and stuffed them into her luggage. She didn't appear to be making any distinction between her clothes and her mother's.

"Which one of you?" I repeated, and lack of sleep put a sharper edge on my voice than I had intended.

Marilyn winced, then rallied enough to grab an armful of shoes out of the closet. "I don't have time for this, Jo," she said hastily. "If Mom and I leave now, we can get to Shannon before the late night flight home." And she elbowed me out of the way so she could yank open the dresser.

"*You* attacked Sean," I said. "You're running from the law."

"I'm running, all right," Marilyn agreed as she burrowed in the underwear stacked in the bureau, "but not from the law."

"That's not what it looks like to me."

"Oh, for God's sake, Jo," Marilyn snapped, "use your head. Patty's cracked. First Sandra, now an Irish cop. I'm not waiting around for her to come after me and Mom, too." And she slammed the drawer shut.

I allowed myself a moment of weary puzzlement. "What Irish cop?"

"Don't be coy, Jo. We saw Sean flash his badge. What is he? Under cover?"

I plopped onto Mrs. DeWitt's unoccupied bed. "Oh, my God."

"You didn't think we'd find out?" Marilyn smirked, momentarily her old superior self.

I stared at her. "You attacked Sean because you *saw a badge*?"

Marilyn raised her hands. "I didn't touch him. That was all Patty. It's *always* been Patty."

"Sean's not a cop," I said angrily. "The badge was his dad's – a keepsake. Sean has *nothing* to do with the police."

Marilyn froze for a moment as she evaluated my information, then shook all regret out of her head. "Well, too bad for him. Patty thought he was a cop and he had to be stopped."

"That's absurd," I sputtered. "Why would Patty want to hurt him?"

Marilyn looked at me with complete sincerity. "Because she's fucking nuts." And she yanked another suitcase from the closet.

I squeezed my eyes shut. Both Marilyn and Patty had disappeared from our party at the pub the night before. Either one of them could have sneaked up behind Sean and smashed him in the back of the head. Marilyn blamed Patty, but why couldn't Marilyn be the assailant?

"Because I was giving a French banker a hand job," Marilyn said when I challenged her.

I rolled my eyes.

"Right where you're sitting," she insisted, pointing at the bed. "He didn't have a condom and I wasn't going to fuck him without one."

"Jesus, Marilyn," I gagged, and hopped off the bed.

"At least I practice safe sex," Marilyn said self-righteously. "What about you and your Irish boyfriend?"

That knocked me off center. "Sean and I never – "

"Spare me, please," Marilyn sniffed. "Of course you did."

I opened my mouth to protest, but realized that persisting in an argument over my virtue wouldn't solve anything. So I forced myself to backtrack. "Why did you care that Sean might be a cop?"

"*I* didn't," Marilyn stressed as she dumped cosmetics on top of her underwear, "but *Patty* did. She said if you were hooking up with a local cop, then you'd figured out Sandra, and you and Sean would try to arrest us."

"Did you and Patty do something to Sandra?"

"Don't try to play me," Marilyn snapped. "You *know* Sandra wasn't an accident. Patty killed her."

"How do you know that?" My mind was swirling, but I forced myself to speak calmly. If Marilyn wasn't handing me a line of bullshit, I didn't want to spook her with attitude.

"I *know*," Marilyn huffed as she tried to stuff a jacket into the first suitcase, "because I was there. I *saw* Patty shove Sandra out into the street."

"And you didn't report it to the police?"

Marilyn leveled weary eyes on me. "Patty has been hurting people since she was a little girl. I've covered for her all her life. She'd *kill* me if I told."

"I don't believe this," I pushed back. "I don't believe Patty is a homicidal maniac."

"Then you're a fool," Marilyn said, and she stopped her packing long enough to dig a cigarette out of her pocket. I gaped as she lit up.

"See what the bitch has done to me?" she said, and she inhaled deeply.

I shook my head. "Take me back to Sandra. Why would Patty kill her?"

"Well, wouldn't you?" Marilyn asked as she offered me the pack. "She was *so* annoying."

It had been a long night in the waiting room, and my vows to get clean disintegrated. I fished a cigarette out of Marilyn's pack and greedily accepted a light.

The rush of nicotine fired up my blood pressure but bathed my brain in a false sense of calm. Only Dave would be able to break my habit now.

I exhaled luxuriously. "Annoying isn't justification for murder."

"It is if you're Patty," Marilyn said ominously.

"I'm not following."

"Because you have your head up your ass," Marilyn said as she resumed squeezing items into the suitcases. "Sandra was making too much noise about dead Girl Scouts – first at the reunion and then as she dug into death certificates and insurance policies. She signed her own death warrant when she insisted on talking to the remaining Scouts about girls who had died."

I remembered how irritated Patty had been because Sandra had accosted her at the drugstore about dead Scouts, and I felt myself tuning into Marilyn's story.

"Patty went kinda crazy when she was young," Marilyn conceded as she tugged hard at the zipper on the second suitcase. "People got hurt because of her. But then something really *unexpected* and *bad* happened – " Marilyn looked at me, then swiftly looked away – "and Patty cleaned up her act. She didn't hurt *anybody*. For *years*. And then that stupid Sandra started raising questions about dead people." And Marilyn shook her head in disgust.

"Are you saying Sandra got what she deserved?" I asked, mildly appalled.

"I'm saying if Sandra hadn't been so curious, sticking her nose where it didn't belong, she wouldn't be dead," Marilyn admitted.

"Enlighten me," I prodded.

"Give me immunity," Marilyn countered.

"We're in a foreign country. I can't give you a thing."

"Then I have nothing more to say."

I grabbed her arm. "You've said enough already to make you a material witness. I can have you detained at customs."

I didn't have any such powers, but Marilyn didn't know that. She blanched.

"If I tell you everything, will you let me and Mom go home?"

I tilted my head to make it look like I was giving her proposal serious thought. Then I nodded. "You get a pass," I lied.

Marilyn licked her lips. "This is bad," she warned me.

I nodded sagely. "I can take it."

Marilyn's eyes darted nervously around the room, then hesitated at the door I had locked. "You gotta protect me, Jo. You gotta let me and Mom go home."

"I'll do what I can."

Marilyn weighed her options, then abruptly caved. "Patty made Nikki Hocevar crash her car. She could've killed all of us instead of just Nikki." Despite the horror of what she was saying, Marilyn's voice took on the bored tone of recitation. "Then she helped Debbie Gauer overdose. And she was there when Becky Freeman died, days before anyone expected. Then she had an affair and her lover ended up dying in a fire. Patty was always around when people died, and Sandra had started to figure it out. So Sandra had to go."

"How do you know all this?"

"I'm Patty's best friend," Marilyn said dully. "She confides in me."

"She doesn't think you'd turn her in?"

Marilyn shook her head. "I love her madly. She's the sister I never had, and I'll never turn on her."

"But you're talking to me," I pointed out. "That's turning on Patty."

Marilyn snorted. "You'll never be able to use it against her. She'll get to you first."

"That's ridiculous. I'll have her in jail by nightfall for attacking Sean."

"And your mother will be dead," Marilyn said flatly.

I froze. I had lost touch with Mother. I hadn't seen her since the night before at the pub.

Marilyn shook her head. "You still don't get it, do you?"

I stared at her in a rising fog of fear.

"For God's sake, Jo, she killed your husband and your daughter. Do you think she'll balk at killing your mother, too?"

My mouth was dry. "How do I know you're telling the truth?" I managed. "How do I know you aren't playing me so you can run away with your mother?"

"Because Patty's a lunatic!" Marilyn said frantically. "She was screwing your husband, but he told her to get lost and *no one* dumps Patty. She set the fire to teach Steve a lesson, only it got out of control and Steve and your little girl died. It scared Patty into going straight for *years*."

I stared at Marilyn in bewilderment. I had never, ever considered such a scenario before. Why should I?

Because Mrs. DeWitt believed Steve had been running around.

And Mother believed it, too.

And as Marilyn tugged madly at the zippers on her suitcases, a scene in the cemetery after Sandra's funeral flashed into my head.

"Scooter should have never died," Patty had said.

Except she shouldn't have known that nickname for Elizabeth. It was one Steve and I had used because of our baby girl's early ability to scoot across a room on her hands and knees. It was a name we had never shared with anyone else.

Well, *I* hadn't shared it, except years later with Dave.

But had *Steve*?

"Where is Patty?" I asked as dread worked up my spine.

"Out touring with your mother," Marilyn said with a malicious little bite to her tone.

That scared the crap out of me, and I responded by crowding Marilyn against the wall. "Where did they go? What is Patty doing to my mother?"

"Nothing good," Marilyn conceded. "Patty hates your guts, for obvious reasons."

I pushed Marilyn harder into the wall. "And you let my mother go with her? Knowing Patty is a murderer?"

"Murderer is a bit harsh, Jo," Marilyn protested.

I growled.

"Okay, it isn't an overstatement, but I gotta take care of my mother and me. My Number One priority is getting us to Shannon before Patty gets back."

"And my mother?" I demanded as I pressed my arm across Marilyn's throat.

Marilyn gagged. I couldn't understand her, so I eased up a little on her windpipe.

"Collateral damage," she wheezed.

I slammed her upside the head. She sank to the floor with a pitiful moan. I ran out of the room to find Mother.

CHAPTER FIFTY

Mrs. DeWitt said Mother and Patty had gone out to tour the Dingle Peninsula, but both rental cars were still parked on the road outside the B&B. That gave me hope – that Marilyn was wrong about Patty taking off with Mother and that any moment, Mother would wander back with a sack full of apples from the local market. But then the landlady heard me talking to Mrs. DeWitt and volunteered that Mother and Patty had gone off on the local tour bus, which circled the peninsula.

The landlady thought I'd be relieved to know where Mother had gone, but I was frantic. The farther Mother was out on the peninsula, the longer it would take me to get to her – and the more time Patty would have to hurt her.

But the landlady had pamphlets that included a map of the tour bus route.

"Where would they be now?" I asked, jabbing the map with my finger.

"It depends," the landlady hedged. "If they went west first, they'd be heading to the old fort at Dunbeg. If they went north, they'd be at the Oratory about now."

"So which is it?" I demanded. "North or west?"

The landlady shrugged. "Either one. They're both lovely this time of year."

I growled and shoved the map into my purse. I had a 50-50 chance of heading in the right direction. So I fired up the rental car and pointed it toward Dunbeg. It was only thirty minutes away. It was my easiest shot.

The morning was brilliantly clear, so much so that the sun glinting off the bay was nearly blinding. But thankfully the two-lane highway veered inland, and I could floor the accelerator with little fear of sailing off a cliff into the ocean.

And I had time to think debilitating thoughts.

It had been hellish coming to grips with the idea that my little girl had died because of careless smoking, that I had lost her to something so *stupid*. It had torn a hole in my heart, and the mere mention of my dead husband's name had been intolerable. But eventually – thanks in large part to Bradley – I had learned to live with my loss.

Hearing that my daughter had died because of my husband's *mistress* was turning my world upside down again. I had almost forgiven Steve for falling asleep with a lighted cigarette in his hand. He had paid for his carelessness with not only our daughter's life but also his own. Now hearing that Patty had purposely set the fire unleashed an old vitriolic anger against all the forces that had conspired to kill my baby girl. Resentment against Steve returned with such strength, I nearly lost control of the car. The only thing that kept me solidly on the road was the thought of finding Patty and sinking my nails into her throat.

Fortunately, Dunbeg was coming up on my left.

* * *

Dunbeg is a fort dating from the Iron Age, sitting high up on the cliffs overlooking Dingle Bay. The fort is across the road from another favorite tourist stop, the beehive huts where early Christian pilgrims apparently hung out. Neither spot was a surefire attraction for a 20th-century grandmother, so I had to take my chances: primitive huts made out of stone or a primitive fort overlooking the ocean?

I chose the huts, thinking right, right, right like an American driver, but Ireland's mad highway system funneled me to the fort on the left instead. And parked in the middle of the fort's gravel lot was the Dingle tour bus.

The car bucked and swerved over the gravel because, after a night of no sleep, I was in no shape to drive, but I wrestled the steering wheel and stomped on the brakes until the car squealed to a stop inches from the bonnet of the bus. “Bus” was a generous description. It was more like a big van, with ads for the Dingle tour bolted to its sides.

I scrambled from the car and gagged on the dust I had raised. Across the parking lot, a couple of respectable tourists were staring at me, and a man dressed like a farmer was running down the driveway toward me, shouting and shaking his fist. I might have neglected to pay him when I jerked the car off the highway and descended toward the fort.

I yanked open the passenger door on the bus, but all I saw were surprisingly plush but empty seats. So I turned toward the fort and shaded my eyes against the glare of the sun.

A couple dozen tourists were wandering around the fort's inner rampart, its single intact clochan, or hut, and the stone walls holding the curious back from the black cliffs and the sea. I squinted but I didn't know what Mother and Patty were wearing, and none of the people roaming the earthworks looked familiar. However, there were walls leaning here and there, and Mother could easily be standing behind one of them, hidden from my view.

And my protection.

“Mother!” I shouted uselessly, and ran down the path toward the fort's central causeway.

No one answered, although a couple of folks were startled enough to back out of my way. If I'd been on the job, I'd have drawn my gun by then. My hand twitched without it.

I darted looks each way as I cleared the first ramparts. No tightly waved gray wig in sight.

"Mother!" I yelled again.

And perhaps I heard a querulous shout in return, down by the sea wall and the cliffs.

I sprinted around two fat tourists fumbling with their cameras, skidded across a narrow swath of lush grass and slammed to a halt at the waist-high sea wall. It could have been the boundary of a pleasant Irish garden – except, when I planted my hands on the top of the wall and leaned over to look, the world dropped straight away to roaring white waves smashing against jagged black rocks ninety feet below.

I shuddered as sea water sprayed my face and whirled back toward the fort.

And found Patty smirking from barely a yard away.

"Where's Mother?" I demanded hoarsely.

Patty shrugged. "She came to see the ocean." And she looked over my shoulder at the angry bay.

I wasn't a cop in Ireland. I was a tourist who had lost her mother. And forgetting everything Bradley had ever taught me, I turned back to the sea, irrationally leaned over the wall and looked for Mother.

Until a 150-pound weight smashed into my butt and knocked me over the wall.

I squawked and furiously flapped my arms.

But I couldn't fly.

CHAPTER FIFTY-ONE

I tumbled and rolled over ancient black rock, and I could feel the skin on my arms and shins split apart as I fell toward the crashing waves. But then I bounced onto a narrow ledge and before gravity pulled me over its insubstantial lip, I frantically dug my fingers into the rock and wedged my toes into any hold they could find, and for a breathless moment, my plunge into the sea was halted.

I shakily looked up. I had fallen only six feet or so. No bones were broken. I was bleeding here and there, but not badly. If I didn't slip on the slime, I could climb back up the rocks to the wall and safety.

But then a head blocked the sunlight slanting over the wall.

Patty leaned over the stone wall six feet above my head. "I'm truly sorry about Scooter," she shouted into the Irish wind. "She wasn't meant to die."

Then she heaved a rock over the wall, and it smashed onto my left hand.

I jerked in pain, lost my grip and slipped toward the angry gray waters of the North Atlantic.

*   *   *

More scraping skin. More pain. I wanted to scream, but it was more important to breathe.

And then I slammed my head against a rock and everything was gone.

*   *   *

I dreamed of a muffled scream and a mass plummeting past me to the pointed rocks below. I clung to wet stone and licked salt off my lips.

And passed out.

*   *   *

"Lassie?" a male voice shouted. "Can you hear me?"

I peered through the salt spray and saw a red-haired leprechaun dangling on a rope.

Ireland is so delightful.

I passed out again.

*   *   *

Rough hands poked and shoved at me.

I squawked awake and grasped desperately at the rocks. Another layer of fingernails ripped away.

"It's all right, lass," said the prickly red-haired mouth pressed against my ear, "I'm here to save you. Now stop your fussin' and let me get on with it."

I looked wildly past his beard. I was lying precariously on an even smaller ledge much too close to whirlpools, undertows and deadly waves. The climb up was impossible. The plunge down was swift and inevitable.

But my leprechaun was dressed in a very efficient harness, and he was diligently trying to tie me to it, too.

"I've had too much Guinness," I blathered.

"No such thing as too much," he laughed, and a rope that had magically appeared around my arms and legs was firmly clipped to his own life line. "Next round is on you." And he tugged on the rope.

There was a painful jerk, I gasped, and we slowly rose. I hugged my leprechaun as we caromed against rock, gouging a few more holes in my hide, but we were steadily hauled up from the waves by hands trained to save silly tourists who get too close to the edge. I should have told my savior to be on the lookout for a madwoman roaming the fort, but all I could do was concentrate on breathing. I was afraid that if I did anything else, the Celtic gods would be displeased and send me back to the rocks.

We bumped up the jagged wall around the fort, and hands reached out to haul us back onto firm ground – gnarled old shepherd's hands, calloused farmer's hands, soft tourist hands. The cliff was crowded with rescuers and well-intentioned wannabes.

But all I wanted to see was one disheveled wig.

And as my leprechaun unceremoniously pushed me over the top of the wall, Mother shoved her way through the crowd and caught me as I landed.

She cupped my face in her hands. "Are you still with me, Jo?" she demanded. "Dave and Adam would never forgive me if I let you drown in the sea."

Her wig was damp and her face was haggard. As soon as I was freed from the harness, I crushed her against my chest. "I'm okay," I gasped. "Everything is okay."

My leprechaun delicately extricated himself from our tangle of ropes. "I have another retrieval," he said, and sketched a salute before loping down the path to a jagged point in the wall about ten feet beyond us and launching himself over the side again.

I looked inquisitively at Mother.

"We lost Patty," she said, and she brushed my frizzled bangs off my forehead.

I remembered the muffled scream and the body flying past me as I clung to the cliff. Patty had fallen, too?

I staggered to the cliff's edge and leaned over the wall. Mother wasn't happy, but stoically followed, patting my hand as I gazed at the rocks below. A crumpled mass lay about 10 feet above the surf. It had definitely once been human. I had to take Mother's word that it was Patty. The face was crushed beyond recognition.

I shook my head as I turned away. “I don't understand,” I said. “She shoved me over the edge. She was free. How did she fall?”

Mother carefully draped a blanket across my shivering shoulders.

“It's simple, dear,” she said. “I pushed her.”